For every reader who believed in me and waited so patiently for me to find myself again.

BLURB
AN UNEXPECTED CLAIM: NATHAN & PEYTON #1

A one night stand.
A runaway shifter.
An unexpected claim...

I never thought I'd see her again after our primal, passion filled night together. But finding Peyton's nearly lifeless body on my land sends a shock to my system. She's on the run from a serial killer and looking for an ally... not a mate.

Danger.
Protect.
Mine.

My blood calls for her.
My mind screams to protect her.
My body aches to posses her.
Make her mine.

But Peyton is a loner, and she will never truly belong to anyone.

CHAPTER ONE

PEYTON

A shiver skittered down my spine as I set a few mixed drinks onto the glossy wooden table of the booth in front of me. The patrons nodded their thanks as I turned away and headed to the bar.

My body temperature spiked and an electric current sizzled on my skin, causing my panther to pace restlessly.

In a club filled with shifters, who were highly sexual creatures, I might have chalked it up to the atmosphere. Especially with the full moon tomorrow. The days leading up to it heightened our base desires and made us…well, horny as hell.

Essentially, our animals went into heat, except it also amplified our human hormones. And since the only time we could get pregnant was during a full moon, it was usually preceded by a couple of days of nonstop fucking. It had also been a couple of months since I'd blown off—pun intended—some steam doing the horizontal mambo.

And yeah, he definitely returned the favor.

But something about my body's reaction felt different this

time, more intense than ever before, though I couldn't explain why. My eyes swept around the club as I threaded my way through the high-top tables surrounding the dance floor. The patrons at The Spot—where I waitressed at night—were almost all shifters, with the exception of one or two human mates. The owner, Sam, a leopard shifter, had jokingly named it with a double meaning. It was "the spot" for shifters to congregate for a good time as well as a reference to his spotted fur. No matter how much we all teased him, he still thought it was hilarious.

He'd built it inside one of the smaller, old cathedrals on the Upper West Side, and spared no expense when he repurposed it as a nightclub. He'd taken care to restore a lot of the original wood and stonework, while still creating a modern feel. People entered through a set of enormous, wooden double doors and from the lobby and the luxurious, yet laid-back atmosphere impressed everyone.

Inside the main room, two of the walls were lined with black walnut paneling and high-backed, button-tufted, black leather booths. Each booth was illuminated by a single pendant light hanging from above to create a little privacy, while the bar and stage took up the other two walls. Bodies packed the dance floor in the middle of the room, moving sensuously to the heavy beat of the music.

Finally, my gaze landed on a table in the back corner, near the bar. Three large men sat on stools, drinking beer and talking, but only one drew my complete focus. Every single thing about him, from his countenance to his broad stature, radiated power. His imposing presence was heady, and my panther purred in admiration while I squeezed my legs together for a moment, trying to quell the rush of desire that throbbed there.

He was the cause of the heat flushing my body. His potent stare felt like a caress, everywhere and all at once. *Would he surround me as completely if we were naked in bed? Mmmhmm. My guess is yes.* As soon as the thought popped into my head, his stare intensified, making me wonder if he knew, somehow, what I'd been thinking. Odd. Then again, I hadn't made an effort to hide my interest in him.

My steps slowed, and my gaze traveled over him from head to toe. Even seated, I could tell he was at least six and a half feet tall and would tower over my five-foot-nine height. He wore a white, short-sleeved T-shirt that showed off huge biceps and strong, veiny forearms—one of which was marred with claw marks. The scars were old, but for them to still be visible despite his rapid healing, they had to have been very deep. Every one of his sculpted muscles rippled when he moved, and I clenched my thighs again, barely restraining myself from licking my lips. From what I could see, the rest of his body fit the same description.

Big, hard, and sexy as hell.

He wore a trimmed, full beard over a firm, square jaw, and had light brown-blond hair that was long enough for a man-bun high on the back of his head. I didn't normally like long hair on guys, but on this man…

He was fucking hot.

H.O.T. *Hot.*

And he lit up my body like the Fourth of July. I desperately wanted to know if his facial hair was as silky as it appeared and if it would leave burn marks between my thighs.

Dirty scenarios filled my mind, creating a porn montage. *When the hell did I become such a nympho?*

I'd experienced overwhelming desire before as well as unbelievably hot, toe-curling sex, but none of that compared to the pull from this man's gaze. As I passed his table, I felt as if I were on the verge of an orgasm even from a few feet away.

My cat urged me to make a beeline for the cause of our

explosive libido. She didn't understand the complexities of human behavior. As an animal, her comprehension of the situation was simple—feel desire, act on that desire, walk away satisfied.

I wasn't wholly opposed to her view, but I still had a job to do, so I tried to ignore my rapidly deepening hunger for this man.

"Peyton," Sam called from the end of the bar.

My eyes snapped away from the sexy stranger to my boss. Startled at his presence, I picked up my step and tried to focus on my job rather than the electricity humming over my skin.

"Hey," I greeted him with a smile when I arrived. "You're working the bar tonight?"

The leopard shifter was unusual for his breed. Like black panthers, they rarely mated and settled down, which wasn't entirely surprising since we were technically of the same species. Although I was in the jaguar family, rather than leopard.

Sam had not only opened a business, he also had a mate—Linette—and they were expecting their first cub in a month. Since cats of our breed had only six-month pregnancies, he'd handed most of the responsibilities of running the business to his manager and taken time off to be with his mate. Which meant I hadn't seen him at the club much, especially not at night.

Sam rolled his eyes. "Apparently, I hover."

I stifled a chuckle, having heard a rant from Linette earlier in the day when I'd stopped by to check on my sweet friend.

Unlike my boss, staying in one place wasn't in my nature. I always felt antsy after a time, needing to breathe new air and see new places, even as a kid. It meant I had few friends and formed no deep attachments, but I didn't mind it. I preferred to be alone, free to do as I pleased, unfettered by the opinion of others. No matter how well-meaning.

But Sam and Linette had somehow wormed their way into my life, deeper than anyone ever had.

I'd worked at The Spot while putting myself through college at NYU. I'd left immediately after but kept in touch with them. After roaming around the world for the last ten years, I'd felt the desire to return to New York, though I didn't know why. It had been particularly odd because I'd realized during college that I didn't enjoy city life for more than a short period of time.

When Linette called to tell me about the pregnancy, she asked me to come stay until the baby was born. At first, I'd assumed that had been the reason for my odd urge to return, but it hadn't sat well with me and I was still trying to figure it out.

Since I'd come back, I'd spent enough time with Linette and Sam to see why she needed a break. Seeing him behind the bar suddenly made much more sense.

"You? Hover?" I asked innocently.

He narrowed his gaze on me, and I smiled brightly. After a second, he huffed and grabbed two shot glasses from under the bar. "Anyway, she kicked me out for a while, so I figured I'd come in." He turned around and pulled a bottle of expensive tequila off a shelf, then did an about-face. He poured two jiggers and pushed one toward me before lifting the other.

"Welcome home, kid," he toasted before tossing back the shot. I laughed and brought the glass to my lips, pausing in confusion when a strange burn raced through my body. My eyes were drawn to the stranger once again, but this time, his expression had a dark edge as he observed Sam and me.

Is he jealous? I wondered. *No, we don't even know each other.*

I tore my gaze away and threw back my drink, wishing the alcohol would dim some of the pulsing need inside me, since I still had a couple of hours left on my shift. It wouldn't happen though because it took a hell of a lot of alcohol to get a shifter drunk, and the buzz didn't last long. Our bodies spit out toxins and healed much faster than humans. We also felt emotions more deeply, our physical reactions were stronger, we were harder to kill, and some of us were immortal (depending on heritage and breed).

Sam raised a brow along with the tequila bottle, and I shook my head. "I need to get back to work."

He scoffed but didn't say anything else as he returned the bottle to its place and washed the glasses.

Yeah, yeah, I thought. We both knew I didn't need the money. I'd accumulated a very nice nest egg over the last decade. I'd been into computers in high school, and it had quickly become apparent that I could tackle just about anything involved with them. My degree had opened the doors for me to establish myself as a freelance ethical hacker or white hat hacker, although I occasionally slipped on hats of another color.

So, no, I didn't need to waitress at The Spot, but I was in between jobs and it passed the time.

I glanced at the sexy giant once more and knew without doubt that I would be spending the night with him. Now I had a whole new appreciation for my current employment.

Leila, another waitress, hurried up to the bar, cutting into my line of sight and bringing me back to the present. "Another round for table three," she told Sam as she handed him a few receipts. My ears perked up at the sound of the stranger's table number.

"I'll take it over," I announced.

Leila frowned and I mentally rolled my eyes. "You'll still get the tip."

She studied me for a minute, then shrugged. "Okay."

She put in another drink order and Sam waved over the other bartender to help an approaching customer. Once I had a tray laden with three shots and three beers, I weaved my way over to table three.

As I moved closer, I gained a better view of the men sitting around it, and the amount of gorgeous packed around one table stunned me. They looked nothing alike, but each of them could grace the cover of a magazine, particularly the ones with "World's Sexiest…" lists.

Their conversation halted when I walked up to the table and set their drinks in front of them. Their scent broke through all of the others mixed together in the club and I frowned.

Shit. They were wolves.

As a rule, I avoided wolves whenever possible and normally I would have shot in the opposite direction like my ass was on fire. But damn this sexy-as-fuck wolf! I'd never been so hot and needy for someone in my entire life. And I couldn't see any other option for dealing with it than to give in and get it out of my system.

Three sets of eyes peered at me, but after a second, a low growl rumbled from the wolf currently making my panther beg for a good, hard fucking. At the sound, the other two men dropped their gazes and their necks tilted minutely to the side.

The breath in my lungs stalled as memories I kept buried flashed to the surface for a second. I'd seen that reaction before, the automatic acquiescence and show of submission.

Hive mind.

This wolf was clearly their Alpha.

I knew there were other shifters in the world whose packs,

leaps, prides, colonies—whatever their family was called—shared a "hive mind" with their leader. But I'd only ever experienced it with one pack and that had been enough. Just another reason why I enjoyed being a lone shifter. Ultimate freedom.

Alpha females did not give up control easily, even more so for a solitary animal like me. It was something I could only ever see a mate earning from me. But a mate would be like a chain around my neck, so I intended to take a hard pass on that.

My instincts told me this Alpha would demand it. He'd be in for a shock when I refused, and I could definitely picture him limping off without one of his testicles. I hadn't been a fan of the possessive growl, essentially his way of stating "dibs." My panther snorted at my lie. *Okay, so it was kind of hot.*

"I'm Nathan King," the wolf introduced himself, his expression unreadable, though his eyes—a melted silver color—were still dark and intense. Alpha vibes were pulsing from him, cloaking me in a shroud of desire that I felt over every inch of my body.

Still, the evidence of his hold on his pack made me hesitant. I debated for a beat, then mentally shrugged. A night of hot sex didn't mean I'd be joining his pack, so what did I care how this Alpha ruled?

My panther vibrated excitedly, feeling my own anticipation heighten now that I'd made my decision. She was clearly in favor of my choice.

"Peyton Dyer," I responded as I placed a napkin beside each drink.

"Asher," one of the other wolves piped up. He had thick brown hair and piercing blue eyes that were currently filled with playful laughter.

"Jase," the other man said—a tall, dark-haired wolf with blue eyes and a leaner build than the other two.

"What time do you get off, beautiful?" Asher asked with a

wiggle of his eyebrows. I couldn't help chuckling. Especially when his blue orbs flashed with a knowing look at his Alpha and his smile turned a little wicked. "Never mind, I'll just tell you when I'm going to get you—"

"Asher," Nathan interrupted. One word, but it was loaded with Alpha energy and aggression.

But instead of submitting like before, Asher winked at me and held his hands up in a surrender motion. "Well, I've got shit to do. Nathan, I won't wait up for you. Nice to meet you, Peyton." Then he grabbed Jase, who had been staring at me thoughtfully, by the arm and dragged him away from the table.

Confused by the exchange, I watched them leave until I couldn't resist the pull of Nathan's dedicated attention. I hadn't noticed that I'd moved closer until I turned and found myself standing between his legs.

Up close, I noticed that the flashes in his eyes were subtle changes in the shape of his pupils, alerting me that his wolf hovered near the surface. It was unusual for a shifter and their animal to share the same eye color, but I sensed there was little about Nathan that was common or expected.

His wolf stared back at me with the same penetrating concentration as his human half. My panther nudged me, wanting to be freed to meet his wolf. When Nathan raised a single brown-blond brow, I guessed that the emerald color of my irises had begun to turn yellow-gold.

I felt a jolt when my panther pushed even harder, demanding to be released.

Damn, girl. Chill. I didn't know what to make of her reaction. She'd never responded to another shifter like this. *Seriously?* I scolded her. *A wolf?* She sniffed with annoyance and backed off for the moment.

Someone called my name and broke the spell Nathan had me under. I glanced at one of my regular tables and waved to let them know I'd be right there. Nathan took hold of my arm and his hard gaze suggested I not leave yet. "What time?"

My skin burned where he touched it and I almost melted into a puddle on the floor when he glided his rough, calloused palm down to my hand.

It wouldn't make a difference in my decision, but for some reason, I wanted him to answer a question for me first. "You forced your pack's submission before, how come you didn't when Asher needled you by flirting with me?"

Nathan's mouth curved down and his brow furrowed. *Whoa.* With unreadable features, he was intimidating enough, but with clear displeasure in his expression, I imagined he terrified people.

Apparently, my panther and I had no real sense of self-preservation because we were both aroused by it. Nathan's nose flared and his pupils dilated, the sliver of his irises turning molten, telling me he smelled my reaction; however, he answered my question.

"I didn't force Asher's or Jase's submission. I warned them off, but they made the choice to show allegiance and respect. I would never require it." He must have read the puzzlement on my face because he tilted his head and studied me. "This surprises you. Why?"

I wiped my expression of anything except the attraction consuming me. "Just curious," I said, shrugging a shoulder. He looked as though he might argue, but I placed my hand on his bulging biceps—*oh, damn.* Every bit as hard as he seemed—and locked eyes with him. "Midnight."

He nodded and it amazed me that one single gesture conveyed so much. I felt as if I'd been commanded and caressed all at once. He clearly had no doubt I would come to him at the end of my shift.

Arrogant, yes, but not wrong.

With one last glance, I returned to my job.

His eyes followed me everywhere throughout the night. Whenever I had the opportunity, I'd meet his heavy-lidded gaze, and the dark promise of passion in them had me wishing time would speed the fuck up.

CHAPTER TWO

NATHAN

I'd lived over two millennia and in all that time, I'd never encountered an attraction so explosive—almost uncontrollable.

As the Alpha of the powerful Silver Lake Pack, the owner of a freelance black ops agency, and the head of the SCA—the Shifter Council that presided over the Americas—and the ISC—Interspecies Council—it was damn disconcerting.

But Peyton was sexy as hell. The way she moved, the sound of her voice, everything about her was alluring, drawing me in. I'd mused over the possibility that she might be a vampire or a siren, but when she'd come close enough for me to scent her, I'd immediately smelled her feline—a panther, if I had to guess. And I was rarely wrong. She even reminded me of her jungle cat with her sleek, toned build and her graceful, confident stature.

However, more important than her breed, there had been no mistaking the arousal effusing from her body. The first moment our eyes met, I'd felt something snap between us like a string tethering us together. One so taut it vibrated through my whole body and bounced around in my mind a couple of times. I didn't understand the pull between us, nor did I care.

With the full moon approaching, the need to fuck grew more forceful, and I fully intended to sate my lust in Peyton's body. My wolf brushed his fur under my skin and emitted a low rumble of approval.

I tore my eyes away from her to check my watch before they returned to the sway of her sexy ass as she moved from table to table. *Two hours.*

Certain circumstances in my life had instilled nearly endless patience and an ironclad control over myself. But tonight, those attributes had gone up in flames, and with every second that I didn't have Peyton beneath me, I felt aggression building inside me.

Our gazes collided frequently and the potency between us acted like non-verbal foreplay. A rare smile curved my lips when her body tightened as if to stem a rush of passion.

Though my eyes stayed on Peyton, my thoughts drifted to the events that brought me out this evening. Asher, my head enforcer, and Jase, another of my enforcers, had dragged me out to The Spot after a particularly shitty day at the Council HQ.

I hated the city, preferring the rural setting of my Silver Lake home in upstate New York. But, if I was in the mood to find satisfaction with a woman, I would never do so with a member of my pack, so I stuck to the city. I'd been sure this wasn't what I needed after finding more evidence that the divide developing within the Councils appeared to be a deliberate plot.

Now, I'd have to give those assholes credit for the idea because my intuition told me that this night with Peyton would be more incredible than anything I'd ever experienced. And that said a lot considering my age.

A night together didn't require us to know anything about each other, which was generally the way my hookups went. However, Peyton's surprise that I hadn't used my ability as the Alpha to force submission from my packmates piqued my curiosity. I knew there were packs whose Alphas abused their telepathic power—often referred to as a hive mind—and I had some knowledge of most of them through my connections. But to have experienced it, Peyton would have had to be a member of their pack, which didn't fit with my assessment of her. Not only did her breed of cat choose not to live in packs or settle down with a mate, but I sensed the restlessness of a lone shifter inside her.

Her attitude toward the hive mind hinted at it, but there was also an edginess about her that told me she was used to being on the move. I could see how a nomadic existence came naturally to her. It meant she was strong and capable because shifters without a pack were easier targets.

It also made her an ideal partner for a one-night adventure, so I ignored any interest in her beyond her delicious body.

While I watched her, I perused her features. Black hair hung in long, silky waves to her round ass. Every time she tucked strands of it behind her ears, she brought my attention to her bright green, intelligent eyes flecked with gold and framed with thick, black lashes. I avoided lingering on her plump, red mouth as it inspired thoughts that had the potential to break my control.

As the night progressed, the air in the club became increasingly saturated with pheromones. The couples on the dance floor were grinding against each other while others were outright fucking in booths or dark corners. Shifters were not shy about sex, one of the traits that marked us as part animal.

My wolf pushed against me again, demanding to be set free.

He wanted Peyton almost as much as I did. The glimpse of her cat when the yellow-gold bled into her emerald eyes hadn't helped the situation. But I forced him to back off.

At ten to midnight, Peyton glanced at me one last time before disappearing into the employee area behind the bar. I debated following her but ultimately chose to wait and let her come to me.

I'd known instantly that she wasn't a submissive shifter and as an Alpha wolf it was my natural inclination to dominate. Although I preferred partners who didn't immediately capitulate to my power. Something told me that Peyton wouldn't easily submit, but the fight would be hot as hell.

Peyton reappeared still wearing the fitted leather pants she'd had on all night, but she'd swapped her black tank with the club's logo for a one-shouldered black top that hugged her body. The outfit showcased her full breasts, athletic limbs, flat stomach and slender hips. She had a birthmark on her shoulder that was similar to the one on my biceps, except hers was shaped like the paw of a panther with extended claws. There was also a tattoo of a butterfly on her wrist. I licked my lips in anticipation of putting my hands and mouth all over her smooth skin and losing myself inside her.

When she reached my table, she ran her hands through her hair, pushing it back, giving me a glimpse of her ears, each with four jeweled studs. Uncommon for a shifter since they would remain in her animal's ears when she changed form, but it fit her. As her hands fell to her side again, a ring glimmered on her right thumb, a gold band with an engraving I couldn't read.

This woman continually intrigued me. Under different circumstances, I might have tried to delve in and discover her secrets. But my life had too many moving parts already. I didn't need another complication.

Tonight was about one thing. We both knew where this was

going, and the anticipation made the air around us flammable. One spark and we'd go up in flames.

"Do you want to dance?" Peyton asked in a husky voice that sent bolts of lust through me. I raised a brow, and a tiny smirk played on her red lips. "Horizontal mambo," she said with a laugh.

My mouth curled up in a wicked grin as I stood. "Excellent idea."

I delved my hand into her hair and cupped her neck, pulling her forward as I bent my head and captured her mouth. My tongue immediately plunged in and explored before tangling with hers. She moaned and stepped closer, pressing her body against mine as I tilted her head and deepened the kiss. She tasted sweet, as though she'd been sucking on candy, and it made me even hungrier for her. My mouth watered from her scent—like honey and cloves.

I used both hands to palm her ass and boost her up, urging her to put her legs around my waist, and fitting our centers together. Groaning into her mouth, I ground the large bulge in my jeans between her thighs. When her head dropped back and she cried out, I was at the end of my restraint.

My first instinct was to do as the other patrons had done and find a dark corner to sate our lust, but I knew once with Peyton wouldn't be enough. I wanted to find a bed where I could keep her naked and screaming until the sun came up.

Peyton panted as she raised her head and met my gaze with equal fervor. "My apartment is two blocks from here."

Perfect. I debated for a second on whether to carry her there—no one on a New York City street would give us a second look. But when she wiggled her hot little body, I knew if I continued to hold her, the friction with each step would torture me the entire way and might derail my control.

Reluctantly, I set her down and gestured for her to lead the way. At least it provided a spectacular view for the walk.

Peyton didn't waste any time in heading to the exit and power-walking the two blocks until she reached a red brick building that rose up five floors. She unlocked the front door, and we entered an old, but clean, tiled hallway. Then she opened the first door on the right before spinning around and snaking a finger into one of my belt loops. She yanked as she walked backward, and I let her pull me into the apartment.

My eyes never left Peyton as she pulled me across the room to another door, through which I glimpsed the only item that interested me. A bed.

I allowed her to be in charge until we crossed the threshold, then I took over. A second later, she was in my arms again, her legs around my waist and her back pressed against a wall. "I hope you're prepared for what's about to happen, Peyton," I muttered gruffly. "Because it's too fucking late to change your mind."

"I can take it," she said with as much conviction as she could through choppy breaths, her body trembling, and on the edge of release.

"You're close," I grunted smugly. All the eye-fucking we'd done had clearly primed her.

"Yesss," she hissed as I rocked my hips into her. Her hands delved into my hair, dislodging the bun so it tumbled down around my face. She fisted the strands and held on as if it were the only thing keeping her from being carried away.

Peyton's head fell back against the wall, exposing a naked expanse of her elegant throat, and my canines descended. My wolf fought for control and I wrestled him back, trying to fight the need to sink my fangs into her. It would enhance her orgasm, but I'd made it a rule a long time ago not to bite women during sex. It was an intimate action and would only complicate things that were meant to be simple.

Instead, I sucked on the delicate skin and sped up my movements. She gasped, and her body went taut before she cried out as she shattered. I couldn't help it—I dragged the sharp tip of one fang along her neck. But no matter how tempted I was, I didn't break the skin.

I lifted my head and watched her as she rode out her climax. I hadn't thought Peyton could be any more gorgeous, but holy shit. In the throes of orgasm, she was like nothing I'd ever seen, and the sight imprinted itself on my brain, never to be forgotten.

"Wow," she breathed when her orgasm ebbed. She released my hair and her arms flopped down to her sides as she opened her eyes. The deep emerald swirled with gold and my wolf responded to the peek at her panther with a hungry growl. Apparently, our animals were feeling a bond as well. But freeing them to play in the city wouldn't end well.

"It's only going to get better, baby," I grunted as I moved to the bed and dropped her onto the mattress.

"Put your money where your mouth is, Nathan," she taunted with a half-smile.

I extended a claw and sliced down the center of her shirt and pants. "How about I put my mouth where your pussy is?"

Peyton's pulse visibly fluttered at the base of her throat before increasing in speed, and the scent of her desire thickened between her legs.

Pulling apart the fabric of her pants, I tugged them down until they were completely off, then tossed them aside before her shirt met the same fate.

I dragged her to the edge of the bed and knelt between her legs. My hands smoothed over the soft skin on her thighs, and I grappled with the urge to bite her again. I snarled at my wolf, assuming the impulse was being projected from him, and he snapped at me in return. Ignoring him, I refocused on Peyton.

Her center was pink and wet, and I lowered my head to taste it, groaning when the delicious flavor burst on my tongue. Peyton's hands dove into my hair again and I grunted when she yanked hard enough to cause pain. She was severely testing my control, something I hadn't lost my grip on for centuries. But in that moment, I didn't care. Hunger consumed my mind, gaining strength the closer we drew to the full moon.

Peyton's body practically vibrated with each lash of my tongue, her need as potent as mine, and when I pushed her over the edge, she screamed in ecstasy. I became obsessed with the sound and made it a personal goal to draw it out of her as many times as possible throughout the night.

I trailed the tip of my tongue along her body as I moved up until I was covering her from head to toe before crushing my mouth over hers. While our tongues tangled together, my hands caressed her breasts until she reached the edge once more. I'd been waiting all fucking night to bury myself in Peyton's heat and I slid my hands under her ass, lifting her pelvis as I teased her entrance with the tip of my cock.

One swift punch of my hips sent her spiraling into another climax. Her muscles clenched around me and though I was only about halfway in, I nearly lost it. But I held fast to my control and dragged my shaft out of her channel, fighting her grip the whole way. Once I'd pulled out almost to the tip, I growled, "Open your eyes, Peyton."

She slowly parted her eyelids and stared up at me, her deep green orbs with their flecks of gold swirling with desire. I kept our eyes locked while I drove into her fast and hard, fully sheathing myself this time. Peyton cried out and her back arched as her hands clutched my biceps. I groaned at the tight fit and bent my head to steal another deep kiss before I began to move.

At the club, I'd known we would be explosive, but I hadn't expected the degree to which we burned. The first time I exploded inside her, the inferno cremated my intention to keep my true cravings inside, and my darker, dangerous impulses were exposed.

My need to dominate consumed me, and I pinned Peyton to the bed as I pulled out before I'd finished, releasing the rest of my seed onto her flat stomach.

Peyton's eyes narrowed; she knew exactly what I was doing. Marking her, establishing myself as the Alpha, and demanding that she submit. My wolf pushed heavy, powerful vibes through me that pulsed in the room, helping me to stay in control.

She started struggling against my hold, and I growled in approval. The harder she fought me, the more excited I became, knowing that when I finally won, I would rule her body and soul.

My iron grip on her wrists kept her hands above her head and I used my weight to push her deeper into the mattress. She bucked her hips, trying to throw me off, and I grunted at the streaks of pleasure that shot through my body when our centers collided.

"Get off of me, you asshole!" she snapped and bucked again. But her attitude was ruined by the cloud of lust that filled her emerald eyes.

"I can smell your need, Peyton. You long to be dominated, forced to submit."

Another flare of desire contradicted the streak of curses that spilled from her mouth. "Bullshit," she seethed, her claws extending as she continued to struggle.

I smirked when she glared at me because gold had eclipsed

her green irises for a beat, and I saw her panther's appreciation of my power and acceptance of my worthiness as an Alpha. She wanted Peyton to give in, but the emerald returned, filled with fury and determination.

Suddenly, Peyton's legs wrapped around my waist and she clamped them so hard it forced the breath out of my lungs unexpectedly. I reared back less than an inch, but it was all she needed. She yanked on the strands of my hair and used the sliver of leverage to twist her body, managing to push me off of her enough to wiggle away. I still had her wrists shackled, but she curled her fingers and her claws dug into the soft skin between my fingers.

"Shit!" I released her but grasped her waist before she was able to scoot off the bed. Instead, we rolled off together and crashed onto the floor. We tussled, each of us determined to subjugate the other. "Fuck," I grunted when she dragged her claws down my chest, drawing blood. "You fight like a wildcat, baby." I meant it as a compliment, but she didn't appear to be in the mood to receive it.

We continued to fight, both of us leaving our marks in cuts and bruises. Peyton even bit me a couple of times, but I kept my vow and my teeth away from her.

I had no clue how long it went on, but I ultimately gained the upper hand and trapped Peyton on her knees in front of me, facing away, with her arms locked behind her back. In this position, I could mount her like my wolf would do to her panther. My wolf urged me to stake our claim with such force that he managed to push me aside mentally and took over our actions.

Peyton fought to extricate herself and I growled low and menacing, wrapping the long strands of her midnight hair around my fist before plunging inside her. I released a sharp howl when she cried out in pleasure. I took control from my wolf again, but we battled it out even as we took Peyton fiercely, forcing her closer and closer to climax no matter how hard she fought it.

"You come when I tell you to, baby," I ordered.

She threw me a mutinous glare, but then her eyes rolled back into her head and she cried out in ecstasy. When she reached the pinnacle and tipped over the edge, I yanked her back against me and sank my teeth into her shoulder. She screamed in rapture and my orgasm detonated, taking me to a level of ecstasy that I'd never experienced before.

As we spiraled down to reality, my wolf finally retreated, satisfied with our actions, and I hastily removed my fangs from her flesh. Peyton tried to move away, but I held her tightly as I stared at the mark I'd created. To my surprise, I felt no regret at breaking my rule…in fact, the idea of it remaining there appealed to me. Not that I was in any way interested in keeping Peyton, but seeing the mark proved that I'd gained a certain level of submission from her. I chalked it up to male pride and all that shit. Besides, with Peyton being a lone shifter and my ambivalence to the idea of a mate, I had no doubt that she wouldn't accept the mark and start the mating process.

"I can't believe you bit me," Peyton snarled.

A wicked grin split my face and I released her, allowing her to scramble away and stand. "Don't pretend it didn't get you off even harder, baby."

Peyton growled, but I smelled the spicy aroma of her arousal. She stomped to the bed and bent down to snatch my clothes off the floor, then tossed them at me.

My eyes narrowed with warning and she met them without a shred of alarm. As a powerful Alpha, it was rare for anyone to stand up to me, and even more rare for someone to stand before me without even the smallest amount of fear. It was incredibly hot, but it also pricked at the darker desires inside me. I wanted *her* to fear me, to bow for her Alpha. In the light of day, she had no pack and therefore no one to answer to. But for this one night, I would own her, make her beg, make her crawl.

CHAPTER THREE

PEYTON

"Damn," I muttered the next morning when my body protested as I tried to move over in bed to avoid the sunlight streaming through the window. I kept myself in peak condition, but I'd used muscles I didn't even know I had the night before. My lips curled up at the memories of some seriously hot fucking.

Nathan was a bastard, but he sure as hell knew what to do in the bedroom. I'd been livid at his forced submission and yet I'd let him dominate me over and over without killing him afterward because…he'd been right. *The jerk.*

I craved it, but only if the male had earned the right. And he had. Although I'd never given in completely and Nathan had only pushed to a certain point, seeming to respect my hard limits.

Speak of the devil.

I smelled his delicious scent, a mixture of woodsy and spicy. Then a thick, muscular arm curled around me and dragged me back, plastering me up against a hard body. My panther purred and stretched contentedly.

"Last night was hot as fuck, Peyton," Nathan grunted before

turning my head by the chin and taking my mouth in a deep, hungry kiss.

"I agree. But you're still an asshole."

A low chuckle vibrated in his chest. "Let's see if I can change your mind."

Two hours later, I lay in my bed practically boneless and completely satisfied, with my opinion of him somewhat altered. My panther hadn't needed convincing as she hadn't agreed with my assessment of him in the first place. She poked me with her nose in an "I told you so" kind of way, but I was too blissed out to care.

He'd proven he could go soft and slow, but he'd still tortured me before allowing me to come. I couldn't totally blame him, though, because it meant a harder climax when he finally gave me what I needed.

Nathan appeared at the side of the bed, showered and fully dressed; his long honey-colored strands once again pulled up into a man-bun. It still surprised me that I found it so damn sexy on him. He bent over me and pressed his fists into the mattress on both sides of my head. "I need to go. I have work to do, then I'm headed home."

I nodded and neither of us asked or offered more information.

"Thanks for last night," I murmured when he leaned down to kiss me.

"My pleasure." When he pulled back, he stared at me for a minute, his silver eyes contemplating. Then they cleared and he gave me a chin lift. "Maybe I'll see you around sometime. If you're ever in town again, Sam knows how to get in touch with me."

My brow creeped up in surprise. I'd never had a repeat performance, mostly because I moved around so much. But breaking that streak with Nathan didn't sound like such a bad idea. Something else to anticipate the next time I visited Sam and Linette. My panther picked up on the vibe between us and she preened as if it would convince him to come back.

"Maybe," I conceded with a smirk.

He planted one last hard kiss on my mouth then strode from the room and, after a minute, I heard my front door closing.

I smiled and rolled over in bed, stretching my sore muscles as I checked the clock. Just after eight, which meant I had some time to rest. Spent, I snuggled into my covers and pillow until I was super comfy and fell back asleep.

My alarm went off a couple of hours later and I sighed, feeling no less tired and worn out after my nap. I practically peeled my eyelids back before climbing out of bed and stumbling to the bathroom. My panther snarled at being woken up, then curled up and pouted. *Such a diva.*

The woman staring back at me in the mirror was a hot mess. And yet the corners of my mouth were tilted up because I looked like I'd been thoroughly fucked. Bed head, swollen lips, and—I raised a brow—a bite mark on my neck. I'd forgotten about that. I knew I should be pissed about it, but honestly, it was kind of hot.

However, my nose wrinkled at the smell of alcohol, sweat, and sex that clung to me. Probably should have showered before I jumped his bones. *Not that he had any objections last night,* I thought smugly.

I trudged to the shower and twisted the handle to start the spray, then stepped under it without waiting for it to warm up. A shriek escaped when the icy water pelted me, but it did as I intended and jolted me awake. It warmed up quickly and I took my time washing, shaking my head at the increased sensitivity of my breasts. Unusual after-effect of sex, but Nathan had certainly given them plenty of attention last night.

Once I'd finished, I shut off the faucet and slid the shower curtain open before pulling my towel off the rack. Wrapping it around me, I stepped out onto the bathmat, but had to put my hand on the wall to steady myself when a wave of dizziness hit me. My panther yipped and shook her head, trying to find her equilibrium as well. Then my stomach lurched, and I dropped to the ground in front of the toilet just in time to lose what little food was in my stomach. I dry-heaved for another couple of minutes before falling onto my butt and leaning against the cool, tiled wall. The towel had pooled at my feet and I leaned slightly forward—so I wouldn't aggravate my stomach—and used two fingers to catch hold of it and drag it to me. My face dropped into the damp fabric for a moment before I used it to wipe away the beads of moisture that had formed on my forehead.

What the hell is happening? Shifters weren't susceptible to bacteria or viral infections. The towel fell into my lap as I considered my circumstances. I closed my eyes and slowly inhaled, trying to relax and think rationally. *There has to be a reasonable explanation*—My thought process halted, and I drew in another deep breath. When the scent that had given me pause hit me again, my head reared back, slamming into the wall the way reality had just slammed into me.

My scent had changed.

No. *No, no, no. It's not a full moon!*

But there was no mistaking it.

I smelled pregnant.

It can't be. Right?

My panther was effervescing with joy at the idea while I sucked in lungfuls of air and tried not to panic.

The nausea had passed, so I carefully stood and made my way into the single bedroom in my compact apartment. I went straight to the nightstand and grabbed my phone. After opening a web browser, I searched for the exact time the full moon had risen. People always assumed it happened at night, but in reality, the moon rose at different times every month, even in the morning. The sun just kept us from seeing it until night. And somehow, I'd forgotten all about it the night before.

6:52 AM.

Shit. Shit, shit, shit!

How could I be so damn stupid?

I groaned and collapsed onto the bed, immediately rolling over and burying my face in my pillow. I usually kicked guys out after we burned up the sheets—mainly because I liked to sleep like a starfish and take up the whole bed.

But I'd forgotten all about it with Nathan and had even indulged in morning sex before he left.

And where's that landed me?

Knocked up by a random, a hot-as-fuck shifter I'd probably never see again.

CHAPTER FOUR

NATHAN

Though my wolf hadn't been very happy to leave a gorgeous, naked Peyton behind, I was unusually relaxed as I strode into my office at the Council headquarters and went straight to the large desk on the opposite wall from the entrance. The room was full of glossy oak from the desk to the chairs and bookshelves. It had all been handcrafted by a packmate, and friend, Jax, and he'd given each piece the kind of character that made it seem older. It gave the room a rustic feel and reminded me of my cabin in Silver Lake. I hated the city, so this little pocket of home helped me focus on the work that needed to be done whenever I was required to be here in person.

After dropping into my brown leather chair, I rifled through the messages my assistant, Willa, had left for me. One in particular made me smile, though this one was on a different stationery with someone else's handwriting.

It contained a chess move. Chuckling, I stood and walked to a small table set between two chairs. A beautiful, wooden chess set sat on top. Each piece had been meticulously carved, and the edge of the board had wolves running in packs carved all around it. It was the second chess set that Jax had made for me, as the first had disappeared one day, with the exception of a single pawn. The next time I'd arrived at HQ after Jax had delivered the replacement set, I'd found one of my new pawns missing and a note with a chess move.

I adjusted the board, the opponent's bishop displacing one of my pawns, and deliberated as I stared at the board. Before I could make a decision, a knock on my door drew my attention.

"Enter."

Willa pushed open one of the double doors and came inside carrying a stack of folders. "Still playing with your ghost?" she asked, her golden eyes twinkling. They stood out against her dark complexion and jet-black hair.

Willa was only half shifter since her mother was a witch, but she'd inherited traits from both of her parents. She also had a great sense of humor, which boded well for her since her animal was a black cat. She'd heard no shortage of jokes about the witch who shifted into a black cat.

"Always," I replied. Only Tanner, my Beta, Asher, my head enforcer, and I knew the identity of my otherworldly opponent, but Willa liked to refer to him as a ghost since the notes seemed to just appear out of nowhere. He'd even made the moves himself from time to time, always when no-one was here to see him.

I moved one of my knights into position, then returned to my desk just in time for her to drop the pile right in front of me.

"These are the ones you asked for," she informed me before leaving me to my work.

Grunting, I flipped through them and the aftereffects of morning sex quickly wore off, causing my mood to go to shit. Sensing the change, my wolf perked up, on alert for danger.

When he didn't find anything except Willa, he flopped back down and went to sleep.

The packets contained the information for possible packs, covens, and other supernatural groups that might be responsible for the disappearance of a Council member. Beau, a tiger shifter from a streak in Chile—who sat on the SCA and ISC—reportedly hadn't arrived home after our last meeting.

He'd been an unbiased, level-headed voice and while there were other options, my gut told me he'd been snatched or killed to keep his voice out of Council decisions.

Unlike vampires and fae, witches and shifters didn't have royalty. The SC consisted entirely of shifters that oversaw all packs within a designated territory—the term "pack" was used to encompass all shifter breeds for the sake of expediency. Our main purpose was advising on pack business and mediating situations to avoid escalations. However, even if the packs chose to go to war, we didn't step in unless rules were violated.

The ISC however, was a group of representatives from most supernatural races, and a few humans. It was created to keep the peace between the different species, and to protect the secret of our existence.

Trouble had been brewing a little hotter lately, both within the packs—who'd been squabbling like spoiled children—and within the other species' ranks. And there'd been more discord than usual among the members of the SCA and ISC.

The whole situation gave me a headache, but as the head of both Councils, I had obligations to fulfill. Besides, having lived through and fought in countless wars, rebellions, uprisings, and many other conflicts, I was well equipped to deal with all the bullshit, as well as legitimate issues.

The fact that I ran a well-known security company, King Black Ops Consulting, or KBO, didn't hurt either. We also had a division that developed new technology for weapons and protective gear. My contacts extended farther than most people believed possible.

I set the stack aside and worked for another couple of hours before buzzing Willa's intercom.

When she came into the office, I separated two folders and handed them to her. "I need to get home and back to work, but I want to meet with those two first. Later this week. We can do it via teleconference, but I want them on HQ premises when it happens. I just need a couple of days to run a more thorough sweep on them at KBO. I'll take the rest with me and we can work our way through the pile,"

"Got it." Willa nodded and took the proffered folders, then pivoted on her heel and glided across the room. She exited into our waiting area and turned left to head to her office, which was two doors down from mine.

Wandering over to the chessboard, I stared at the configuration while deep in thought. Finally, I returned to my desk and scribbled a note before gathering my things. On my way out the door, I dropped the note onto the table by the game.

Walking to the parking lot, my mind drifted back to my time with Peyton and one corner of my mouth inched up. Last night —and this morning—had been seriously hot. The best sex I'd ever had. In another world, I might have chased her sexy ass until she agreed to be my mate. But despite our compatibility in bed, our personalities clashed. Still, she'd been on the periphery of my mind all day. My wolf pushed at me, wanting more of her. Something about her was sticking with us, but I didn't know what.

CHAPTER 4

"TANNER," I greeted my Beta as I opened the front door to my house. I'd been on my way to the kitchen when I'd spotted him coming up the stonework steps and went to meet him at the door.

"Alpha. Welcome back."

I grunted and stepped aside to allow him to enter. He waited while I shut the door, then followed me to the large, open kitchen where I tossed him a beer from the refrigerator. As I popped the top of my bottle and took a swig, I studied Tanner. He was almost as tall as me, but that was where any similarities ended. His short black hair, dark brown eyes, and muscular—but not bulky—build were pretty much my complete opposite. However, we meshed well as Alpha and Beta, and also as friends.

At that moment, he looked agitated, though I doubted most would've picked up on it. I didn't need to tap into his mind to tell, either. I was very good at reading people, an ability that had served me well in my lifetime. I preferred not to dig around in the minds of my pack, giving them their privacy, just as I had mine. I mostly used it to communicate with my enforcers, though there were times when it became necessary to use it in other ways.

I motioned for Tanner to follow me once more and led him to the side of the cabin that housed my home office. He sat on a couch that faced my desk—one of two in the room because I often had long meetings, particularly with my enforcers. There were also a couple of comfortable leather chairs and I dropped into one of those. I took another drink and lifted a foot to rest the ankle on the opposite knee. I held my bottle on the bent leg and scrutinized my Beta.

"Report." I'd only been gone three days, but I still liked to keep on top of anything I might have missed.

"Nothing new in the pack. But there's been some chatter about issues between the Castile and Rossberg packs again."

"What's that asshole up to now?" I growled.

Xavier Castile had been a pain in the ass since he became the pack Alpha at twenty. Sixty-five years and he'd only become more of a problem. I'd never liked him as a person, but he'd gone off the fucking deep end a little over thirty years ago when his daughter, and only child, had died. I'd heard it was during childbirth, but there were no reports of a grandchild and he'd never confirmed one way or the other. Just the mention of the Castile pack sent my wolf into a fit of growling and gnashing his teeth. He'd wanted a bite out of the son of a bitch for a long time. I placated him with the promise that we'd get our claws in him eventually.

"His usual bullshit." Tanner downed the rest of his beer and set the bottle on a table next to the couch. "Mainly border disputes. You know how power hungry he is. However, my sources tell me that a few more packs in the area have lost members to 'hunting accidents'."

My brow furrowed as I absorbed the information. Reports of shifters being killed by hunters were not new to me, especially when said shifters resided in areas like the South where the activity thrived. Upstate New York didn't exactly have a plethora of places for hunting, nor was it a big sport here. It did happen sporadically, but there had been at least ten in the last four months, which was double the amount we'd ever had in a single year. The majority had been members of packs that were within miles of the Castile wolves. My gut told me Xavier was involved, but so far, I'd been unable to link him to the incidents in any way other than proximity.

The Castile pack had built a reputation for their prejudice and overly harsh punishments by the Alpha. Around twenty years ago, word had reached me about a child who'd been treated as an outcast within the pack. I would have attempted to step in, but by the time I heard about it, the kid had vanished. Once again, no one would confirm or deny the child's existence. I'd dug around, but the trail had been so thoroughly swept away that even my best people hadn't managed to pick up on it. After that, I'd kept a much closer eye on the Alpha and his pack members. Unfortunately, I hadn't been able to justify ridding the world of Xavier. *Yet.*

He was exactly the type of scum I spent my life trying to destroy. My wolf approved wholeheartedly, brushing his fur against my skin in solidarity.

I'd grown up in privilege, my father being *dvoryanstvo*—Russian nobility. But he'd taught me to be open-minded, to see all people as my equal, and to fight for those who faced injustice.

My activities in the pursuit of freedom for the oppressed had eventually driven us from our home and country to settle in upstate New York and establish the Silver Lake Pack. It hadn't stopped me, though. Even the nearly fatal wound that had left me with the scar on my arm hadn't been able to stop me from fighting. Over the years, I'd continued to protect and defend—establishing KBO had a great deal to do with my desire to right the wrongs of the world. When I'd taken over from my father as Alpha, it had given me the tools I needed to continue working toward a higher cause without abandoning my pack. I'd developed my own moral compass along the way, and sometimes fighting for justice meant crossing lines. I had plenty of blood on my hands, but it hadn't been spilt arbitrarily. I never did things on impulse, so, although each incident stained my soul a little more, I had no regrets.

Peyton filtered through my mind again as I swallowed down the rest of my beer. But I moved on from thoughts of her when Tanner brought up KBO business. He'd been with me from the beginning and held the position of COO. There was no one I trusted more to lead both the pack and the company whenever I was needed elsewhere.

"I emailed you the dossiers of some possible recruits," Tanner started. "As well as for the IT position we need filled." The Information Technology department was the label we gave to our computer specialists—or hackers.

I grunted as I stood and rounded my desk to sit down, setting my empty bottle off to the side. Finding new recruits was a task I actually enjoyed. However, finding a replacement for our best hacker—who'd retired at the ripe old age of twenty-five—had been impossible. Not one of the candidates had even been able to break through the KBO firewall. We'd put out feelers on the dark web, but so far, none of the cyberpunks were willing to tie themselves to one company.

I opened the files on my computer and we began to go through them one by one, but were interrupted by my phone vibrating in my pocket. I dug it out and glanced at the screen, not at all happy to see the name Dana Klimmer on the screen. The Assistant Chief Medical Examiner of New York never called with good news. My wolf rumbled and pushed against me, picking up on the darkening of my mood.

Though most humans were unaware of our existence, the ones on the ISC had established relationships with some high-ranking officials in major cities and the federal government to make sure it stayed that way. Dana's boss happened to be one of them and since Dana was a wolf shifter, supernatural cases were handed off to her.

"Dana," I answered in a neutral tone.

She sighed. "Do you always have to sound like you just received a terminal diagnosis when I call?"

One corner of my mouth kicked up. "When you call me

with positive news, perhaps I'll answer the phone with glee next time."

Dana snorted. "I'm surprised you even know the word 'glee,' Nathan. I doubt you'd know it if you felt it."

I shrugged even though she couldn't see it, but Tanner chuckled, his shifter hearing picking up on the whole conversation. "If it ever happens, I'll be sure to text you so you can call and hear me answer with—never mind." I cut myself off because the idea of me experiencing "glee" was ridiculous. "Moving on, what's happening?"

"Another body came in this afternoon, a woman. Same MO as the last four, and right on schedule. I'm officially labeling this guy a serial killer."

Dana had called me four months ago, concerned about a potential pattern after a third murder victim had shown up with the same wounds and within a similar window of time—four to six weeks between each. They were all shifters and they'd all been clawed so deeply that even their enhanced healing hadn't been able to save them before they bled out.

Their sexual organs had been particularly mangled—though this was done postmortem—and their other wounds had matched as well; tongues removed, clothes discarded, and while there was never any sign of sexual assault, they'd found semen on the bodies—men and women alike. Despite the excess of evidence, they couldn't match the DNA to anyone in the system, so all we knew about the killer was his gender.

The only reason she had hesitated to label him a serial killer prior to this murder was because she hadn't seen a pattern in the victims' appearances. But after the first five, it became clear that there was, in fact, a connection. All of the women were blonde, and the men were dark-haired. They were all mid-thirties and extremely healthy. However, these links still didn't shed enough light on the killer's motivation or any other clues that would give us a place to start digging into his possible background and identity.

Because the targets had all been shifters, I'd agreed to give her access to some KBO resources, but without more to go on, and no highly-skilled hackers on my payroll, there hadn't been much we could do. We needed to collect more data, so we'd started digging into the victim's lives, trying to find similarities between them, but we hadn't discovered any further threads that tied them all together.

I hated that the motherfucker had struck again because I hadn't been able to stop him. "Send me everything you have on her and the location where she was found."

"Already done," she replied. "I was just calling to give you a heads up."

"Thanks." We hung up and I tossed my phone down with an angry snarl. I hated when things were beyond my control.

"You think your chess buddy would help us out?" Tanner asked suddenly.

I contemplated his question, then shook my head. "He's dealing with enough bullshit in his part of the universe."

Tanner ran a hand through his hair and raised his eyes to the ceiling as he thought for a moment before returning his gaze to my face. "What about the witch?"

I frowned, thinking about Sapphire, the confusing witch who talked in riddles and seemed to live in the clouds. One of my old friends, Jean-Marc de la Croix—a spy and member of the French vampire royal family, the *Monarchie du Sang*—had had dealings with her in the past. He did his best to stay away from her because she drove him fucking crazy. However, I'd met her when Marc teamed up with Makayla, a member of my pack who used to work for KBO before going freelance, to help him rescue Sapphire. I'd understood his frustration with the blue-haired witch immediately.

Before I could answer Tanner, my doorbell rang, and I scowled at being interrupted yet again. Grumbling, I stalked to the front door and yanked it open.

"Well, speak of the she-devil," I drawled at my unexpected visitor.

CHAPTER FIVE

NATHAN

When I opened the door, I had to look down, *way down*, to see the pixie of a woman with long, flowing blue hair and a dreamy expression on her face standing on my porch.

"Sapphire."

"Hmm?" She blinked big blue eyes at me that were the same color as her hair. Then she tilted her head to the side, her expression one of wonder. "Oh, right." She shook her head. "Two seconds early. How strange. I should learn to count better. Or maybe your steps are… too long." She glanced down, then shrugged. "But yes, yes, I'll come in," she said airily as she slipped between me and the doorway to step inside.

Narrowing my eyes, I shored up my reserves of patience, which were always necessary when dealing with a woman who lived in a universe of her own making and spoke in riddles. I shut the door and followed her as she wandered into my living room. She made herself comfortable in my favorite recliner and I chose to stand by the large fireplace across from her.

"Isn't this a twist of fate?" I drawled, slipping into my

native Russian, aware that she could understand it and about a dozen other languages. I used the phrase about *fate* to needle her because as a seer, Sapphire knew a great deal about the future—and had a penchant for meddling in it. Something my oldest friend, Dimitri Ivanov, muttered about from time to time when we spoke.

It was my understanding that they had struck a deal, though I didn't know the particulars. Just that he was using her to help with his plan to regain his rightful place as the king of the Royal Vampire Dynasty—which ruled over the vampires in Eastern Europe. I'd only interacted with her a handful of times, but it didn't take more than a few words from this enigma to understand Dimitri and Marc's frustration with the little witch.

"Twist of fate?" She considered the term. "I prefer to think of them as crossed, not twisted. Although your fate might be a little unexpected. Rawr."

I frowned, unhappy with her implication. My voice was low and dark when I growled, "Don't even think about—"

She interjected with a tsk. "You're the one who brought up fate, Alpha. Such a foolish thing to say to a foreseer, hmm? But the crossing isn't related to you. Someone like you, perhaps. Stubborn. Strong. Although I do think you handle news quite differently." Her gaze took on a faraway gleam as she nodded. "Yes, differently indeed. By the way, how do you feel about children?"

I ignored her question as I knew better than to encourage her predictions. I simply crossed my arms over my chest and stared at her, patiently waiting for her to get to the purpose for her visit. If I knew anything about this little witch, it was that she took her own damn time coming to a point and no one else's.

She smiled after a beat. "Yes, I do believe you'll be fine."

She fished in one pocket of her dress, then another, then a third before her expression lit up with triumph. She held up an amulet with a large, dark red stone in the center. "For you."

Raising an eyebrow, I leaned back against the mantel, then grunted, "Not really my style." Neither was the one with the topaz stone that I kept locked in a safe at the Council HQ and very rarely used. They opened up a network of portals throughout our universe, as well as ones that would take the wearer to another realm—the one my chess set had likely disappeared into.

A tinkling of laughter drifted from her mouth. It reminded me of a wind-chime, pretty and a little bewitching. "Consider it a good-luck token for your next game of chess. You're going to need it to save your Bishop."

I tensed and my wolf brushed under my skin, suddenly alert. Madame Bishop—the code name for one of my former operatives, and Asher's sister—Makayla Laurier. She'd gone freelance a couple of years ago thanks to Marc—who'd become her mentor when he stole her from my ranks. I still hadn't completely forgiven him for that. However, as her Alpha, I kept tabs on her. Usually using my otherworldly chess opponent, Jude, whom Sapphire had referred to as The Rook. As of the last mission Makayla had accepted, he would know better than I where to find her. The pack link only extended so far, and since Makayla had traversed realms—something I only did when absolutely necessary—I relied on him for updates. Her brother Asher would be up my ass about it if I didn't assure him of her safety regularly.

My brow furrowed in concern. "Has Makayla's ring stopped working?" Like the amulet Sapphire had brought to me, Makayla's ring held a bewitched jewel that allowed her to use the portals to travel from our universe to the other. If something interfered with the ring's enchantment, it could lead to Makayla being stranded in the other realm.

Sapphire waved her hand in a fluttery motion. "Depends on your definition of functionality. But I would get this to her sooner rather than later. Perhaps use it yourself for a visit in, say, four weeks' time?" She glanced down at my legs again. "Maybe three weeks instead. You move faster than you should. Of course, I think she'll like that quite a bit about you."

I almost asked who would like it but bit my tongue at the last second. Even if she did answer me, it would just be more incomprehensible gibberish that I was too tired to try and translate. A low growl of frustration resonated in my chest. "Why exactly do you need me to deliver it for you, *malen'kaya ved'ma?*" I asked the little witch tiredly.

I pulled off the elastic band holding my hair up and let it down, hoping it would stave off my building headache. I hadn't slept much the night before—not that I had any complaints about it—and it had been a long fucking day. "I don't have time to play your games. If you're not here to help with—"

"I'm always here to help," she chirped with a mischievous grin. "I'm quite fond of your Bishop, as you know. Perhaps talk to the other chessmaster soon? He might have details about your next play."

"Jude." I clarified, referring to my constant "opponent."

"Jude, who?" she asked with an innocent blink, dangling the amulet. "Trust me, or don't, but you will need this, Alpha."

I held out my hand and she dropped the amulet into my palm with a pleased smile. Closing my fingers around it, I frowned when it felt different from the others I'd encountered. I briefly considered the idea that Sapphire might have a sinister purpose, but Dimitri trusted her and that was no easy feat, so it was good enough for me.

"I'll be back in the city in a week," I informed her. If she asked me to make a special trip, it was possible I'd wring her neck.

"Might I suggest moving the Rook to E5?" she suggested.

Another reference to Jude, the director of E.V.I.E. I narrowed my gaze. "How do you know the positions of the pieces on my chessboard?"

She blinked again, that damn innocent expression on display once more. "What chessboard?"

"Alpha."

I turned to see Tanner strolling out of my office, his expression filled with annoyance. "I need to deal with some bullshit at KBO. One of the techs hacked into the wrong server and created a fucking mess."

"Do you need help cleaning it up?" I asked in English.

All of the employees in our internet division were highly talented, or they wouldn't work for KBO. But none of them were at a level that didn't require supervision and more training. Tanner and I were only people in the company with the necessary skills to run the IT department, but we were too fucking busy running the whole damn business.

He jerked his thumb back toward the door he'd exited. "Just take a look at those candidates so I don't have to babysit the toddlers anymore."

I nodded and he lifted his chin in farewell before leaving out the kitchen door. "I need a vacation," I groused as I swung my focus back to—no-one. The place where Sapphire had been sitting was empty and I knew from previous experience that I wouldn't find her anywhere if I went searching.

Muttering a curse, I pressed my fingers to my temples and rubbed in circles, loosening some of the tension. I needed a shower and some sleep, but with Tanner busy at KBO, I had pack issues to handle.

After meeting with my head enforcer to assess his current

trainees, I dealt with a property dispute between two pack mates, checked in with the security team assigned to town safety and monitoring human activity, as well as completing a few other duties. By the time I showered and crawled naked into my large, comfortable bed, it was close to one in the morning.

I PICKED up the pawn that didn't quite match my chess set and placed it on a specific square on the board before returning to my desk and settling in to go over reports from Council members. A meeting was scheduled for the afternoon and I had plans to meet up with Asher and Jax for a drink that night.

It took about two hours, but finally, the pawn fell to its side and a portal opened up in the wall. A tall man in a custom-tailored suit and Italian loafers strolled through it. His lips were pursed, as they always were when he was stressed, causing slight wrinkles on his forehead and lines around his mouth. He had short, dark hair, a close-cropped Van Dyke, and intense brown eyes that were always assessing his surroundings. Makayla called him debonair.

He appeared to be in his early forties. However, his actual age was a mystery, even to me, and I'd known him a long, long time—in many shapes and names. He'd spent lives in both realms, but the other world most often, as he did now. I had a feeling he would be sticking with his current identity indefinitely.

He'd worked his way through the ranks of a slayer organization known as Eliminate Vampiric Influences Everywhere, or E.V.I.E. Now he ran the place, which came in very handy for me at times. We'd also traded favors here and there. Although, his price usually included a peek at whatever technology we were developing at KBO.

"Jude," I greeted as I leaned back in my chair with a smirk.

His mouth curled down into a deeper frown, a rare show of emotion for my cool, collected friend. Jude hated being summoned as much as I did and if it weren't for the chess pieces—Jude being the jackass who'd stolen the first set without permission—I doubted we'd get anything done because neither of us would capitulate. For that reason, we'd set up the pawns as a truce and agreed that if I sent the signal, he would come to me and vice versa. It didn't stop us from testing each other though, hence the two-hour wait for him to appear.

I gestured for him to take a seat in front of my desk, but he just folded his arms and watched me with narrowed eyes. It didn't bother me whether he stood or sat, so I just shrugged and got down to business.

"Sapphire paid me a visit," I told him as I reached into my shirt and pulled out the amulet before drawing the chain over my head.

Jude's cheek creased slightly, and his brown eyes glittered with amusement. I didn't think he'd met the perplexing witch, but he'd heard about her from Makayla and Marc.

Nobody despised Sapphire more than Marc, but he'd still saved her ass on multiple occasions and every time she ran him in circles. I watched with satisfaction because it served him fucking right for poaching Makayla from me.

"She asked me to pass this along to Makayla. I assume you're aware of the job she took in your universe."

Jude gave me a dry look and I grinned because I'd succeeded in getting a reaction from him. Nothing happened in "his city" that he didn't know about. It was arrogant, but true.

"I'm not your errand boy, Nathan," he said smoothly. "However, it just so happens that her mate"—my eyebrows shot up at that—"and I have some business, so I'll be sure to take care of it."

"Mate?"

"Her story to tell," he replied.

I wouldn't get anything out of him that he didn't want to share, so I let it go. I stood and walked over to hand him the enchanted necklace. "Thanks."

He nodded, then glanced at the chessboard and snatched up the pawn before replacing it on the square from where I'd taken it to draw him here. He moved one of his knights, captured a rook, then tsked as he shook his head. "Checkmate. So quickly, Nathan? Your game is slipping."

"I believe it was you who lost the last two games," I deadpanned.

"Hmmm. But I put up a good fight."

I didn't bother replying to his comment and switched subjects. "Let me know if Makayla needs anything."

We shook hands, and he disappeared into the portal.

It wasn't until I sat back at my desk that I noticed I was short a rook. "Asshole," I muttered, shaking my head. Taking the piece was his way of telling me to come to him next time.

I went back to work and attended my meeting in the afternoon, emerging incredibly frustrated because tensions were growing high between supernats. Whenthat happened, it risked exposing us to humans. I also felt something stirring. It had been gaining strength lately, but I had no clue what was causing the unsettling feeling. Perhaps I'd be able to relax while having drinks with Asher and Jax. My mind wandered from there to Peyton, and I wondered if she would be working tonight. Another night in her bed would definitely give me a reprieve from reality.

A knock on my door drew my attention and I called for them to enter.

Willa stuck her head in. "You might want to deal with something in the lobby."

I frowned. I'd given a directive not to disturb me and to tell anyone who asked, other than Jax or Asher, that I'd left for the day. "Security can't handle it?"

"Trust my intuition, boss," Willa stated. It was not a request.

I did trust her instincts, so I tossed my pen onto my desktop before pushing my chair back and standing. Willa's head disappeared, but she was waiting for me when I reached the elevator. "Want to explain this to me?" I asked.

"You'll see," she said with a shake of her head.

When the doors opened to the lobby of the building, I immediately understood Willa's insistence.

Marley, one of my security guards, was being talked at—not to—by a girl with long silvery lavender hair, her hands moving agitatedly while she spoke. Though I doubted most could see it, she had a faint purple shimmer around her that told me she was a witch, but I sensed her magic was tightly leashed. Her body was small, but her black clothes didn't hide the fact that she was toned and muscular, or that she was actually a woman, not a girl. A very small woman, particularly to someone as big as me because she had to be at least a foot and a half shorter than my six-foot-five height. However, she carried herself with a confident air and pulsed with power. The combination almost made her petite stature easy to forget. And my instincts told me she would be deadly in the right circumstances. She practically vibrated with pent-up energy, and if the witch let go of her tightly leashed control, I didn't want her attention directed at Marley.

As I approached, Marley flinched under the witch's hard

glare. Damn, one of my toughest, most badass employees flinched under the stare of this tiny ball of fire.

Marley's voice held some hesitancy as she told her, "I'm sorry, but you can't just demand a meeting with Nathan King. You don't have an appointment, and even if he were here—"

"*Ne pizdi*," the purple-haired witch snapped in an accusatory tone.

Her use of a Russian expletive, with a clearly native accent, intrigued me.

Apparently, Marley's confused expression clued the woman in to the fact that she'd spoken another language. "Bullshit," she snapped. "I know he's here."

Marley sputtered, and I elected to step in. I stood just behind the witch's right shoulder and said, "I'll take care of this, Marley. Just get back to work."

The pixie-sized woman spun around, and her head dropped back as far as it would go in order for her to see my face. "*Nichyevo sebe*," she breathed, her eyes—the same lavender shade as her hair—full of awe.

I raised an eyebrow at her quiet exclamation that was roughly equivalent to "wow."

She shook her head, breaking from the trance-like state and clearing her throat, all business. "Nathan King, I presume?"

"*Da, eto ya. Shto ya mogu cdyelat dlya vas?*" I responded in my native tongue, informing her that she was correct and asking what I could do for her.

Her expression turned serene in an attempt to hide her thoughts and emotions, but I could see that her smile was forced. "Can we speak in private, please?"

She attempted to keep her tone pleasant, but the demanding undercurrent had my wolf bristling, and her carefully composed mask slipped for a half-second when she saw him through my eyes. Alphas did not respond well to commands; however, I had more control over myself than my wolf.

I studied her in calculating silence, working things out in my mind, not unaware that it made her feel awkward and restless.

"It's incredibly important. Life or death," she insisted.

Finally, I ceased my contemplation of her and glanced over her shoulder, where Willa was patiently waiting. I lifted my chin at her, and she started toward us. "Willa, please show Ms. —" I broke off and raised my brow at her in question.

"Rowan."

I waited a beat for her to divulge her last name, but when it was clear she didn't intend to share it, I sighed and glanced at Willa once more. "Escort Rowan to my office, please."

After the pair walked away, I stepped up to the counter and Marley ducked her head, clearly embarrassed at having been intimidated by Rowan. "Calling me to come deal with this situation was the right move," I told her. "Next time, don't wait for Willa to step in."

Marley turned a little green and stared at me as if I were about to sentence her to death.

"Relax, Marley. I'm not disciplining or firing you. I'm telling you this to help you the next time you find yourself in a situation like this. That witch is incredibly powerful, and I suspect a little unstable. Not someone I want my staff trying to handle. I expect you to learn from this and take the correct steps in the future." My tone wasn't harsh, but it was firm. I understood that people made mistakes, but I had no tolerance if they didn't learn from them.

Marley's muscles seemed to uncoil, and she nodded, her face awash with relief. "Thank you, sir."

"Jax should be here in a few minutes. Tell him I'm running late." I rapped my knuckles on the counter and nodded before striding to the elevator to face the newest she-devil in my life. What was it with tiny witches? They all seemed to be missing a few links in their chain.

Once I was back in my office, I sat in my chair while Rowan paced the floor. She launched into an explanation of a vampire she was hunting. It seemed this Dorian had been targeting witches in search of something or someone only they could give him.

She startled me when she claimed to work for E.V.I.E., but I remained quiet and gave nothing away in my demeanor or expression.

Then she brought up the subject of the amulets and—assuming I had no knowledge of the bespelled stones—gave me a summary of their abilities. She glossed over a lot, but with what I already knew, I filled in the blanks. Then she mentioned Dorian being connected to a Russian slayer bloodline, confirming my suspicions about her.

The way this little witch danced around her history, the slight Russian accent, and her knowledge of the amulets hinted that she might possess the power to create them.

Until the latter half of this century, these amulets had been nearly impossible to acquire. They'd been created only for vampire slayers—ones who'd been born from the right bloodlines. Not all witches had the ability to create them, and the ones who could came from certain bloodlines, just like the slayers.

Recently, the witches who created them had found ways to make them for most anyone, adding in new spells and enchantments to suit their situation, even turning them into jewelry other than amulets, such as Makayla's ring.

Although, from Rowan's explanation, it sounded as though she was unaware that they had evolved. While the amulets didn't give the wearer all the abilities they would for a slayer, they could be used by anyone to travel through portals, and they gave the wearer immortality.

Something about her was rolling around in the back of my brain, but I couldn't place it, and until I could, I would play things close to the vest. I kept my knowledge of portals and amulets to myself, wanting to speak with Jude about her before divulging anything.

However, E.V.I.E. slayer or not, she needed help tracking down her target and trying to figure out how he'd been able to evade her for so long.

I was willing to do so, but she hadn't yet explained exactly what she needed from the ISC.

I waited until she appeared to be finished, then rested my elbows on the arms of my chair and steepled my fingers. "And how exactly were you hoping we could help?"

"I'm assuming you have contacts all over within the supernatural world."

I nodded but stayed silent as I waited for her to make her point.

She stopped pacing and stood in front of my desk with her hands on her hips as she glared at me in exasperation.

I almost smiled. She certainly had a big presence for such a small thing.

"I would think you'd be just as interested in ridding the world of this psycho as I am," she huffed. "I mean, it could be shifters next. And I happened to notice you own a worldwide security company. You could tap into those resources as well."

I continued to study her before finally responding. "You have a point," I conceded. "What you're saying sounds rather improbable, but better to be safe than sorry." I doubted my resources were the help she needed, but I would do some digging for her anyway.

I stroked my beard and leaned back in my seat. The amulets

were created by witches, so it seemed like that avenue would yield the most help. "You know, your best bet would be to go to the head of the Witch Council with this," I suggested. They were located near Russia, and taking her heritage into account, it surprised me that she didn't already have a contact on the Council. Then again, she'd been residing in another realm for a long time.

She stiffened for a fraction of a second before dissolving into a relaxed, easy state. Her ability to hide her thoughts and emotions behind a mask of serenity was impressive. "Maybe I'll do that," she replied with a noncommittal shrug.

"Alright," I agreed as I stood. "While I'm not confident that I'll be able to find out anything that you wouldn't learn faster from them, I'll look into it."

"Thank you."

"Of course." A thought occurred to me. If this vampire was using NYC portals, perhaps the king of the *Monarchie du Sang* —the French vampire dynasty—would be able to help her in her search. Despite living in France the majority of the time, Lucien owned a nightclub in the city—The Crimson *Calice*. His brother Phillipé resided here most of the time though, and nothing happened in this city without their knowledge. Still… she was a slayer, so I didn't know how she'd react to my suggestion. "Have you thought about reaching out to the vampires here in New York?" I asked, being deliberately vague.

Panic flared in her eyes for a moment before it disappeared behind her wall. "I'd rather not deal with any more of the living dead than is strictly necessary." She smiled sweetly—not fooling me for a second—and added, "'Strictly necessary' being the equivalent of a stake to the heart."

My eyebrows rose as I fought not to smile. I'd never met anyone quite like this witch. I stroked my beard again, continuing to assess her. "You are very unique, Rowan."

She tossed her head and flicked her long, purple hair over her shoulder, then smiled and winked. "You bet your ass, baby. There's no one like me."

"So I've noticed," I said with a chuckle. "Come on, I'll walk you down. I'm meeting a friend for a drink."

CHAPTER SIX

NATHAN

I grunted in frustration as I shoved another file aside and opened a new one, ignoring my fatigue. Tanner dropped the files off a month ago, and I still hadn't found a decent replacement for the open position at KBO. Not that I'd had an abundance of spare time.

After my meeting with Rowan, I'd met Jax in the lobby and almost had my head ripped off for holding him back when he tried to follow the witch. Until he'd made it clear that she was his true mate, at which point I'd had no choice but to let him go. I'd warned him that her situation was complicated and, from the time I'd spent with her, I had a very strong feeling that she wouldn't be very receptive to the idea of a mate. Particularly a possessive, jealous, overly protective shifter.

However, I understood his determination. Finding one's true mate was a rarity.

For our breed of shifters—born, not bitten—we didn't have "fated mates." Thankfully, because once bitten shifters met their other half, their physical desires were solely directed at their mate. The male lost the use of his equipment unless he was using it with his mate. If one rejected the other, that was it. Their lives became lonely and celibate.

Luckily, born shifters, like my pack, were given the ability to choose our mate. Even though each of us was created specifically for a "true mate", that didn't mean we would find love with them, assuming we even crossed paths with them in this giant universe. We had the ability to mate and imprint with someone else, choosing who we loved and who we fucked.

Most of the time though, when true mates met and both were single, the physical and emotional pull between them was impossible not to explore. Not that I'd had experience with it myself, but I'd seen it. My parents were true mates, and their devotion had never wavered.

I appreciated what they had between them, but I had no interest in finding a mate. I wouldn't know what the hell to do with one—other than fucking.

However, considering the evidence, I hadn't been surprised when Jax and Rowan showed up in Silver Lake a few days later, already in the early stages of the mating process. They'd brought her friend, Emerald, here to protect her from the vamp Rowan was hunting and only stayed a few days.

I'd confirmed her story and identity with Jude and continued to reach out to my contacts for any information that might help her. But I knew she was holding back a lot, and my blind spots made it harder because I didn't know exactly what to search for.

All the while we'd been developing new tech at KBO. We always were, but we'd run into some glitches on a project creating special headgear. We'd smoothed them out just in time because only a few days later, I'd received a message from Sapphire that the beacon from Makayla's new amulet had been activated.

Asher and I had loaded up and used my stone to cross

realms. We'd discovered that Makayla had been chasing down a trafficking ring but had uncovered an entire conspiracy involving experimentation on shifters in an attempt to create some kind of super-soldier. Jude had sent the signal—because the asshole had still had the amulet—when he, Makayla, and her new mate had all managed to land themselves in the hands of the enemy.

After rescuing them, I'd asked my father—the former Silver Lake Alpha—to take care of the pack so I could spend a couple of weeks in the other realm helping Jude to clean up the last of the organization. When I'd returned, I'd brought a new wolf to my pack, a broken woman who needed a fresh start. There was another reason involving Asher, but I wasn't going to interfere unless absolutely necessary.

Now I blew out a frustrated breath and ran my hands through my loose hair before twisting it up in a bun. My wolf growled and pushed against me, urging me to go for the run I'd promised him, and I acknowledged that we could both use it. A glance at my watch revealed that I had two hours until my teleconference with an Alpha in Anchorage who was also on the SC. The supernatural community was growing more restless, especially as the votes coming up split or with unexpected results increased. The missing members—now up to two—still hadn't been found. And I'd heard chatter about anti-shifter activity, though we hadn't been able to pin down who or where. It was all speculation at the moment.

Yeah, I needed a run.

A knock on my door made me scowl and my mood dipped even further when I opened it to find Tanner wearing a similar expression. "I'm going to kill him," I growled. Even without the pack link, I knew why Tanner had come. Only one person pissed him off this much lately.

"Not if I do it first," Tanner replied, his tone murderous.

"How long?"

"Lisa called me five minutes ago. She noticed the hole in the system right away, but he screwed up so thoroughly that she could only patch it while she tried to figure out exactly what he did."

"Get his ass in my office, deactivate his security badge, and wipe his computer."

I retrieved my wallet and keys from the dresser in my bedroom, then stomped out to my SUV. I drove it to KBO headquarters, housed in a plain, gray cinder block building in the middle of hundreds of acres, which the company owned to keep it isolated.

The drive only took ten minutes, but by the time I arrived, my anger had escalated to absolute fury. This was the second time that Dexter, one of our newer techs, had punched a hole in our security. The kid had a lot of potential, but he liked shortcuts. Most of them didn't cause big problems when he tried them out, but eventually one of his experiments had caused a major vulnerability to our system and it was an entire day before someone noticed because the kid hadn't even been aware that he'd done it. Of course, our most sensitive information was stored in a SCIF room that only a handful of people could access.

After that, I'd forbidden him from cutting corners and tasked the other techs to keep an eye on him, which was how Lisa had caught the mistake so fast.

Once we arrived, Tanner hauled Dexter to my office while Lisa took me through everything. She certainly hadn't been exaggerating the situation. I sent an email to the Alpha in Anchorage and rescheduled our meeting before getting to work. It took me the rest of the day and late into the night to straighten it out and fix what Dexter had broken.

When it was done, I went to deal with the punk who'd

created the problem. Tanner had already begun interrogating Dexter when I arrived to take over. By the time the kid was escorted from the building, I was confident that he hadn't been in anyone's pocket. All of my employees signed NDAs and a whole stack of other legal documents that protected the company, so I wasn't concerned about him running his mouth, but I still scared the fuck out of him. Just to be sure. And because it gave me an outlet for my aggression without killing him.

When I returned home, I debated just falling into bed and passing out, but I'd promised my wolf a run and I knew I'd feel less tense afterward, which meant I'd sleep harder. I undressed and shifted, letting my wolf take over.

CHAPTER SEVEN

PEYTON

"Are you sure you should be here?" Sam asked, eyeing me disapprovingly.

I frowned right back at him and snapped, "I'm sure. Now stop treating me like a fucking invalid." Four weeks of Sam babying me had made me extra irritable.

Sam merely rolled his eyes at my outburst, used to the moods of a pregnant shifter. He took my tray from my hands and set it on the bar before shoving my hoodie—which he'd obviously stolen from my locker—into my hands. "Go home, Peyton. You're dead on your feet."

An involuntary hiss escaped my mouth, but Sam ignored the warning and gently pushed me toward the door that said "Employees Only" on a silver plaque. I decided not to fight him anymore and stomped to the back because he was right, I was fucking exhausted. The growing cub in my stomach had sapped all of my energy but being idle made me crazy. I needed something to do while I figured out what to do next.

My panther was curled up contentedly inside me, as she'd been most of the time since the morning I learned I was pregnant. She only popped her head up when she sensed danger to us or our cub.

It didn't surprise me that my girl had only one care in the world. Panther males were notorious for knocking up a female and taking off, leaving the mother to raise the cub, or cubs, on her own. My father had been no exception. I didn't think he'd even stuck around long enough after sleeping with my mother to find out she was pregnant. And that said a lot since shifters could smell it almost immediately.

Raising our cubs on our own was supposedly built into our DNA and my panther seemed to have a natural maternal instinct. *One I evidently lack.*

I wasn't unhappy about the baby, but I did feel a little lost and unsure—two feelings I hadn't experienced since my childhood, and they were as unwelcome now as they were then. Could I raise a cub with my nomadic lifestyle? It could be cool to grow up that way. I would have loved it, so maybe my baby would, too.

The biggest headache I faced was the human side of things. Sure, my panther and I preferred to be on our own and hated the idea of being stuck somewhere...caged in. We were just fine moving on with our life and raising our little cub alone.

Unfortunately, my human half also had a stupid conscience and it kept poking at me, reminding me that keeping the baby a secret from Nathan was wrong. I'd obtained Nathan's number from Sam right after I realized I was pregnant, but it had been burning a hole in my pocket since then. He deserved to know about his son or daughter, but the idea of telling him made my free spirit quiver. How would it work if he wanted to be a part of the baby's life? I'd never leave my child, nor was I capable of settling down in one place with someone all up in my space all the time. An involuntary shudder raced through my body. *I'd probably pull my hair out in frustration or kill him...or both.*

I suddenly felt nauseated, although I wasn't sure if the morning sickness had struck again or the idea of giving up my sleeping habit of starfishing had brought it on.

I had to pass through the kitchen to get to the back exit, so after shoving my keys, phone, and tiny wallet in my pockets, I hit up the pantry for some crackers on my way out. By the time I reached the door, I felt much better.

Even though the October weather had grown quite cool, like all shifters (unless they were cold-blooded), I ran hot. But I slipped on my hoodie as an extra precaution because I was only wearing a tank top and pregnancy made us slightly more susceptible to sickness.

I pushed open the thick metal door and as I stepped into the alley, I took a deep breath of the crisp autumn air, only to begin choking on the quickly rising vomit in my esophagus. The streets of New York City weren't known for their pleasant smells, but I'd never been so overwhelmed by the rusty scent of blood. It permeated every inch of the alley and my stomach was not handling it well.

My panther jumped to her feet and it caused me to stumble forward a bit, so the door slammed shut behind me. I was about to dash to the right, heading for the opening that spilled out onto a sidewalk, when I heard a muffled sound coming from the darkness that shrouded everything to my left. My head automatically turned toward it and I knew it held the source of the smell.

I picked up another muffled sound and this time, I was almost positive it was a person. My instincts were all over the place. One part of me shouted to run and protect my cub and the other demanded I investigate because someone obviously needed help. There was a scuffle in the darkness and right that moment, a car turned at the intersection where the alley ended. The headlights bared a portion of the darkened alley and a pair of terrified, pain-filled blue eyes met mine and my fight-or-flight response kicked in.

A man—no, a wolf shifter—was holding a female shifter from behind, one arm around her neck and his claws extended from the other, threateningly poised over her chest. Her mouth was bleeding profusely, and tears poured down her cheek as her body trembled in terror. She tried to say something, but it came out gargled, and when I realized why...my gut flipped again. *Holy fuck! Shit! Fucking son of a bitch!* I was silently yelling at the rolling in my stomach, as well as the evil son of a bitch who'd cut out the woman's tongue.

The claws at her chest tightened, the tips pressing into the flesh, but not quite breaking the skin yet. My panther hissed and spat, sensing the situation posed a threat to her cub.

"Don't say a word, puss," a smooth, melodic voice commanded.

I finally turned my gaze to the woman's captor as I slowly approached them. While he would normally be considered handsome with his boyish features, artfully unruly hair, and dimples, the pure evil in his brown eyes and the twisted smile on his lips made me feel like I'd been coated in oil. "Walk away. I'm giving you one chance to leave. Protect your little pussycat."

His words sent a sharp slice of fear through me. I couldn't walk away from his victim, but terror at the possible harm to my baby had me frozen. Then the tips of his claws pricked her skin and my mind emptied of everything except rage. My panther took it as a sign that this man was trying to harm our baby and she leapt inside me, pushing me forward and almost bowling me over in her attempt to be freed.

Before I could regain my footing, he shoved his victim out of the way and lunged for me. The bastard was too fucking fast and before I could shift, he had his claws clamped around my throat. I struggled to breathe while trying to keep still because I could already feel rivulets of blood dripping down my neck. But it wasn't my inability to breathe or my sliced flesh that kept me from shifting and caused terror to roll over my skin. His other hand was poised over my stomach, the tips of his claws putting just enough pressure to cause pinpricks of pain. My panther didn't know what to make of my volatile emotions, but she must have sensed the danger to our cub because she stopped trying to get out and started whining while brushing her fur comfortingly under my skin.

"You aren't really my type," he said in his smooth voice. He sounded tranquil and friendly, as if he was recommending a restaurant. "But you've given me no choice. Besides, you're two for the price of one."

I gasped while my fingers worked at my throat, trying to pry his hand away without pushing his claws deeper into my skin. When he increased the pressure, just slightly, at my stomach, I'd had enough. I put my fingertips in the soft area between his digits and extended my claws. With my other hand, I punched his biceps tendon on the arm threatening my cub, causing the reflex to kick in and bend. At the same time, I twisted my body so that as his arm retracted, his claws leaving only scrapes on my hip and narrowly missing my stomach.

The evil asshole let out a blood-curdling scream that rang in my ears as he released me. I sucked in deep, raspy breaths in between harsh coughs. He shook his hand, trying to dislodge my claws, but I'd extended them directly into the muscle, sending them deep. Grasping his wrist with my free hand, I used it as leverage to kick him in the groin, sending him stumbling backward so that when I released him, my claws tore his flesh.

I immediately shifted and let my cat out to fight. He glared at me as he did the same and then I was facing the scowling yellow eyes of a big-ass black wolf. He had quite a bit of size on me, which was unusual. I was small for a black panther, but I was still pretty evenly matched with most wolves. This guy had a good fifty pounds on me, but I'd always been quick and had outmaneuvered plenty of my giant instructors at school.

My panther moved to circle him, and he stared at us as he did the same. After a beat, I feinted right before swiping a paw over his face and leaving a nice, bloody gash on his nose. He growled menacingly and my girl responded in kind.

Red and blue lights flashed in my peripheral as sirens blared. I hadn't noticed at first because sirens were basically white noise in the city. But they were traveling down the road that this alley crossed and there was an ambulance, which had a much higher-pitched, harder-to-ignore siren. The wolf and my panther were momentarily distracted, but he managed to refocus faster than her and in the next second, he had her pinned to the ground. He raised a claw and snarled, drool oozing from his mouth and landing in her fur. Pissed at herself for letting him get the upper hand—claw or whatever—my panther swiped again as she hissed and spat angrily. She was a special breed of Jaguar and at the top of the food chain. We were not often threatened by other shifters, so the fact that this wolf had managed to get the drop on her made her livid.

Suddenly, the sirens and lights came to a stop at the mouth of the alley. He growled in their direction as we heard doors slamming and people shouting, giving my girl a chance to shove him off and roll away. But his yellow eyes swung back to her and he pounced, pinning her again, but on her stomach this time, so his paws landed hard on her upper back. Then his claws dragged down from neck to hindquarters.

He tore through the muscles, creating deep wounds. I screamed inside my panther and she emitted a similar sound as we nearly blacked out from the pain. Still, she fought like hell to get him off of her. Then they both froze as the shouting of people rose in volume; they were headed right to us. The wolf grunted, but then his weight lifted, and she was free, but my panther and I could barely move from the pain.

My wounds would have been much worse if I'd been human, but while they hurt like a motherfucker, I'd heal. I was pretty sure. Although, if the slashes were as deep as they felt, it would take longer. And as a lone shifter, I didn't have a pack link, or a mate, to draw energy from.

My gut told me that the only reason the wolf had taken off without injuring me further was because he'd assumed I'd die. But I told myself I just needed to find somewhere to rest where I could stay in my panther form. Not easy to do in a bustling city. I couldn't exactly wander into my apartment building—a big black cat with deep, bleeding gashes on her back. I couldn't let any human find me in panther form. They'd call animal control.

Shit, with these injuries, they'd probably put me down.

I closed my eyes, and my cat began to withdraw, allowing me to the surface, but with every second of the shift, we were in excruciating pain. It didn't matter whether it was my human side or my panther who was hurt, we shared the injuries. Which meant that once it was complete, my human body sported the deep wounds and I screamed in agony because the pain was so much worse in this form.

Someone dropped to their knees beside me and started asking me questions, gauging my grade of awareness. I answered as best I could, but when cool air hit my wounds as they cut away my shirt, I couldn't focus anymore, and tears streamed from my eyes.

"Holy shit," the person next to me whispered. No doubt they thought I couldn't hear their comments, but my shifter hearing didn't miss a thing. They checked my pulse, breathing, and blood pressure, then yelled, "I need a trauma transfer board!" I winced when their elevated volume caused the pounding in my head to become sharp stabs.

My confidence in my healing ability faltered.

Pressure on my back ripped another scream from my throat as they applied bandages to minimize the bleeding. It hurt like a motherfucking bitch.

As multiple footsteps ran up to me, I felt a pinprick in each arm. They spoke for a few seconds, but I had begun to feel a little sluggish and didn't bother to listen. Several hands lifted me and set me on a board before strapping me in and placing an oxygen mask over my face.

Being imprisoned or strapped down—unable to move—was uncomfortable for humans, often panic-inducing. But for shifters, who are half animals, it was a living nightmare. My panther was freaking out, but thankfully, she understood enough not to push for freedom so as not to increase my pain. Still, hysteria bubbled up inside me and I fought to keep it contained. The effort drained me and the next thing I knew, I woke up in the back of an ambulance.

CHAPTER EIGHT

PEYTON

I passed out? Whoa. It was definitely worse than I'd thought. I shut my eyes again and whimpered at the feel of hands probing my back. When I opened them the next time, a female paramedic sitting opposite me met my gaze, her brown eyes brimming with sympathy. She took my hand and introduced herself as Kathy before softly asking me a few more questions. My responses were carefully worded because I couldn't exactly explain that I was half animal, I needed to shift, then find a place to curl up and rest undisturbed.

"Peyton?"

My eyes flew to Kathy, wondering how the hell she knew my name. If I ever had to do something humanish like go to a hospital, I used a pseudonym to avoid follow-ups, which would make things even more complicated. Especially if they examined my blood closely enough to see the minor differences from human blood.

Wallet. Shit. They had to have searched me for identification while I was unconscious.

"Are you allergic to anything?"

"No."

A minute later I shouted obscenities at myself for saying something so stupid. They'd hooked up an IV before securing me on the stretcher. I hadn't noticed the medicine trickling into my bloodstream at first, but now I felt the effects in my system, making me uncomfortable. Medications were essentially useless for shifters, unless they were specifically designed for us. If we had to pop an aspirin every once in a while, to keep up appearances, it was no big deal. But being pumped with high amounts of heavy drugs—such as the blood pressure medicine and painkillers being administered to me—put our bodies into healing mode.

It fought to expel the medicine, essentially seeing the foreign substance as a sickness or disease. The harder the body fought, the more uncomfortable we were, and eventually, it could become extremely painful. With the agony I was currently experiencing, adding the meds only made things rougher. But worst of all, they made it difficult to shift.

I glared at the bag full of medicine, wishing I could telepathically make it explode or something. But after a minute, my hard stare aggravated the pain in my head and everything around me blurred. Kathy kept changing my dressing, indicating that I was still losing copious amounts of blood. Between that and the meds, I was seriously woozy.

At least I knew none of this would hurt my baby. Shifter babies were even more immune to drugs and sickness than fully grown adults, and since it was pretty much the size of a peanut, it wouldn't experience the pain. I thought about telling them I was pregnant, but it wouldn't stop them from giving me painkillers. Plus, the pregnancy wouldn't show up in human tests for another month or so. Shifter blood already made doctors scratch their heads with our odd DNA sequences and all that stuff. These were all reasons why we tried to stick to doctors who were, or knew about, supernaturals. It wasn't always possible though, *i.e., my current situation.*

Trying to take my mind off the drugs, I listened to everything happening around me. One of the paramedics called in the injuries to the hospital while the driver groaned and swore under his breath as he tried to navigate NYC traffic. This city wasn't somewhere people ever wanted to take an ambulance ride. I'd seen more ambulances stuck in gridlock in one month than most people would see in their town ever.

"Another animal attack?" the medic in the passenger seat asked the driver.

Another? Great. Just fucking great. The last thing we needed were more reports of wild animals in the city.

"This is my third call for one, but I've heard there were more over the last year," the driver replied.

"Did you see those slashes? Her spine and ribs were visible," the passenger medic whispered. "It'll be a fucking miracle if she survives."

Way to stay upbeat, man.

"I've seen some amazing recoveries in my years on the job. You never know."

Exactly. Thank you.

I mentally high-fived the driver, then grimaced. How did moving my body in my mind hurt too?

Kathy continued talking softly to me, trying to make me feel safe and keep my mind occupied. Sweet gesture, sure, but I really wanted to shout at her to pull over and let me out. *Because that wouldn't arouse suspicion at all…*

The siren shut off as the truck pulled up to the designated entrance and the back doors flew open, then I was being transported again.

Apparently, my blood pressure was low and my heart rate elevated, so they rushed me right into an OR. I bit back the desire to holler at them in frustration. I didn't want them to misinterpret it and up the dosage of meds flooding my body.

A doctor entered and came to stand by the head of the table they'd transferred me onto.

"Hello, Peyton. I'm Dr. Cannon. We're going to take good care of you."

I barely resisted the urge to roll my eyes and instead gave him a trembling smile. I didn't have to fake the quiver because the next couple hours were going to fucking suck. Starting with the IV of blood they hooked up.

Human and shifter blood didn't mix well any more than B- mixed with A+. So, despite being O+, the burning started out small, but after a few minutes it felt like magma slithering through my veins. The heat caused chills to race through me and nausea churned in my stomach. My panther curled up in a frightened ball, and I wished I could do the same.

As they unwrapped the bandages and prepped me, the doctor explained the procedure. He said something about stitching layer by layer, but with my level of pain, it made it hard to concentrate, so I wasn't really listening. Until he mentioned anesthesia. My loopy brain debated making a run for it, except that even if I had the strength to move on my own, I doubted I could walk a straight line.

Go ahead. Just pile on the drugs that do nothing but bog down my system so I can't heal faster.

A nurse walked up to the doctor and whispered something in his ear, making them both glance at me with worried expressions. The meds and blood loss were obviously starting to get to me, because my shifter ears should have picked up what she'd said. But it just sounded garbled.

"Let's get started."

I closed my eyes and tried to ignore the building pressure from everything coursing through my veins. They asked me to count backwards from one hundred and I trailed off at ninety-three knowing they expected me to be asleep. If only... Instead, I had to lie completely still and...

Actually...it's not so...what was I thinking?

Is it cold in here? That's odd...

I feel funny...I fleel fubby. Fubby? Is that a worb? I mean. Wooorb. No. Wooooooooorb. It still doesn't sound right.

"Damn it!" someone shouted. "Where is all that blood coming from?"

Uh-oh. Sounds bab. Um, baaa-D. Yes!

I'm col-D...and so sleeeeeepy.

"We're losing her!"

Am I lost? But I didn't hibe yet! Worst gabe of hibe-and-seek ever. Cheaters.

I quib. Quiiib...t...qui-iiit.

Hmmm. Time for a nap.

CHAPTER NINE

PEYTON

"Here's your paperwork, sweetie," Nurse Fawn said as she entered my hospital room with a spring in her step. She smiled and dimples popped in her kind, round face. Fawn had been the only part of my excruciating five-day recovery that made it bearable. It helped that she was a shifter, too. Otherwise, I would've been like those patients in movies who pitch their Jell-O cups at stupid people and curse constantly. *Loudly and a lot.*

To be fair, although I hated it, I understood why I had to be there so long. At first glance, it appeared as though the damage was limited to the skin and muscle, but it turned out the son of a bitch had also injured my liver and a vessel had been bleeding. Not to mention the other cuts, bruises, and broken ribs. Rather than healing, my stubborn ass would have curled up and died if they hadn't found me and taken me to the hospital.

Nurse Fawn had also found out what happened to the attacker's other victim. It turned out she'd saved my life every bit as much as the medical professionals. While the wolf and my panther had been fighting, she'd managed to call 9-1-1 and through yes or no questions and beeps from the keys on her cell, they'd dispatched help. It broke my heart to find out that she'd been declared dead on arrival at the hospital.

After the state her killer had left me in, I knew physically hunting him down wouldn't be the smartest route for me. But my skills would lead me to the evil bastard eventually, and then I'd pass the evidence off to the people who would finish the job.

Nurse Fawn drew me from my thoughts when she held out the sheaf of papers. "Thanks," I replied with a smile. I waited until she'd left to cringe as I glanced over everything. Even being a nomad, I needed a place to claim as home so I could have a driver's license. I used New York as my home base and even kept a P.O. box—under another name and social security number—Sam checked it for me from time to time. When I'd arrived for this stay, my license had been about to expire, so I'd renewed it with my current address. I'd given them my real social security number while I was loopy and even Sam and Linette's information as my emergency contacts. Now the hospital had me in their system.

It would probably seem crazy to other people that I cared about something so inane, but I'd spent my life being invisible. I'd learned at a very young age how to hide who and what I truly was, then I'd discovered my talents with a computer. I'd long since wiped out any records that tied me to my childhood before boarding school. And now, my job depended on leaving no digital trail, which was easier to do without a physical one. Knowing one existed literally made my brain feel itchy.

So yeah, it irked me to see the records, but I'd clean it up later.

I grabbed the jacket Linette had brought with my change of clothes the day before and slipped it on. The skin on my back stretched a little tighter than normal because of the scars marring my flesh. Being in the hospital meant that I couldn't shift—which had made my panther every bit as pissed about it as me—and they'd given me an intravenous antibiotic, so I'd healed even slower (still faster than humans) while my body tried to deal with the drug and my injuries.

There were several doctors in the facility who were shifters, but unfortunately, I'd been assigned to someone else, and they hadn't been able to sway him into altering my treatment plan. At least he didn't fight removing my stitches after only a day, but by then the damage had been done and I now sported very visible claw marks on my back from my neck to just above my ass. Given enough time, they would become less and less prominent, but they would never disappear completely.

The claw marks on Nathan's arm popped into my head, and I wondered how he'd received them, and if they remained because of similar circumstances. Ugh. I hated when I had random thoughts about Nathan. It reminded me of the decision I'd been putting off and that the longer I did it, the harder it would be. Yet I pushed them away and stuck my head in the sand. My panther didn't care for my strategy though, and she gnashed her teeth at me whenever I forced images of Nathan from my mind.

I picked up the bag the hospital had given me that held my belongings from the night I'd arrived, fished out my wallet and keys, and tied the handles in a knot. After slipping the items into my pockets, I stared out the window, absently fiddling with the ring on my right thumb.

"Are you ready?" Linette chirped as she waddled into the room.

"What are you doing here?" I asked, my tone exasperated. "You shouldn't be on your feet!"

She shrugged and pointedly ignored Sam, who glared as he walked in after her. "She insisted she'd be coming whether I helped or not."

I sighed and threw Linette a wink before saying, "Sam, can't you control your woman?"

Linette giggled as her mate turned his scowl on me. "Hardy-har. Let's go." Then he pivoted and stalked out the door, muttering about having to deal with two pregnant women.

With one last look to make sure I'd grabbed everything, I exited the room to find Sam waiting next to the door. He put his arm out for Linette to hold and guided her down the hall.

Hospital rules required me to be wheeled out, but we were making a break for it before a nurse showed up with a wheelchair.

I smiled as I watched the two mates whisper to each other and occasionally chuckle. Seeing their love and devotion always made me happy, but it had never inspired a sense of longing to have it for myself. Even with my cub growing inside me, I couldn't see myself in their shoes. However, I did feel a rush of tenderness and excitement at the bond I would forge with this little one. I couldn't wait to cuddle my baby, share our own secrets, and laugh at our private jokes.

I'd never desired much human contact beyond sating my sexual needs and time spent with Sam and Linette. So the emotions shocked me. At the same time, they were a huge relief. I'd been a little worried that I'd never be able to connect with my cub the way a mother should. The lack of experience had built me this way, but it had never bothered me before. I hadn't missed what I'd never had. Even seeing it all around me, I'd just felt...ambivalent to it all. Then this cub had come along and suddenly I craved the deep, loving relationships I saw between other mothers and their children. Perhaps I wouldn't be the crappy mother I'd feared when I'd first discovered my pregnancy.

I rubbed my stomach thoughtfully, and my panther purred with bliss as she picked up on my emotional revelation. There had been no doubt in my mind that she would be a perfect maternal figure to our cub, but the baby certainly couldn't be raised solely by my panther.

A gust of wind broke through my thoughts when a glass door slid open so we could exit the building. The days were shortening quickly this time of year and the sun had almost completely set, though it was barely five o'clock. Sam used the app on his phone to call for a ride and a few minutes later a yellow cab pulled to a stop in front of us. We maneuvered between two of the parallel cars parked along the curb of the one-way street—a feat I swore only a New Yorker could manage with a belly as big as Linette's—and climbed into the back seat.

Linette insisted, begged, cajoled, and even demanded that I come stay with them, but I just wanted to be in my own space and collapse on my bed, then sleep for a couple of days. *I don't care what anyone says, "resting" in the hospital is tiring.*

They dropped me at my apartment building before heading home, and I trudged inside and unlocked my door before dragging my ass over the threshold. I hung my keys on a hook by the entrance and flipped the lock.

I went directly to my minuscule kitchen and dumped the bag with my torn, bloody clothes into the trash. The refrigerator called to me and my stomach growled, knowing it held the fixings for a sandwich. But in the end, I wanted to sleep more than eat.

However, I did take the time for a hot shower. After using the hospital bathroom for almost a week—which was smaller than the tiniest bathroom I'd ever seen in this city—it was the first time I felt truly clean since the morning of the attack.

I used my towel to dry my hair before I hung it back on the rack, then I padded over to my bed and dropped onto the mattress face down. I breathed in the scent of my fabric softener, another thing I'd missed when everything smelled like antiseptic, except their fabric, which smelled like nothing. *Literally nothing. How does one make something that lacks any kind of smell? And to a shifter nose, in particular.*

Inhaling once more, I turned my head to the side and remembered another delicious scent that had lingered on my sheets for days. I would never admit it to anyone, but I'd waited to wash them again until Nathan's woodsy, slightly spicy scent had disappeared.

Damn it. I'm way too weary to think about the Nathan situation. My panther hissed at me but settled down quickly because she was tired, too.

Pulling the coverlet up to my chin, I sighed and drifted to sleep.

My eyes popped open a second later when I heard a creak in the living room. A glance at the clock told me it hadn't been only a second, I'd been knocked out for over eight hours. I remained motionless, listening carefully. Creaks and groans were not unusual in these old buildings, but there had been something about this one that put me on alert. My cat jumped to her feet before going still, in hunter mode.

I heard the sound again, closer to my bedroom, and then the soft sucking sound of rubber soles on my hardwood floor. *Shit!*

The doorway suddenly filled with a large, dark shape and there was no mistaking the glint of a knife in their hand. They must have sensed my increased breathing pattern and deduced that I was awake because they spoke. "Time to finish the job, puss." The familiar, evil voice sent chills down my spine, and I immediately shifted. "We're going to fight like cats and dogs, huh?" He laughed at his own joke, until my panther hissed and gnashed her teeth in warning.

He shifted and I found myself once more staring at the wolf who'd nearly killed me. My cat growled and he responded in kind, then they both lunged at the same time. They wrestled and swiped their claws, both making their marks, neither of them gaining the upper hand. Until he landed a blow to our stomach and my panther curled in on herself for a moment. It was just long enough for him to clamp his jaws around her neck.

My cat was good and pissed, but the wolf outweighed us, and we were still exhausted and more cautious because of the baby. We needed to fight our natural fight instinct and go with flight instead.

Because of the position my panther had taken, the wolf's bite was at an odd angle, so before he could move into a better one and rip her throat out, she used the advantage to roll over and smash his head into the corner of the dresser. The blow stunned him long enough for her to wiggle out of his grasp and take off. She flew out of the bedroom and through the front door that he'd left open before smashing through the glass pane that blocked the exit.

We only had a few seconds' lead, but she was typically much faster than a wolf and she flew down the street like a bat out of hell. She couldn't top out her speed with all the cars, pedestrians, and other obstacles, but it was likely that we would outrun the wolf as long as we didn't stop.

For the first time, I didn't care one bit if we freaked out some city-dwellers, I encouraged my girl to keep going, to weave her way through the streets and alleys in hopes that our scent would be more difficult to follow.

When we reached the Hudson, she stopped and played through the options in her mind. She and I both loved the water, but we had no plan, and no idea where to go. It wouldn't be long before the evil son of a bitch caught up to us and our best bet was to get to a less populated area where she could run as fast as possible. Her top speed could hit fifty miles per hour if we were in shape, but in our current state, I worried about being able to outrun the wolf if he managed to pick up our trail.

I mentally shrugged and she chuffed at me in agreement, right before she flew off of the pier and dove into the water.

Swim fast, I thought. *Too much time in the Muddy Huddy and we'll probably start glowing. But it will definitely help with masking our scent.*

My girl swam gracefully across the river until we reached the other side. A wolf howled as we were making our way onto the shore and we bolted.

Not long after, we left the busy cities and bustling towns behind. Despite how tired and hungry we were, it felt a little freeing to be able to let everything go and purely run. We usually went for long runs, walks, and climbs a few times a week, but since being back in the city without a car, it made it a lot harder to find open or wooded areas where we could roam free, much less run and play. Over the years, whenever we'd settled in one place for a while, it tended to be near densely wooded areas.

Without a destination in mind, I let my panther take charge and follow her instincts. We stopped from time to time to drink from a stream or catch a squirrel—she'd been very vocal about the pathetic excuse for a meal. However, we both knew we had to feed the cub—but we never stayed in place for more than ten to fifteen minutes. We'd been running for a little over eight hours when she ran out of fuel, the adrenaline having long since worn off. My cat stopped next to a beautiful lake, the still water glistening in the morning sunshine. Slowly, she padded toward the enticing pool, but before she could take even a single sip, her legs gave out and she collapsed. Neither of us had the energy to shift and my eyes felt heavy, so I closed them for a moment. The soft sounds of the water and distant laughter of children lulled me into a dream-like state. Even though I knew we should get up and try to keep going, something about this place made me feel peaceful and safe. I mentally curled my arms around my stomach and whispered to my little cub that I would always protect them right before the darkness swallowed me.

CHAPTER TEN

NATHAN

After running for a couple of hours in the forests around Silver Lake, it was just after eight A.M. and I couldn't wait to get back to my bed. However, I decided to do a quick perimeter run before returning home. My wolf lifted his chin in greeting when we encountered the members of the pack who were currently on patrol but kept moving until we'd come full circle.

My cabin backed up to the water and my wolf trotted over for a drink, but stopped short when an almost familiar scent reached his nose. Sweet and spicy.

He followed his nose to investigate and that was when we spotted the black ball of fur near the tree line to my property. I knew right away that it was a shifter, but we still approached with caution. As we crept closer, we guessed that the animal was either asleep or unconscious, but it was impossible to miss the smell of fright wafting off of them. And the other scent...I knew it from somewhere.

We stopped a few feet away and were surprised to find that the shifter was a black jaguar—a panther. We didn't see many of those around here because they tended to be introverted, solitary creatures who typically avoided heavily populated areas. Silver Lake certainly wasn't like the city—it was out in the country and spread out, but still inhabited by more shifters and humans than they generally interacted with.

An instant later it hit me.

Honey and cloves.

Black panther.

Peyton.

It couldn't be.

My wolf had come to the same tentative conclusion and he sidled up to the big cat. He inhaled deeply and while it definitely smelled like Peyton, something was different.

Her breath shuddered for a moment, drawing my attention to her physical state. After the pause, her breathing became steady, but very shallow and I didn't like it. I suspected she was unconscious rather than asleep, which could be damaging the longer it went on.

I nudged my wolf to let me through and quickly shifted into my human form. I knelt beside her, eyeing her sharp claws and hoping she didn't wake up swinging.

First, I put my hand on her left side, just behind her front leg, and checked her pulse. It was on the low end, but still considered normal.

"Peyton," I murmured. I received no response, so I tried again a little louder. Still nothing.

Careful to avoid any injuries I couldn't see; I nudged her and called her name again. "Peyton. Baby, wake up."

Her cat stirred, emitting a little moan, before going still again.

Progress.

This time, I shouted her name at the top of my lungs and her panther let out a hiss as she opened her eyes into slits and stared at me with hostility.

My wolf pushed near to the surface and Peyton's animal seemed to get caught in his gaze. Something passed between them and the panther lost some of her tension. Then she sniffed and her ears perked up as she rolled over and rested on all four limbs. She sniffed again before chuffing and dropping her head onto my lap.

Interesting. Once she'd calmed down, she'd recognized my scent and apparently, Peyton's panther was a fan. Slowly, I ran a few fingers from her forehead to her nose and she purred. When her golden eyes met mine, there was no sign of Peyton's emerald irises.

I petted her again before asking, "Can I talk to Peyton?"

She lifted her head and stared at me for a long moment, then began to retreat into herself. Fur became skin and bones cracked as they moved to accommodate another shape. After a few seconds, Peyton lay naked on the ground in front of me. Since she was still unconscious, her head had fallen into my lap and her warm breath bathed the skin of my thigh. My body tightened and I firmly gripped my control, commanding it to behave.

Putting a finger under Peyton's chin, I tilted her head back an inch so I could see her face. My lips curled down at the sight of her sunken eyes and the deep purple skin underneath. She appeared worn out and her expression held hints of the fear I'd smelled on her.

Something inside me roared to life, a desperate need to track down whoever she was running from and rip their throats out. I reared back, physically reacting to the unexpected surge of violent energy. I cared deeply for the people and creatures I protected, but I'd never experienced anything like this. My wolf was gnashing his teeth and growling, his desire to hunt and kill anyone who'd ever hurt her seeping into my own emotional well. I firmly instructed him to back down. We needed to take care of Peyton first. He acquiesced and retreated, but continued to make disgruntled sounds.

I gently shook her again. "Peyton. Wake up." My jaw hardened in frustration when she didn't do as I'd ordered, but I took it as a good sign that her heart rate sped up a couple of beats per minute. I tapped her cheeks before lifting one of her eyelids. Gold stared back at me. "I don't suppose you're willing to help me out here?" I asked her cat. The gold turned molten before green began to bleed into it.

Finally, Peyton gasped, and her eyes flew open. Her gaze bounced around wildly before she scrambled backward in a crab walk. "Who the hell are you? Don't come any closer."

"Relax, Peyton," I said in a low tone. I'd been going for soothing, but soft and cuddly wasn't really my nature, so it came out sounding like a demand. *Yeah, this is going to go well,* I thought dryly.

She reacted as I expected and bristled at my tone, her eyes filling with fire.

I kept my eyes averted from her chest as much as I could, ignoring the way her breasts bounced with each angry breath. I couldn't exactly hide her effect on me while kneeling on the ground without a stitch of clothing. The last thing we needed was for her to see my large, hard shaft and run away screaming because she came to the wrong conclusion. Granted, she'd had my cock between her legs several times before, but it seemed as if she was a little foggy from being unconscious.

"Who are you?" she growled as she altered her position into a low crouch, her claws extended slightly and molten gold seeping into her eyes, showing me flashes of her panther.

I remained still, trying not to spook her, and placidly answered her question. "Nathan King. We only had one night together, but I have to say, it's a hit to my ego that you've forgotten me already."

She cocked her head to the side and studied the features of my face. Recognition flared in her eyes and I slowly rose to my feet. "How did you find me?" she asked as she mimicked my actions.

"I think that's my question, Peyton." I stood with my feet braced apart and my arms crossed over my chest. It was my natural stance, but the fact that it was an intimidating one came in handy. I was pleased when Peyton didn't seem affected by my aggressive, Alpha vibes and "don't fuck with me or I'll end you" stance. Her strength had impressed me when we first met, and I liked that she didn't cower before me now, either. I'd seen glimpses of that backbone when we fought for control in bed, but the full force of it was unbelievably alluring.

"Pardon?" Peyton queried as she put her hands on her hips, drawing my gaze down before I could stop myself. I quickly averted my eyes by returning them to her face to find her glaring at me with narrowed eyes. I shrugged. She was naked and fucking gorgeous, what did she expect?

"This is my land, sweetheart."

Peyton frowned and glanced around. "Your...?"

I nodded. "Mine." The word felt heavy with a meaning I didn't understand. A low purr rumbled in my chest and I raised a mental eyebrow at my wolf, wondering at his strange reaction. He was ignoring me, focused on Peyton, so I did the same.

"How did I end up here?" Her tone indicated that the question was rhetorical, so I countered with one of my own.

"What are you running from, Peyton?" Not one to play games, I got straight to the point.

"What makes you think I'm running from someone?" she snapped defensively. "Maybe I just needed a change of scenery." She almost succeeded in disguising the tremble in her voice.

"The desire for a change of scenery put those dark circles under your eyes and left you unconscious on my property?"

"Yes!' she bit out.

I nearly smiled at her display of fire.

"Okay," I agreed, placating her for the moment. "Would you like something to eat?"

"I'm fine."

Her stomach growled and my lips curled up smugly. "A glass of water?"

Peyton huffed for a moment, but the weariness she was trying to hide slid over her features before stubbornly disappearing. "Fine. Some water would be great. Thank you."

I offered her my hand, but she shook her head and slowly walked toward me. After a few steps, she stumbled, and I lost my patience—something that only seemed to happen around her. I swept her up into my arms before heading back to the house.

"What the hell?" she yelped.

"Enough," I scolded.

She opened her mouth, no doubt preparing to argue, but shut it when her eyes met mine and she saw my wolf staring back at her. He'd been demanding that I care for her and was irritated with her for resisting. Her deep green irises had melted into gold for a moment, and my wolf and I were satisfied that even if her human side was being obstinate, her panther was receptive to our attention.

"We can discuss what has you running"—I gave her a pointed look—"and we *will* be discussing it, but it can wait until you've had something to eat and drink." As an afterthought I added, "You're safe here."

Peyton's expression was half resignation and half relief. She relaxed in my arms and let me carry her to the house and into the living room where I gently set her on the couch.

I knelt beside her and my eyes swept down her form—ignoring the shot of arousal that zipped through my body—searching for obvious injuries. Unable to control my reaction completely, I gave in to an urge and inhaled her scent. The subtle difference hit me again, except this time I recognized it and a shockwave shook the earth beneath me.

Pregnant.

Her scent had mixed with the baby's. Although I didn't smell another man on her, which was most likely why I hadn't recognized her altered aroma at first.

The thought that the cub was mine drifted through my mind, but I quickly dismissed it. We hadn't been together during the full moon. Which meant she'd slept with someone else right after I'd left her bed.

White-hot rage burst to life inside me, catching me off-guard, and my wolf gnashed his teeth while snarling in fury. *What the fuck?*

A menacing growl rumbled in my chest and Peyton cocked her head and stared at me, her expression quizzical.

My brow furrowed low, and I tried to corral the sudden desire to rip out the throat of any man who'd ever touched Peyton. It took some fierce wrestling, but I managed to shove the urges back.

I had no idea where that had come from and not a fucking clue what to do with it. It wasn't as if I'd never had multiple partners in one night…or at the same time. And I'd never felt more than fleeting passion for a woman and certainly not possession.

Perhaps I needed to work her out of my system. That seemed the most likely scenario—one I had no problem following through. Although my wolf was strangely discontented with the idea, while still pushing me to take her.

The inexplicable feelings Peyton inspired were a problem I

didn't have time to analyze. And her naked body was a distraction I didn't need. I swiftly rose to my feet and grabbed a quilt from a basket beside the sofa, before throwing it over her.

As my mind cleared, I began to assess our situation. Not helping Peyton wasn't an option, but I had enough shit going on without piling her problems on top of it. Especially if she was going to be difficult, which I suspected would be the case.

Lifting my eyes to the ceiling, I rolled my neck and shoulders before running a hand through my hair. My frustration at the situation put an unintended edge in my tone, but hurting her feelings was the least of my concerns. "I'm going to put some clothes on, then I'll bring you something to eat,"—I pointed at her and narrowed my eyes—"Don't move," I said sharply.

Peyton glared at me, the gold swirling in her green pools telling me that her panther didn't appreciate the command any more than she did.

Whether she liked it or not, I expected to be obeyed, so I turned and crossed the room to the hallway that led to my bedroom. Once there, I dressed in a pair of athletic shorts and a black T-shirt while the cogs in my brain rotated, trying to work out my next steps.

My wolf made it hard to focus with his agitated pacing. His anxiousness to return to Peyton suggested an abnormal attachment, but I chalked it up to overtiredness and our natural instinct to protect.

I debated on what to give her to wear because she'd be swallowed whole by my clothes. Since I didn't have a sister, and I never invited any of the women I slept with into my home, so there were no random items of female clothing in my house. After searching through my belongings, I found an old KBO T-shirt that had shrunk enough to where I thought it might stay on her slender frame. Item in hand, I headed back into the living room and scowled when I spotted Peyton sitting in one of my recliners, the quilt wrapped around her like a sari.

"Are you always this stubborn?" I growled.

A corner of her mouth lifted into a crooked smirk. "Usually."

I paced over and dropped the shirt into her lap. "I suggest you learn to heel before you find yourself bent over my knee for a spanking."

Peyton gasped and I expected her to yell at me, but she squinted and snarked, "Cats don't heel, dog."

"True enough," I conceded with a nod. A small smile crept onto my lips as I turned toward the kitchen. "But if you don't tame the wildcat, I will."

"Over your dead body," Peyton muttered.

I shook my head, the curve of my lips deepening, as I walked into the kitchen area.

After putting together a stack of sandwiches, I piled them onto a plate and set them on the granite countertop of the large island. I filled two glasses with water and set them beside it. Last, I added a bowl of mixed fruit. "Come eat."

Peyton hesitated and I nearly rolled my eyes. I understood the nature of an independent Alpha female, but her automatic instincts to buck authority were learned, not innate. And incredibly irritating.

After a beat, she stood, letting the quilt fall on the ground, and put on the T-shirt that hung to well below her knees. She shuffled over to a bar stool and paused, her expression one of consternation. When a determined glint entered her eyes, it occurred to me that she might be in too much pain to climb onto one of them. Before she could protest, I rounded the island and picked her up, then set her gently in the tall chair.

"I could have done it," she grumbled. Her lips curved a little and she added, "But it would have taken me a week and hurt like hell. So…thank you."

I swallowed my surprise at her admission and simply nodded. "Eat."

While we ate, I tried to warm her up by asking her questions about herself. She managed to dodge or deflect every question that went deeper than something like her favorite food. Eventually I gave up and we finished in silence until the stack of sandwiches had been demolished and the bowl of fruit emptied. The amount of food she'd put away had been pretty impressive for someone so petite. Then again, she was eating for two. The reminder of her romp with another man sent my mood tumbling down again and I decided it was time for her to come clean.

I gathered the dishes and took them to the sink, then turned around and faced her from across the island, leaning forward with my hands braced apart. "Talk," I commanded.

"About what?" Peyton asked in a wary tone, her body tensing, which caused her to wince. I noticed her absently twisting the gold ring around her thumb, and briefly wondered about its significance.

"You're obviously in some kind of trouble."

"What makes you say that?" She brushed some imaginary lint from her shirt before returning her gaze to my face, her expression carefully blank.

I bent over the island, pinning her with a hard stare. "I found you passed out on my land, starving, dehydrated, dirty, and terrified. Trust me, Peyton. I know when someone is on the run."

Her eyes swirled with gold as she contemplated how to answer. Her cat studied me without any of Peyton's reluctance. I wondered if she and her panther were in agreement or if Peyton was overruling her animal's inclination to trust me.

I waited patiently for her to make a choice. The silence grew heavy, as did the weight of my stare, and after a few minutes, she shifted her position on the stool. "I'm not going to deny it," she finally admitted. "But the details are not important. So, you might as well stop trying to intimidate the story out of me." She passed a hand absently over her stomach before folding it into the other and resting them on the countertop.

The small action spurred a theory. "Is it the baby's father?" I asked coldly.

CHAPTER ELEVEN

PEYTON

My body stilled at Nathan's query. I wasn't surprised that he'd picked up on the pregnancy, although since he hadn't yet mentioned it, part of me had begun to wonder how he hadn't smelled it. I couldn't hide the scent—our potent blood spilled many of our secrets to the keen nose of another shifter.

His assumption that the cub belonged to someone else astonished me. The baby's scent wouldn't reflect its father's for a few more weeks yet, but still…then I remembered my own revelation the morning I found out I was pregnant. Nathan obviously hadn't discovered that we'd been together after the full moon had risen. Given his ignorance, his assumption made more sense.

Although I couldn't say I was all that flattered by his implication that I'd hopped from his bed right into someone else's. And yet…I mentally sighed. Screwing around with multiple partners in the days leading to a full moon was not unusual for our kind. And we barely knew each other. Since I'd been guilty of it plenty of times, I couldn't exactly clutch my pearls and gasp in offense.

"Answer me, Peyton," he ordered, his tone hard and his jaw clenched. The glimpses I kept seeing of his wolf were none too happy, either.

Were they jealous? *No. That's ridiculous.*

"No," I answered calmly. "I'm in no jeopardy from the baby's father." From what I'd seen of Nathan, he had a dark side. He was domineering, a complete asshole, pretty much an Alpha through and through. However, he didn't seem anything like the pack Alphas I'd known in my past and for some crazy reason, I knew he wouldn't physically hurt me. *Except for a spanking*, I thought dryly.

Nathan nodded and crossed his arms over his chest, making his muscles bulge in a way that would have most people cowering, but the pregnancy hormones must have kicked in because it sent a flood of arousal to my core. Without any underwear, I could only hope that I wouldn't leave evidence of my lust in the form of a big, wet spot on my shirt dress.

His nostrils flared and I cursed being a shifter for the first time in my life. What did it matter if I soaked through the fabric when he could smell the way my body was responding to him? Heat simmered in his gaze and he licked his lips, causing a shiver to race down my spine. *Now is not the fucking time,* I silently lectured my lady bits.

I cleared my throat and mumbled, "Um, pregnancy hormones."

Nathan's eyes iced over, and his wolf rumbled in his chest before he looked away and grunted something unintelligible.

My head canted to the side as I studied him, confused by his reaction. The jealousy idea floated through once more, but I grappled for a more plausible explanation because that seemed ludicrous. Okay, not ludicrous so much as terrifying. My panther sniffed haughtily. Unlike me, she found the idea of Nathan being jealous over us intriguing. She wanted me to preen and entice him to claim us again. *Not happening.* She hissed and swiped at me before stomping off to pout.

Without her interference, I returned to my speculation about his attitude. *Maybe he's opposed to cubs altogether.*

That thought both perked me up and depressed me at the same time. *Five more months of roller coaster emotions is going to kill me.*

I didn't like the idea that he would reject his cub. It tugged at old wounds, but I tossed those thoughts away. I was encouraged by the idea of him not wanting children because it meant that he might not try to stop me when it came time to leave.

"Who?" Nathan growled.

I raised an eyebrow in question. "Who is the father or who am I running from?"

He opened his mouth automatically, but his speech halted for a moment before he answered. "Who is chasing you?" Then he quickly added, "And who is the father?"

Biting my lip, I assessed him and mulled over my options. In the end, I kept both answers vague. I didn't want to drag Nathan or his pack into my mess, possibly putting them in danger from the lunatic trying to kill me. In addition, what did I really know about Nathan? I didn't believe he would hurt me, but could I trust him? I twisted the ring on my thumb as I pondered.

I didn't feel quite ready to share my child's paternity with him, but I would tell him eventually. I wanted him to admit he didn't want kids first so that I could leave without any guilt hanging over me.

I faked a yawn, but it turned into a real one as fatigue spread through my limbs like a wildfire in a dry field. "Can we talk another time?" I asked sleepily. Damn, that had happened fast. I could barely hold myself up and I swayed in my seat.

The next thing I knew, Nathan was there to catch me as I pitched sideways. He scooped me into his arms, and I rested my cheek on his warm chest, my heavy eyelids falling shut. Warmth surrounded me and I sighed, feeling safe for the first time in over a week.

"Get some rest, baby. You can tell me everything later."

CHAPTER TWELVE

NATHAN

Peyton slept through the entire day and night. I checked on her multiple times after I'd taken a nap, but she'd been sleeping deeply each time.

I thought about waking her to make her eat, but I could see that she needed rest and if she became hungry enough, it would rouse her. When I rose in the morning, she still hadn't moved. Her ability to sleep like the dead was impressive.

I was working on KBO business when she knocked on my open office door.

The sight of her in my shirt, her toned legs on display and her long, black hair mussed from sleep, sent a jolt of lust through me. Peyton must have felt my slow, burning perusal of her body because she shivered and shifted her weight from foot to foot. I was tempted, so tempted to take her right back to bed and spend the rest of the day inside her…but it wasn't the right time. It didn't help that she was practically devouring the sight of my naked chest.

My wolf perked up at her presence and his possessiveness of Peyton flared. I bluntly reminded him that she wasn't ours and he needed to stop acting like it. He growled menacingly in disagreement and I gave up trying to convince him. He could have his little fantasy, as long as it didn't affect *my* feelings and actions.

"Good morning," I murmured as I leaned back in my seat, resting one elbow on the arm while fiddling with a pen. My residual irritation with my wolf caused my tone to be a little rougher than I intended.

Peyton frowned and muttered, "Is it? Could have fooled me."

I chuckled, her candor lightening my mood. "You have a point. How are you feeling?"

A small smile graced her pink lips and she sighed. "Much better, thank you." Then she tugged on the T-shirt and grimaced. "I could really use a shower, though. And, um, I should probably find some better clothes."

It was on the tip of my tongue to tell her she could only wear my clothes, but the logical part of my brain knew it was a ridiculous notion and beat back the possessiveness bleeding from my wolf's emotions.

"I'm sure I can find you something. The bathroom is the door between my office and your room. Go ahead and shower while I make breakfast and scrounge up something for you to wear." I smirked as my eyes trailed down her gorgeous legs. "Not that you don't look good in what you have on."

Peyton rolled her eyes, but one corner of her mouth lifted as she turned and strolled from the room.

I watched her sexy ass sway as she left, and my body tightened painfully. I had to fight like hell to subdue the urge to join her in the shower. The fierceness with which I craved her perplexed me. Our night together had been extraordinary, the best sex I'd ever had. But I couldn't fathom one night resulting in this level of hunger for her. Not to mention the way my wolf was reacting.

Our chemistry had an element of wildness, something beyond my control. And it pissed me the fuck off because I was always in control. *Always.*

I shook off my thoughts—or shoved them into a corner to ignore—and picked up my phone from where it had been resting beside my keyboard. I tapped my mother's number and put it on speaker as I stood from my chair and headed to the kitchen.

"Nate! To what do I owe the pleasure, *moy malysh?*"

I smiled at the sound of her voice, filled with warm affection and a very slight Russian accent. Thousands of years old and she still referred to me as her baby boy—she was the only woman in the world who could get away with shit like that.

"Hello, *Mamen'ka*," I said as I opened the refrigerator and took out the items I would need to cook breakfast. "I need a favor."

"Of course," she responded immediately.

"I found a woman collapsed by the stream in my backyard yesterday," I told her as I chopped vegetables and put them in a large bowl. "She's in trouble and will be staying until we can figure out how to solve the problem."

"Oh, dear. How can I help?"

"She was in her shifter form, so she didn't have any clothes with her. Would you find her a few things to wear until we have a chance to buy her some new clothes?"

"Absolutely. Tell me about her size, so I know who to ask."

As I cracked some eggs into another bowl and whisked them together, I filled her in on Peyton's features and vaguely answered a few more of her questions. My mother assured me she'd be by soon and said goodbye.

Peyton padded into the living room just as I was taking our omelets off of the stove. I smelled her first, the shower having made her honey and clove scent stronger. Surprisingly, the idea of her carrying another man's cub filled me with jealousy, but the scent of her pregnancy aroused me. When I glanced over my shoulder and saw her, the desire simmering inside me burst free.

She'd piled her wet hair on her head and a few tendrils hung enticingly around her slender neck. Her skin was pink from being scrubbed, and she was wrapped in a navy-blue bath sheet. I'd seen plenty of women in clothing that covered a whole lot less than that towel. And yet her outfit was hot as fuck and all I could think about was untwisting the knot holding it together between her breasts and peeling the thick terrycloth away from her beautiful body. It didn't help that I knew exactly what was hiding underneath that scrap of fabric.

Electricity crackled between us, the air suddenly thick with tension.

Peyton's emerald orbs were glued to my back and they did a sweep from top to bottom. She licked her red lips, leaving them glistening, just begging to be kissed.

I attempted to recall the reasons why I was holding back and couldn't come up with a single one. With a quick twist of a knob, I shut off the stove and stalked around the bar. Peyton's eyes widened as I prowled toward her and her breath caught in her throat. I knew she was seeing more beast than man. When it came to her, my need felt raw and animalistic. It was what had driven me to bite her when we'd slept together before. At the reminder, my eyes dropped to her shoulder and the smooth, unmarked skin set off an even greater primal need inside me. I hated that my mark was no longer there.

Peyton backed up a few steps until she bumped into the wall. However, there was no trace of alarm in her gaze. There were hints of wariness, but mostly, her eyes were cloudy with passion. My hands clamped around her waist, holding her in place while I lowered my head and captured her lips.

A groan rumbled up my chest as the sparks between us erupted. My tongue pushed into her mouth and tangled with hers as we tasted each other deeply. She was so petite compared to me that my body encompassed hers, and when I crowded her back against the wall, she had no means of escape. My cock was thick and hard as steel as I pressed it against her stomach. But that wasn't enough. I glided my palms around to her ass and cupped her firm cheeks, boosting her up so our centers fit together perfectly and her legs locked around my hips. The towel split open and the only barrier between us was the thin fabric of my pajama pants. Heat radiated from her sex and enveloped my cock, urging all of the blood in my body to settle in my groin. Her fingernails dug into my flesh where she gripped my biceps, but it only made me hotter.

"Fuck," I grunted against her lips when I pulled back mere centimeters to catch my breath. "I thought I remembered how good it was between us. But nothing compares to the real thing."

I rocked into her and she moaned, her head thumping against the wall when she tried to drop it back. My eyes strayed to the spot just between her shoulder and her neck and my mouth found its way there with a mind of its own. I kissed the creamy skin and dragged my teeth lightly over it.

Suddenly, Peyton went rigid in my arms, as if someone had thrown a bucket of cold water over her. "Don't even think about it," she growled.

My first instinct was to growl right back and tell her it was my fucking right to claim her, but it was as crazy as it was untrue. I blamed my wolf again and instead of marking her, I stepped back and allowed her legs to fall so she could stand on her feet.

But before I let her go completely, I brought our noses close together and stared into her eyes. "Biting aside, this chemistry between us is only getting stronger. Fighting it is an exercise in futility."

"Maybe for you. I have more control over myself," she quipped.

I raised a sardonic eyebrow at her attempt to play it off when her erratic heart rate and choppy breaths said otherwise. "Is that a challenge, baby?" I asked with an arrogant smirk.

Peyton narrowed her eyes, but when they melted into gold for a moment, my smirk spread into a full-blown grin. Her panther stared at me with hunger, begging me to take her, but challenging me to dominate and overpower her, therefore proving my worth as a potential mate. While I had no intention of mating, I had no qualms about showing Peyton who the Alpha was between us and demonstrating the power I wielded over her kitty cat.

"Fact, not challenge," she argued.

With one hand holding her waist, I slipped my index finger of the other into the valley between her breasts and tugged on the knot holding up her towel. It pooled on the ground at her feet, and I inspected her from head to toe. Her thighs glistened with her arousal; her stomach quivered when I drew the tips of my fingers up from her belly button to her full, perfectly shaped globes. I brushed the pad of my thumb over one hard, berry-colored nipple and my lips tipped up in satisfaction when a shudder racked her body. "We'll see."

I released her and walked back to the kitchen in slow measured steps, trying not to wince at the pain from my very stiff cock. Our breakfast had cooled some, but not enough that it needed to be reheated, so I plated them and brought them to the island. I'd also cut up some fruit and set a bowl of it beside each dish. "Come here, Peyton. You need to eat."

Peyton sighed as she wrapped the towel around her once more, then threw me an exasperated scowl. But she didn't argue and took a seat across from me at the bar. She ate every bite of her meal and I made her a second omelet without a word, knowing she wouldn't ask but was still hungry. She took the food with a pleased smile and polished off her seconds.

Like the night before, I asked her leading questions about her background, trying to learn more about her, all while contemplating how to drag her story out of her. I decided to let her get away with avoiding the personal questions for now. But she wasn't going to get out of telling me about what had sent her running this time.

After clearing the dishes, I sat on one of the tall chairs next to her and met her gaze with steely determination. "Tell me what happened to you."

Peyton sighed and leaned her elbows on the granite. She folded her hands together and stared at the cabinets across the kitchen, instead of at me. "It's not your problem, Nathan. I'll handle it." She finally twisted her head in my direction and studied me before adding, "I don't want to bring my trouble to your pack's door."

Something in her tone warned me that there was more to her reluctance to share. "Is that really it, or is it because you don't trust me?"

Peyton pursed her lips as she twisted her ring around and around, then blew out a harsh breath and admitted, "A little of both, I suppose."

I nodded. "Fair enough. But your natural instinct to go at things alone is just going to get you killed."

She frowned and it didn't escape my notice that she very

subtly leaned away from me. I didn't think she was even aware that she'd done it. "How would you know that?"

"Relax, Peyton. I'm not your enemy. I told you, I recognize a person on the run." I pulled a rubber band from my pocket and gathered my hair up on the back of my head. "And the signs all point to something that's threatening your life, or you would have stayed and dealt with the situation on your own."

Her expression didn't let up, but her body stopped trying to put distance between us. "You say that as if you know me."

"I'm perceptive," I replied, tapping my finger on the counter as punctuation.

"You're a cocky asshole," she volleyed back.

I shrugged. "I can be. It doesn't mean I'm not perceptive. Or that I'm wrong."

When she remained stubbornly silent, I clenched my hands into fists to keep from throttling her...or kissing her. I wasn't sure which desire would win if I let my emotions take over.

"Whatever it is, I can protect you," I tried again.

She cocked her head to the side. "Why would you do that? I'm no one to you. Why put yourself in harm's way for a stranger?"

Her question took me off guard, particularly because I could tell that her confusion was sincere. She honestly didn't understand why I wanted to aid someone I didn't know. Well... that fact was somewhat debatable.

My admiring gaze floated down her body and I couldn't stop a wicked smile from forming on my lips. "I don't know about that, Peyton." I cradled the back of her head in my large palm, easily holding her still as I brought my face a breath away from hers. "I know what every inch of your gorgeous body looks like. I know what makes you wet and the spots that give you the most pleasure. And—my favorite thing—I know what you sound like when you come."

Peyton's pupils had dilated to the point that only a sliver of green was visible around them. Her heart was pounding, and her breathing became choppy. It was sexy as fuck and my body burned to take her, to experience the bliss of being inside her again. "We're definitely not strangers, baby."

She scoffed—or tried to, but the sound effect was ruined by her soft panting. "The fact that we had mind-blowing sex make us acquaintances at best," she argued. "Who would stick their neck out for an acquaintance? It's ridiculous. And what about your pack? They need you—"

Her rambling was cut off when I released her head and glided my hand down her back until it slipped under the hem of the towel and I was palming a naked, toned ass cheek. In one smooth movement, I lifted her into my lap, so she was straddling my legs. "Mind-blowing, huh?"

"Seriously? That's all you heard?" she huffed as she pushed against my chest, trying to squirm away. Despite her exasperated tone, I saw a glint in her eyes. She'd known exactly what she was doing, the conniving little feline.

I cupped her ass with both hands and yanked her forward so that our centers were nestled together. The large bulge in my pants made it very clear where my mind had gone. Although, when it came to Peyton, sex always seemed to be on my mind, even if it just hovered in the background. If we hadn't been in the middle of such an important conversation—despite her attempts to derail it—I would have simply carried her to the bedroom, tossed her on the bed, and reminded her just how well we knew each other.

"Don't play games with me, kitty cat," I purred. "I'm well aware of your diversion tactics, but I think perhaps you need a lesson in what happens when you play with fire."

Her eyes grew wide, and she doubled her efforts to wiggle out of my grip, but I didn't budge, and her efforts backfired when she inadvertently rubbed her sex against my shaft. A moan tore from her chest and the towel around her—which had loosened during her struggle—dropped to her waist, exposing her perfect breasts. Maybe we could talk after…

I groaned in displeasure when we were suddenly interrupted.

CHAPTER THIRTEEN

NATHAN

"*Moy malysh*? Nate?" a gentle voice sing-songed from the front porch. My mother rapped smartly before working the key into the lock. *Fuck.* Why the hell had I given my mother a key?

I quickly secured the towel around Peyton and set her back on her chair. Then I rounded the bar in order to hide my body from the waist down. Peyton's expression had gone wild, and she appeared ready to bolt.

"My mother," I told her softly, hoping my tone would help smooth her frayed nerves.

The lock clicked as the mechanisms unlatched and the door swung open. A petite woman with blue eyes, a bright smile, and dimples bounced through the entrance. Her honey-colored hair hung over her shoulder in a long braid, but after dropping an abundance of bags from each hand, she flung the flaxen rope to hang down her back. Her curious gaze swept the room, skipping right over me and locking on Peyton.

"You couldn't have given her something to wear besides a towel, Nate?" my mother admonished me with a shake of her head. "Don't worry, my dear, I brought you plenty to choose from."

Peyton curled into herself, but it was such a small movement that I doubted many would have noticed. However, my mother's smile and bright countenance were infectious. I'd rarely seen anyone who could withstand her sweetness—not that she didn't have a badass side. My mother knew exactly how to scare the living shit out of people with one look, and even the toughest men turned into pups and fell all over themselves to make things right any time she was disappointed in them. Myself included. There weren't many people in the course of my life who'd been able to bend me to their will—it was ingrained in me to fight oppression, which was probably why I ended up fighting with the rebels so often—but my mother led the group. Although there were some secrets I guarded even from her. My hands were far bloodier than she would ever know.

"I'm Lizabeta," my mother said, attracting my attention once more. "But everyone calls me Beth." She gathered up a few of the bags and practically danced over to set them on the island near Peyton. "My son mentioned that you were in need of some clothes. Of course, since he's a man, I figured there were several other items he didn't think of as well."

She beamed at Peyton, who had begun to relax, the tension seeping out of her muscles as she basked in my mother's sunny presence. "I'm Peyton. Um…you didn't have to go through such trouble for me," Peyton insisted, though her curious eyes strayed to the bags. "I'll only be here a couple of days, anyway."

Irritated at the prospect of her leaving, a growl formed in my chest. *Because she needs help*, I lied to myself. I could feel my wolf's disgust with my attitude, and he snarled at me before ignoring me.

"Nonsense," my mother announced. "You'll stay until Nathan helps to take care of whatever is plaguing you, my dear."

"I can take care of myself," Peyton grumbled, though there was no bite in her tone—I assumed because she didn't want to offend my mother.

"Of course, you can. But it never hurts to have a little brute strength on your side. And since he has brains and isn't all brawn, you might as well use him."

I rolled my eyes to the ceiling and took a deep breath. *What a ringing endorsement.*

Peyton placed her hand on my mother's arm, her expression earnest. "I'll pay you back for all of this when I get a chance."

My mother tsked and shook her head. "Nonsense," she stated with finality as she began to unpack one of the bags. Peyton started to say something else, but my mother cut her a look and, like the rest of us would, Peyton shut right up. Mother drew out several pieces of clothing, a hairbrush, and some other female things I recognized, but couldn't name.

Mother chattered about the things she'd brought for Peyton, who listened intently as she played with the soft fabric of a light blue sweater. I sat back and waited until they were finished and my mother had left to continue my argument with Peyton.

I gathered up the bags by the front door and took them to the guest room. After dumping them on the bed, I went to my room and took a shower, leaving my hair down to dry. I exchanged my sleep pants for jeans and a long-sleeved thermal with the three buttons at the top open, then retreated to my office to work.

"I'm off, *moy malysh*," my mother said later as she popped into my office. I glanced at the clock to see that it had been over three hours since she arrived. What the hell had they been doing?

"*Do svidaniya, Mamen'ka*," I murmured as she kissed my cheek. "Thank you for your help with Peyton."

My mother straightened and appraised me with a speculative eye for several moments. "I'm assuming the cub she's carrying is not yours?"

I shook my head, my brows slashing across my eyes as anger burned in my gut.

"I figured you would have told me because I raised you to be a good man," she said with a pat on my back.

I wondered if she would still think that if she knew about all that I'd done in my life. She'd definitely instilled values in me and I lived by a code of conduct. But that code didn't prohibit me from torture or cold-blooded murder if the situation warranted it.

Mother turned but had only taken a single step when she glanced back at me over her shoulder. "Have you considered making that cub yours, Nathan?"

"Pardon?" I asked, taken aback by her question.

"I don't know why her pregnancy makes you angry, but my assumption is that it's born of jealousy. So why don't you mate that sweet girl and give me grandchildren?"

"Mate?" I coughed, choking on the word. "Grandchildren? Mother, what have you been smoking?"

She rolled her eyes and started for the door again. "There is so much darkness in you sometimes, Nathan. You've managed to exclude emotion from your life and it's not healthy." At the door, she halted once more. "I saw something ignite in you when you looked at Peyton. It was the first time in a very long time that I saw a spark of something besides your wolf in your eyes." I started to say something, but she cut me off. "Yelling at sporting events doesn't count." Then she smiled brightly and blew a kiss in my direction. "Just my two cents."

I didn't know what else to say and she didn't seem to expect a response.

"Come to dinner next week. You and your father can yell at the sports people together." I chuckled at the mention of my father and his habit of shouting at the television whenever he was watching a game, one I'd picked up when I was a kid. My mother shook her head as she walked out of my office muttering, "Of all the traits to pass down…"

I turned back to my computer and I sent off one last email before shutting it down and going in search of Peyton. It was long past time to get the truth out of her. I would like to have been more patient with her, given her more time to come around. But my gut was telling me that the threat chasing her would catch up too fast, and I needed to be prepared.

I found her out back, sitting in my favorite rocking chair—a birthday gift from Jax several years ago. She pushed the chair into motion with a foot propped up on the railing that surrounded the large porch. Her eyes were on the river, but they were unfocused, as though she wasn't really seeing what was right in front of her.

My wolf huffed at that thought. *What? I see her.* He pushed against my skin, trying to surface, clearly unhappy with how his human part was handling Peyton. I growled at him to bugger off and he gnashed his teeth, but stopped trying to take over.

Much to my disappointment, she'd exchanged the towel for a maroon, oversized sweatshirt and a pair of black leggings. The stretchy material left little to the imagination, which I appreciated, but she'd have to change if we left the house.

I leaned against the railing, facing her and bracing my hands on either side of me. I watched her for a bit, not bothering to hide my probing gaze as I pondered whether sharing some of my past would urge her to open up a little.

Perhaps that, and maybe telling her about KBO, would give

her more faith in my ability to protect her.

"I hope my mother wasn't too much for you."

Peyton flashed me a tiny smile and shook her head. "She's adorable. I loved her energy."

A smile tugged at my own lips. "She's always been that way. But it wasn't until we left Russia that she felt unrestricted enough to truly be herself. We hadn't realized how much of herself she'd been holding back until she set it free."

Peyton's curious gaze drifted to me, but she didn't say anything at first. I was sure she was pondering whether or not to engage in this conversation. Sometimes questions revealed as much as answers.

"I wondered if you were from Eastern Europe when you spoke Russian to each other." She hesitated, then asked, "Why didn't she feel free to be herself?"

I stroked my beard and studied her carefully. Something in her tone sounded... empathetic. "My father was *dvoryanstvo*, Russian nobility."

"I didn't know Russia had nobility."

"A long, long time ago. In the late sixteenth and early seventeenth centuries, the term for those of high-ranking birth evolved to *dvoryane*—the highest-ranking gentry. Even that eventually turned into wealthy, powerful families, rather than royalty or nobility."

"So, you're a trust fund kid, huh?" she teased.

I listened hard, but there wasn't a single hint of distaste or sarcasm in her tone. *Interesting.*

I shook my head and shrugged, my lips forming a crooked grin. "I suppose you could see it that way. Although my mother likes to think of me as more of the Robin Hood type."

"You're a thief?"

Again, I analyzed her words and tone, but heard only curiosity. No judgment for a thief or a rich kid. That was a bit of a contradiction. Peyton was quite the puzzle and her caginess only made me more determined to assemble the pieces.

"Not a thief, exactly. Although, truth be told, I've done plenty of that in my life. But no, it's because she thinks I've spent my life standing up against corruption. I think my father's choice of description is probably more accurate."

"What does he call you?"

She was listening intently now, and I kept talking in hopes of learning more. "A crusader."

"Like Batman?"

For the first time since I started talking, Peyton showed distaste. I wasn't sure what that was about, the expression on her face was almost comical.

I made a low sound of amusement. "No, he's being literal. As in someone who fought in the Crusades."

Peyton's eyes grew wide. "You"—she pointed at my chest as if she was staring at a cross emblazoned there—"you fought in the Crusades?"

I nodded.

"But—but that would make you—*holy shit*." Her eyes lifted to my face. "How old are you?"

"Thirty-five," I replied with a smirk. Our breed of shifter stopped aging in our late twenties to early thirties.

Peyton rolled her eyes. "Okay, smartass. How long have you been thirty-five?"

I ran a hand through my hair and thought about how to answer. "How many times have I turned thirty-five or how many years since I turned thirty-five the first time?"

"I'll take either, stop stalling."

"Let's see, I've celebrated my thirty-fifth birthday almost fifty-nine times."

Peyton's jaw went slack, and she stared at me, completely still. Except something in her eyes told me she was thinking.

"You were born...damn, Nathan." She shook her head, her expression one of utter disappointment. "I never would've taken you for a cradle robber."

I barked a rare laugh and shrugged helplessly. "It's so hard to find girls my age."

Peyton burst out laughing and like every other time I'd heard it, I enjoyed the musical quality. Not that we'd done much laughing the last time we'd been together.

Her guard was down a little, so I contemplated seeing what I could draw out of her. Before I could, she said, "So you're older than dirt"—ticking her list off each finger—"you fought in the Crusades, you are Russian, and your mother thinks you're Robin Hood."

"I suppose that's one way to sum it up."

"You didn't finish telling me about your mother."

"So I didn't," I acknowledged with a nod. "My father likes to refer to me as a crusader, not because of those specific wars, but because I fight for what's right. It's what he taught me. Which is why he and my mother have never blamed me for being forced to flee our home."

"Why would they? Was it actually your fault or did they just need someone to place the blame on?"

There was a speck of bitterness in her question. She almost succeeded at hiding it and if I hadn't spent thousands of years learning how to read people, I might have missed it. I filed that away with the other things I'd picked up.

"The blame could be placed on me, as it was my actions that sent us into hiding to avoid execution. However, the blame also lies with the government who was suppressing their people. Or you could blame the man who betrayed me. All three are justifiable."

"Suppressing?"

Hmmm... out of all that I'd said, she'd latched onto the

suppression of the people. "Have you heard of the Decembrist Revolt?"

Peyton nodded and I raised an eyebrow in surprise. "I like to read, and I have a knack for remembering things."

"You have an eidetic memory?"

She shifted uncomfortably in her seat. "Yes. So how were you involved? Is that why you had to flee?"

Her avoidance didn't go unnoticed, but I went on as requested. "I was an officer in the Russian army when we went to Europe and marched to Paris to take care of Napoleon. It was a wakeup call to many of us." I ran a hand through my hair and stroked my beard. "We were ages behind them in so many ways. The treatment of our peasant class was…" I gripped the railing tight, containing my fury. "We needed radical changes to the structure of government, to the rights of the people, and so many other things. So we formed…I guess today's best description would be coalitions. All covert, of course. We wanted to limit sovereign power, abolish serfdom, and other deep reforms. We were planning a revolt, but I had gone to help out a friend, intending to be back by the time we executed the plan. Unfortunately, some of the more fanatical members pushed for an earlier date and somehow convinced the others to go with it."

"It wasn't supposed to happen when it did?"

"No. I had a polished, well-thought-out plan that would have all but guaranteed victory. By revolting early, it was poorly planned and many of the Decembrists—as people refer to them now—were hesitant because they wanted to wait until I returned."

"Why didn't they?"

"Someone convinced them that their identities were about to be leaked and if they didn't do it then, they would never have the chance."

"Was it true?"

"In a manner of speaking. The man who led the group that was pushing to move up the plan was the one leaking the names."

"So they would have been betrayed either way." Peyton's tone was flat, and her expression wiped clean. "Had you been there or not, the outcome would have been the same."

I shook my head, and she cocked her head to the side in silent question. "My friend received word of the traitor's name and actions. If they had just waited until I returned, I'd already set up a trap for him and a way to discredit anything he might have shared."

Peyton slouched back in her chair and scowled. "Instead, he won, and people were executed or exiled. And you and your parents had to leave your home, your family, everything behind to save yourself from a firing squad."

I nodded and watched her thoughtfully. "I made sure he faced a fate much worse than a firing squad." I murmured darkly. She eyed me suspiciously and I smoothed out my expression and shrugged. "Right doesn't always win." A subtle tightening around her mouth told me what I wanted to know. "I've certainly learned that after years of revolts, rebellions, wars, and police actions. How did you learn it?"

Peyton immediately closed in on herself. *Fuck.*

I'd learned a little, but if my play to know more about her wasn't working, then it was time to move on to what had brought her here. And I wasn't going to budge or be gentle on this end. Everything came to a halt at one conclusion. I needed to know what I was up against before I could prove to her that she was safe with me and my pack.

She was silent for a long time and I was just about to push her when she murmured, "I still don't understand why you all want to help me."

"Because you need help, and I can provide it." How many times would I have to say this before she understood it?

"Just because you're a giant, and a powerful Alpha, doesn't mean you can assume that."

I didn't reply at first. I pulled a deck chair over next to hers and took a seat, then unfolded my body into a relaxed position before twisting my hair up and securing it with an elastic band. "Tell me, and we'll see if I'm right." I attempted to soften my tone so it didn't come out as an order, which was my natural instinct. I was used to saying "jump" and having the answer be "how high?" But that wouldn't work with Peyton, which was incredibly aggravating.

Peyton's emerald gaze swirled with flecks of gold as she chewed over my request. After a few minutes, she returned to observing the river and rubbed her temples in gentle circles.

I prepared another argument, assuming this had been her way of dismissing me, but instead, she began to talk.

"About a week ago, I left work late one night. When I went into the alley behind The Spot, I smelled blood…a lot of blood." Her breath hitched and gold flashed in her eyes. The reliving of this story wouldn't be easy, and I wasn't surprised to see her panther trying to surface, her instincts to protect Peyton even though the danger was only a memory.

Peyton continued on, telling me that she'd caught a male attacking a woman—both shifters—and that she'd fought him off in an effort to save his victim. A tear streaked down her cheek when she told me the woman had died anyway, but not before calling the authorities, which had saved Peyton's life.

I felt a rush of gratitude for the incredibly brave, nameless woman and determined to do some digging to see if I could find out who she was and make sure she'd been properly laid to rest.

There was something else about her tale that poked at the back of my mind. As if it were familiar.

"He ran off when the police showed up and..." Peyton hesitated and glanced at me furtively. My eyes narrowed in suspicion; she was holding out on me again. "Um, I went back to my apartment—"

"From where?"

Peyton licked her lips and started twisting the ring around her finger again. I'd noticed she did it when she was wary or anxious and it made me wonder at the significance. I hadn't seen it close enough to make out the engraving.

"A friend asked me to stay with them, but I wanted to go home," she finally answered.

Her explanation sounded logical, but in the short time I'd known Peyton, I'd learned a lot of her tells. I'd always been extremely skilled at reading people, but for some reason, I didn't have to try hard with Peyton. And it definitely wasn't because Peyton wore her emotions and thoughts for all to see. No, she'd been closed to my mother, and yet I'd seen past her barriers. Not completely—it wasn't as if I could hear the thoughts in her head—but I had a sixth sense of sorts that had specifically tuned in to Peyton. Currently, it warned me that she was still hiding things. But I would let her finish her tale to see how much she revealed before tackling her secrets.

"Yesterday...wait, no, the day before..." She closed her eyes and shook her head as if to clear it. "I've lost track of the days."

"I found you yesterday morning," I prompted.

Her lips curved slightly, and she nodded in thanks. "Right. So, the night before that, he showed up in my apartment. He came at me and we fought, but I managed to escape. As soon as I hit a safe place, I shifted and just...started running."

My hands balled into fists and my body vibrated with the

force of the rage coursing through me. When I found the evil son of a bitch, I was going to make him bleed. His end would be slow and painful. My wolf growled his agreement and bared his teeth as though we were already facing the villain down.

Peyton lifted her hands at her sides, palms up, and shrugged. "I honestly have no idea how I ended up here." Her hands were trembling, and I could see how hard she'd been trying to keep her emotions in check while relaying the story.

I had no answer for her on that score. "I don't know, but I'm glad you did." I leaned forward and grasped her chin, locking our eyes. "Try to trust me, Peyton. I promise, you're safe here. I will protect you."

"I don't need you to protect me," she said. "But I won't turn down your help anymore."

"You'll stay?" I asked.

She nodded. "I'll stay for a little while."

"Good." I released her face and leaned back in my chair. I put my feet up on the rail, crossed at the ankles, and folded my arms over my chest while observing the clear blue sky.

"If you're determined to take the risk"—she shrugged—"that's your prerogative. Although I'm not sure how your 'brawn,' as your mother put it, will help catch the guy."

"Maybe I'm not as dumb as I look," I drawled, my tone and expression dry. An amused smile broke out on Peyton's face and my breath caught in my lungs for a beat. *Damn, she's beautiful.*

"Touché."

It occurred to me that it might be a good time to tell her about KBO, but my mind kept drifting to something else. That feeling of familiarity still danced around the edges of my mind, but I couldn't grasp it long enough to study it. I needed more information. Dropping my gaze, I connected with Peyton, who had been observing me with an expression that suggested she wasn't quite sure what to make of me. However, my mind was preoccupied so I didn't take time to address her curiosity.

"Tell me everything again," I instructed. "Don't leave out any details. What he said, what he was wearing. Did you notice anything specific about his victim?" I felt like an asshole for making her relive the story multiple times, but I *needed* answers to my questions.

Peyton sighed and settled back into her chair, in a position similar to mine—appearing relaxed, except the fiddling with her ring that gave her away. "Why?"

Not used to explaining myself, I frowned and almost brushed off her question with another command to be obeyed. At the last second, I reasoned with myself that Peyton wasn't a member of my pack and didn't respond well to being ordered. Normally, I didn't care and simply railroaded over any obstacles in my way. But something about Peyton... I had a feeling that if I wanted her to open up and trust me, I needed to make an effort to alter my behavior with her. Easier said than done when you were my age and set in your ways. "Theories are trying to form in my mind, but there are too many holes for any of them to truly take shape. So I'm hoping you'll remember details you missed before by telling it again."

My explanation satisfied her, and she relayed her story a second time. After she finished, the question clanged louder in my head. Could it be the same killer?

"One more time."

Peyton frowned. "Is there some specific detail you're hoping to find?"

"I'm not sure yet," I answered.

After a sigh, she grasped the sides of her chair, squeezing them tight before folding them in her lap. Then she repeated her tale.

As I'd hoped, every time she told it, she remembered new

details and the idea that we might be chasing the same guy strengthened.

My stomach rumbled and a quick peek at my watch showed we'd been talking well into the afternoon and we hadn't eaten since breakfast. I immediately felt like an ass. *She's fucking pregnant, King. Might want to feed her.*

"You must be starving," I stated as I moved to get up.

Peyton waved a hand and curled her tiny frame up in her chair like a little kitten in a box. "I'm not hungry, but you go ahead and eat."

I frowned and put my hands on my knees, leaning toward her. "You're pregnant, Peyton."

Her eyes rounded like saucers and she gasped. "I am? Why didn't you say anything?" The mocking disbelief disappeared as quickly as it had shown up. "I know how to take care of myself. And my baby. I don't need you to hover. It makes me…antsy." Her gaze swept over the forest with longing. "I think I need a run."

"You need to rest," I grunted. The glare she shot my way was ice cold and threatened to cause me pain. "You can't exercise on an empty stomach," I said, trying a different tactic.

Peyton blew out a frustrated breath, smacked her palms onto the arms of the chair and shot to her feet. "Yes, Mother," she snapped before stomping inside.

How am I the bad guy here? I shook my head as I followed her inside. *I will never understand women.*

I entered the kitchen to find Peyton nibbling on an apple. Despite her scowl, I made a quick pasta salad—millennia of being a bachelor had given me excellent skills in the kitchen. Plus, my mother insisted that every man should be able to cook his own food. Peyton ate every bite and asked for seconds. Not wanting to create more tension between us, I bit back my desire to say, "I told you so."

She pushed away her empty bowl and guzzled down the rest of her water, then yawned.

Fortified with food, I was anxious to do some digging into my theories. I jerked my head toward the large couch and suggested, "Why don't you take a nap. I have work to do."

Peyton yawned again, but her attention drifted to the wall of glass that showcased the back porch and the river and forest beyond it.

"Rest," I grunted. "We can go for a run later."

Her eyes returned to my face and she studied me with open curiosity. "You can't help it, can you?"

"Pardon?"

"I'd say you're treating me like a child, except that's not quite right. You just fall naturally into the role of protector. And you're a born leader. It makes you high-handed and honestly… a little condescending. But I'm starting to believe that you're not being intentionally insulting."

My brow puckered as my mouth tightened at the corners. "Of course, I'm not trying to insult you."

Peyton rolled her eyes and hopped down from the chair she'd been perched on at the kitchen island. "Since you are oblivious, let me spell it out for you. I'm willing to work with you as a partner for the moment. If you keep treating me like I'm breakable, I'm going to break you." Then she spun around, marched over to the couch and flopped down onto her back.

I wanted to laugh but swallowed the urge. Her feisty side was sexy as hell and memories of the spitfire she'd been in bed made me hard as fuck. If it hadn't been so obvious that she needed to sleep, I would have taken her to the bedroom and fueled that fire while showing her who was the Alpha here.

Instead, I shuffled off to my office to work on fleshing out our next steps.

CHAPTER FOURTEEN

NATHAN

I picked up my phone and searched for Dana in my contacts, tapping her work number once I found it.

"Nathan," she answered in a harried tone. "I've been meaning to call you, but it's been hectic around here. What did you need?"

"You first." I wanted to know what had been happening lately, hoping she would fill in some of the gaps in my theories so I could weed out anything pointless..

"There's been another attack, but…something is off. Serial killers don't often deviate from their routine and this one…parts of it fit and I would swear it's him, except…"

"Only minor slashes, though they were enough to kill her," I guessed. "No semen. But the timing fits and her tongue was missing?"

Dana didn't speak for a long moment, then asked quietly, "How did you know that?"

"That's not important right now." I wasn't ready to tell anyone about Peyton or the fact that she'd been a witness. "First, tell me more about the victim."

She hesitated, probably deciding whether or not to demand

answers. However, she knew me well enough to know I wouldn't budge, so she didn't push.

As the ME, she didn't have many of the answers, so I asked for the contact information for the officer assigned to the case, Detective Rogers.

Unfortunately, he was a human with no knowledge of shifters, which meant he wouldn't be inclined to share much about the case with me. I didn't want to bother the chief of police, Scott Hamilton—a warlock on the ISC. In the end, I decided the best way for me to ascertain the information I needed would be to do it through electronic back doors.

I blew out a frustrated breath as tension built inside me. A dull throbbing in my head had me yanking the elastic from my hair. I sighed with relief as it tumbled down around me.

I needed to talk to Tanner and preferred to have our conversation in person. Leaning back in my chair, I opened my mind and sorted through all of the voices filling my head. The connection with my Beta and enforcers was stronger than with any other members of my pack, so they were easiest to locate. I could also see into their minds and through their eyes, whereas with other members of my pack, it was mostly just telepathic—hearing their thoughts—and an awareness of their emotions.

When I contacted Tanner, he appeared to be working in his office at KBO. Rather than call him to me, I opted to go see him since I needed KBO resources to move forward anyway.

There's been a...development with the serial case, I informed him. *I'll meet you in your office.*

I'll be here. Still dealing with the effects of Dexter's shitstorm.

I didn't know if he'd even been home since then, so I made a mental note to kick his ass out when we were done sorting through everything and working out a plan.

Slipping my phone in my pocket, I left the office and went

to my bedroom. After putting on socks and a pair of black construction boots, I picked up my keys and wallet as I passed my dresser on my way out of the room. It wasn't until I stood at the garage door that I thought about what Peyton would think when she woke up to find me gone.

I detoured to the kitchen and pulled a pad of paper and a pen from the junk drawer next to the refrigerator. I scribbled a note to let her know I'd gone to my office and wasn't sure when I'd be back. I made sure to add that she should eat and to help herself to anything she wanted.

I wanted to make sure she saw the note, so I dropped it onto the coffee table in front of the couch where she was sleeping deeply. As I turned away, I spied the basket of blankets and the thought that she might be cold pushed me toward it. A soft, crocheted afghan from my mother sat atop the pile and I spread it over Peyton, then adjusted the pillow under her head so she'd be more comfortable. Satisfied with my efforts, I went out and climbed into my SUV, heading toward KBO. My mind lingered on Peyton for the quick drive, but when I parked the car, I set her to the side and focused on the situation with the killer.

I found Tanner still in his office, glaring at his computer and typing furiously.

"Still finding holes in the system?" I asked with a deep frown as I took a seat on the sofa across from his desk. We'd long ago put sofas in our offices after spending way too many nights falling asleep in our chairs.

"No," he growled. "You plugged them all, but someone leaked it to a few clients, so I've been on the phone non-stop trying to reassure people that we aren't compromised." His eyes darted to me and his expression was thunderous. "If that bastard's mistake messes with any of our DOD contracts, I'm going to hunt him down and flay him alive."

"Why haven't you sent them to me, Tanner?" I asked him,

my voice tinged with exasperation. I usually dealt with clients as I had more patience and diplomatic abilities than Tanner. He'd been my Beta for almost three hundred years, but he was still young and impulsive compared to me.

"Word is that you have a houseguest…a very attractive one."

I growled involuntarily, my wolf and I both irked by the idea of someone ogling Peyton. Except the only person who'd met her…

"You've been talking to my mother." It was a flat statement.

A grin split Tanner's face and he relaxed into his seat. "Mama K might have called to grill me about your visitor and ended up telling me all about her."

"When you aren't gossiping like a schoolgirl, tell the clients to contact me," I said firmly.

His smile faded as his mind returned to KBO. "You said there's been a development?"

For some unknown reason, I felt a reluctance to discuss Peyton with Tanner, but I dismissed it because I wanted Tanner's help. And that would require giving him details. "He surfaced again. They found another victim."

Tanner's lips pinched and he growled as he ran a hand through his short hair. "What the fuck are we going to do about this?"

"He was caught this time," I told him. Tanner's mouth opened, but I held up my hand, anticipating his question. "Not by the police. There was a witness. In fact, he only took off because of the police. Probably saved her life."

"The witness?"

I nodded. "His victim didn't make it. But since he was interrupted, they didn't recognize the kill as his at first."

"I assume you have a plan? To find the witness and question her?"

I stroked my beard as I contemplated how to explain the situation with Peyton. "I've already talked to her."

Tanner frowned. "I saw you less than forty-eight hours ago and, in that time, you found out about the murder, discovered there was a witness, found her, and questioned her?"

I leaned forward and rested my elbows on my knees. "She came to me, actually."

"Nathan," Tanner snapped. "Spit it the fuck out."

I stared hard at him and he bent his head, tilting it to the side to bare his neck in submission.

"Apologies, Alpha," he grunted.

I nodded in acceptance before going on. "After I went home the other night, I went for a run and when I returned, she was out cold next to the river behind my cabin."

Tanner's eyebrows rose so high they disappeared into his hairline. "You can't be serious." I stared at him and he shook his head. "Of course you're serious. Holy shit."

"There's more…" I hesitated again, the reluctance to discuss Peyton—outside of her status as the witness—still hovering on the periphery of my mind. My wolf growled in agreement, not wanting to share Peyton. My wolf's reaction was based on animalistic instinct, without any real-world shit affecting it. But my own disinclination confused me because, while I wasn't exactly an open book—okay, more like a vault—I'd never felt so possessive over a woman. My best guess was that I felt an extra layer of protectiveness due to the cub. Even if it wasn't mine, they were both in need of my protection. But one of the reasons I'd come to Tanner was to talk this out and hopefully, put the puzzle pieces together so I could move on.

"I'd already met her before she showed up here. Last month, when I was out with Asher and Jace. I went home with her."

Tanner stared at me in stunned silence.

"I never saw her again, until she showed up on my land yesterday morning."

"How did she know to come to you?" he finally asked when some of the incredulity had worn off.

"According to her, she didn't." I went on to explain about how she'd been attacked in her apartment and went on the run. "She said she let her panther take over and the next thing she knew, I was waking her up."

"Instinct?" Tanner queried as he observed me with an odd glint in his eyes.

"Apparently."

Tanner scratched his chin and continued to scrutinize me. "What aren't you telling me?"

One of the reasons Tanner held the position of Beta was his ability to reason and his detailed perception. It was a very useful skill…until he turned it on me.

I narrowed my eyes and my wolf brushed under my skin, his tolerance of Tanner's probing reaching its limit. "I promised to help her."

Unsurprisingly, Tanner nodded without question, in full agreement with my pledge. His lips pinched as he contemplated something for a few seconds. "Okay, we also have a serial killer to catch. But that's not why you came to talk to me in person."

I scowled and leaned back against the couch, stretching out my legs. "There's more to her story besides what happened with that murder. It's all in little things, but I can't get them to form an actual conclusion. She's damn good at hiding shit and playing her cards close to the vest."

Tanner snorted and I tossed him a dark look of warning. "Are you telling me she's even more closed off than you?"

"That's not the point."

He bit back his smile and nodded. "Okay, what is the point?"

After running my hands through my hair, I folded my arms over my chest and admitted, "I don't know what the fuck to do with her. I've never spent more than a few nights with one woman, let alone had one stay with me."

Tanner threw his head back and howled with laughter.

I understood his humor, even if I didn't appreciate it, so I simply waited for him to let it out.

"I—I don't think I've ever seen you at a loss before, Nate." He chuckled for another minute before finally sobering, though his eyes still shone with amusement. "I'm assuming she's an adult. I don't think you need to do anything with her. Now, if you want to do something *to* her, that's an entirely different ballgame—pun intended."

"Not helping," I growled as I struggled to keep my wolf from shifting and tearing out Tanner's throat.

"She's not open to another roll in the hay?" he asked. Though the humor lingered, his question was earnest.

"I don't think it would take much to convince her."

"Then what's the problem?"

"It's complicated. Not only does she need my protection, but she's pregnant."

Tanner's jaw dropped.

"That was about my reaction too."

"The father…?"

I shook my head. "We were together the morning before the full moon. It's someone else." I frowned. "I have this need to find him and beat the shit out of him for not taking care of her." I dropped my head back against the couch and stroked my beard. "In all my years, through all the wars and rebellions, all the women I've been with, I've never felt so…protective of a woman. It's damn confusing. Why her? And my wolf seems to think he has a claim on her. He's being a real pain in the ass about it."

"Your wolf."

Something in Tanner's tone brought my head up so I could see his face. "Yes. My wolf. He's overly possessive of her and it's bleeding into my actions."

"What about jealousy?"

I studied him in silence for a beat, then admitted, "He's exhibiting some jealousy." *Or a lot.*

"Your wolf."

"Yes, asshole," I snarled. "My wolf."

"Okay," Tanner said, holding up his hands in surrender. "But do you think it's possible…?"

He trailed off and I raised an eyebrow while I waited for him to finish his thought.

"She found her way to you…"

I nodded, then narrowed my eyes in suspicion when one corner of his mouth lifted.

"And the last time you were together was in the morning."

"Yes," I stated, rankled by his rehashing when we both knew he hadn't forgotten a single detail of our conversation. Tanner had an eidetic memory.

The other corner of his lips rose up. "Your wolf is feeling possessive and jealous…"

"For fuck's sake, Tanner," I grunted. "If you don't start finishing your own sentences, I'm going dumpster diving in your brain for answers."

Tanner's mouth curved up even more, forming a smirk. "I know you don't have much use for emotions and shit, but I'm a little surprised it hasn't occurred to you."

My expression darkened and I growled ominously.

"No," he said with a shake of his head as he pushed back his chair and stood. "I'm not going to interfere." A knowing gleam entered his eyes and I almost threatened to take his secret conclusions from his thoughts. Except we both knew I only did that when it was necessary. I avoided invading the privacy of my pack as much as I could and only ever bent their will if it involved their safety, or someone else's. I demanded and expected the loyalty of my pack, I did not force it.

"I'll brief the IT team on the records they need to acquire." Tanner meandered toward the door of his office but stopped before he went through it and twisted around. "You might want to check the lunar clock on the night you met her." Then he sauntered out.

I rolled my eyes and slowly rose to my feet. Tanner had a flair for the dramatic. But I'd only taken a few steps in the direction of the door when my feet steered me over to his computer.

The jackass already had the lunar clock open to that date. Yeah, he definitely...

"Hey, boss man."

I tore my eyes from the calendar before I could take a good look. Lisa was standing in the doorway. She pushed a hand through her short, dark purple curls before jabbing her thumb behind her. "Tanner said I'd find you here. I want to go over the technical details for the Vienna op with you before I give the go-ahead on the surreptitious entry plans."

"Is there a problem?"

Lisa sighed, then explained the issues the op was facing that needed my immediate attention. The full moon took a backseat for the time being and I headed to the command center. Once we arrived, one of the other techs,

My thought process trailed off as I locked in on the morning I'd left Peyton naked and satisfied in bed.

7:23 A.M.

Well, shit.

CHAPTER FIFTEEN

PEYTON

I stretched like a cat as my eyes drifted open. I glanced at the clock on the end table beside me and my eyes went wide. Damn. Eight A.M. I'd slept the rest of yesterday away.

After reliving my experience over and over earlier, I'd been emotionally spent and physically exhausted.

But after my nap, my body was finally starting to feel somewhat normal after so much trauma from the last week. My muscles were still quite stiff, and I tired more easily, especially with the pregnancy adding to my fatigue, but I was steadily healing.

Slowly, I sat up and took in my surroundings. The house was quiet and still, but that didn't necessarily mean I was alone. Nathan was a predator, stealthy despite being a giant. It was possible he was around somewhere. *No doubt ready to pounce*, I thought with a sigh. I'd been a little surprised at his tenacity, wearing me down until I gave in. And all the while he'd been contained and patient, never once losing his temper, though he hadn't always masked his frustration.

I was also surprised that he'd somehow convinced me he

could help me take down the son of a bitch who was after me. And while I could take care of myself, I eventually had to admit that it wasn't just me I was responsible for anymore. I had to do everything in my power to protect my cub.

Nathan's fierceness at protecting me and the cub he thought belonged to someone else had taken me by surprise. Why would he feel the need to put himself in harm's way for a child who wasn't his? In my experience, bastard children—especially those of a different species from their pack—were made to feel like outsiders and treated cruelly. I'd been around enough packs after leaving mine to know that this wasn't always the case. But usually when those children found acceptance, it was because there was a relationship with a profound emotional attachment (usually pairs who were about to, or had already, mated) between the parent and the step-parent.

Nathan and I had a fuck of a lot of lust, but we were missing the emotional aspect. So his commitment to protecting my cub baffled me. A trickle of guilt spread through my veins as I thought about my secret. But if he was this possessive and aggressive with us now, it would be ten times worse if—okay, *when*, because I wasn't a total bitch—he knew the baby was his. Just the thought of it made me feel claustrophobic and long for a run.

After reliving my experience over and over, I'd been emotionally spent and physically drained. A small piece of paper on the expertly crafted, wooden coffee table caught my eye. I picked it up and squinted at the scrawled note, trying to decipher the handwriting. Nathan had a strong hand and clearly wrote with purpose, but he also wrote like a doctor. However, after a minute, I picked up some specific letters and finally made out what it said. I felt a little like I'd just learned a new language and that thought made me chuckle. Apparently, he would be working until who knew when, but I should help myself to anything. I wondered if that included snooping through the whole house...

After reading through the note again, his mention of dinner stood out to me. My brow rose as I glanced at the clock again. Had he been at work all night? I wondered if they'd made some progress on the search for my attacker. My first instinct was to call him, until I remembered I didn't have my cell phone. My eyes drifted to the phone on the kitchen wall—something I hadn't seen since I was a kid—but it wouldn't do me any good since I didn't have his number. Or anyone else's...my eidetic memory wasn't any good when people put their numbers in my phone, and I never looked at them.

Left to my own devices, I went about making myself some breakfast. As he'd said in the message, the kitchen was well stocked. I stared longingly at the bacon in the refrigerator as I gathered all of the items to make eggs and toast. My morning sickness had been manageable, but I'd learned very fast that bacon would be off the diet until after I had my cub. It didn't taste nearly as delicious coming up.

Once I was done cooking, I sat at the island and ate my eggs, then munched on the toast until I'd eaten every crumb, before making myself a couple more slices. With a pleasantly full stomach, I cleaned up my mess and stowed the dishes in the dishwasher.

I had a little more energy after eating, and I knew I should do a little PT if I wanted to get back into shape, so I wandered out to the back porch to do yoga. After thirty minutes, I was laboring, my body protesting all the exercise with a vengeance.

The only time I'd ever been close to this weak was after I'd broken my leg skiing in the Alps. The fracture had taken a couple days to heal, even in cat form. My leg had bugged me for a few months, which shortened my runs and drove me crazy until I was back at one hundred percent.

This situation was so much worse, mixing my injuries, the baby, and the stress of hiding from a serial killer.

Stop whining and move your ass, Peyton.

Growling at myself—*a glowing example of my mental stability, I'm sure*—I forced myself to do another thirty minutes. Then I collapsed on the ground and tried to wish my body back to bed. *Why couldn't I have been born a genie? Although there is an argument as to whether I would be able to grant my own wishes…*

"Oh dear, Peyton. Are you alright?"

I dragged my eyelids open to see Beth standing over me, her brow puckered and her eyes swimming with concern.

"Never better," I panted.

She peered at me dubiously as she held out her hand. I grabbed onto it and blew out a breath as I used her as leverage to stand up.

"Just doing a little PT," I explained. "I need to rebuild my strength. I'm not used to being idle, and I can't hide in the house and rest until I'm permitted to do otherwise." The words were out before I thought about the fact that I was talking about her son, and she might be offended.

Beth nodded. "I've never been one to sit around and do as I'm told either." Her expression was deadpan, and I blinked a couple of times while I tried to decipher if I'd heard her right.

Her eyes creased at the corners, and the blue orbs twinkled before a laugh slipped from between her lips. "Oh, honey. I know exactly how bossy my son is. He learned it from his papa. Sometimes, they are two jackasses in a pen."

By the time she'd finished, I'd already fallen into a deck check while I laughed hysterically. I really did love this woman. If Nathan didn't know how lucky he was to have her for a mother, I'd have to make sure I knocked it into his head before I left.

"I believe you." Shaking my head with a smile, I stood up. "Honestly, I needed the rest, but don't tell Nathan."

Beth chuckled and slipped an arm through one of mine. "My lips are sealed. I came to see how you were doing. Obviously, I arrived just in time."

"I'm just irritable," I admitted. "I really am fine."

"Nonetheless, I have a mothering complex," she teased with a wink, making me smile in return. "I have to take care of people when they are sick. It's a compulsion. And since that happens so rarely around shifters, I have to take advantage."

She led me into the kitchen and set some bags I hadn't noticed she'd been holding in her other hand on the counter. Then she gave me a little push toward the hallway. "Go take a long, hot shower, and when you come back, I'll show you what I mean. And don't hurry back."

I smiled and followed her instructions like an obedient kid...*wow, she really does know how to "mother,"* I thought with a silent laugh.

After loosening my muscles in the shower, my fatigue approached again. But it wasn't the unpleasant, overpowering fatigue I'd been plagued with for the last few days.

I put my hair up in a messy knot and pulled on a pair of sweats before returning to the kitchen. Beth smiled as I walked in and pointed a spatula at the tall chairs in front of the island. "Have a seat, honey. I made you chicken noodle soup and homemade French bread. The soup is ready, but the bread is in the oven."

"Homemade?" My stomach rumbled at the smell wafting from through the kitchen. "I practically grew up in France, and yet, I never learned to make bread," I lamented with a chuckle.

"You grew up in France?" Beth queried as she ladled soup into a bowl and set it in front of me.

I wanted to kick myself. Why had I told her that? Does she have some kind of mom voodoo thing that makes people tell her things? I had no real experience with mothers, just the ones I'd met as acquaintances. And Linette, but she hadn't had the baby yet, so I'd never really seen her as a mother.

"Um, sort of. I went to boarding school there."

An alarm went off, and Beth turned to pull the bread from the oven. She transferred the loaf to a cutting board covered in wax paper and began to slice through it. "Where are you from originally?" she asked as she put the slices on a plate and pushed it toward me with the butter and a knife.

"New York," I divulged after a brief pause. Then I tucked into my food to avoid more answers and because I was starving.

She served herself a portion and sat beside me to eat. She asked a few less personal questions that I happily answered, and it made the atmosphere light and easy. During the meal, she also told me about snippets of her life and a few hilarious stories about Nathan.

When we'd finished, she gathered the dishes and gave me a very stern glare and an order to sit back down when I tried to help. I couldn't help laughing because she was almost comical with her big personality.

"Would you like to learn how to make bread?" she asked after she'd put everything away. She seemed excited by the prospect, and I really had wanted to learn the skill.

"I'd love that," I agreed with a smile.

Beth patted me on the hand and bobbed her head, her blue eyes dancing merrily. "Perfect! How about I come by tomorrow afternoon, and we'll make something for you and Nathan to share during dinner?"

I shrugged a shoulder and grinned. "We'll see how good it is before I agree to share."

Beth laughed and came around the island with fewer bags in hand than when she arrived. She kissed my cheek and promised to be back the next day after lunch. "Now, at the risk of sounding like my somewhat overbearing son, you should rest."

I snorted in wry amusement. "No one is as high-handed and obnoxious as Nathan." I almost clapped my hand over my mouth and wished like hell that I could recall the words.

But Beth threw back her head and belted a laugh. "I'd like to defend my boy, but you're probably right," she admitted when she'd calmed. "Still"—she grasped my hand in a gentle hold and looked deep into my eyes—"despite all his faults, he's a good man. He's worth taking a risk on, Peyton. He'd make a loyal mate and a wonderful father." She released my hand and gave it another pat before walking to the front door. "Just my two cents," she chirped over her shoulder before she disappeared, leaving me speechless.

I padded over to the couch and dropped down onto it. Sitting there for an indeterminate amount of time, I replayed the afternoon in my mind. The time with Beth had been comforting, just as I imagined spending time with my mom would have been. Which only made me like and respect her even more, and I didn't want to hurt her.

Her assessment of Nathan was probably true, but not for me. Unless Nathan up and decided to leave his responsibilities behind and live like a nomad—which wouldn't happen even if Hell froze over—then the risk would be too significant. Learning to bake bread was one thing, but I had no desire to play house, and if I tried, it would only end in disaster. Because eventually, my wanderlust would get the best of me, and I'd leave destruction behind that would eat at me for eternity.

I doubted he'd be receptive to the idea, given that we

seemed to butt heads at every turn. No, Nathan and I were incompatible, and his naturally protective, possessive, and dominant personality would more than likely continue to piss me off.

After a while, my mind and body were too tired to do anything but lay down to take a nap.

CHAPTER SIXTEEN

PEYTON

When I woke up that night, it was after midnight and I realized I'd slept the afternoon and evening away. I wandered into the kitchen to find a plate of food covered in plastic wrap with another note consisting of instructions on how to heat my dinner and that he'd returned to work and expected me to rest.

I scowled at his high-handedness, piqued that he hadn't stayed to talk about our next moves. Did he expect me to just lie around and wait for this guy to find me? The smell of the food distracted me, so I heated up my meal and devoured it. A healthy appetite had never been a problem for me, but in the last couple of weeks, it had become clear that my cub had one too.

My mind was awake after so much sleep. But as I climbed off my chair, my body protested, still tired and tender, and my movements stretched my scars, making me wince. I knew the yoga had been good for me, but damn…

Sighing, I trudged to one of the comfy recliners and plopped down. There was an extremely large television mounted to the wall over the fireplace and I located the remote in the drawer of one of the end tables. I hit the power button and the room filled with sound and bright light. I jabbed the volume button until it finally fell to a respectable decibel level. I hadn't bothered to flip on any lights in the living room, so the brightness of the television screen filled the room and I blinked rapidly, trying to adjust my eyes. A sporting event filled the screen and I watched for a moment, trying to figure out what the athletes were playing. Was that...? *Interesting*, I thought when I determined it was a cricket match. Selecting the button for the guide, I noticed the channel currently broadcasting was a British sports channel. As I scanned the rest of the channels, I slowly raised an eyebrow, then started to laugh.

Clearly, Nathan was a fan of sports. The revelation had me examining the living room with a keener eye. It was furnished in a way that would seat a large group of people with places for drinks and snacks on the strategically placed tables. It wasn't unusual for the Alpha's home to have an open-door policy. I could picture Nathan and a bunch of guys—*or girls*, I thought with a frown—chilling and laughing as they cheered for their respective teams.

The scenario was appealing and for a second, I could see myself amongst the spectators. I'd always enjoyed sports, and although I'd never stayed long enough somewhere to become loyal to a team, I admired those who did. Especially fans who'd waited a century or more for their team to reach the top.

As I settled into a comfortable position, I found a sitcom that made me laugh and allowed myself to relax and continue to recuperate.

It wasn't until a few minutes to midnight that I heard a vehicle pull into the garage. Nathan looked fierce and lost in thought as he entered the house, clearly unhappy with whatever was on his mind. He stopped short when he spotted the television, then his eyes roamed around until they landed on me. He studied me for so long it started to become awkward. "I thought you'd be asleep," he rumbled.

A shiver skittered down my spine at the sound of his deep, gruff voice, and my cat perked up at his presence.

"I've done nothing but sleep," I replied evenly, unable to read him, as usual. In the short time that I'd known him, it had become increasingly frustrating that the only emotion or thought he seemed to wear freely around me was his desire for my body. "I was thinking that maybe I could go—"

"Stay here. You need rest." His tone was hard, and his probing gaze made me want to squirm uncomfortably, but I held myself still. It dropped to take in my body, lingering at my middle for a beat before returning to my face, and there was a flash of something dark, particularly when his wolf pushed to the surface. But he just cocked his head to the side, his silver eyes glittering in the light of the television. "If you're having trouble sleeping, I'd be happy to wear you out."

I managed to keep my expression deadpan, but his intense stare didn't miss my subtle shift or my stiffened nipples suddenly poking through the soft T-shirt I'd put on earlier. "How kind of you to offer," I said dryly.

His mouth tipped into a smirk and my core tightened while my cat purred seductively. "That wasn't a no."

Ugh! Get a grip, Peyton! I mentally shouted at myself.

Nathan watched me closely while I tried to form a response, but he spoke before I succeeded. "You know where to find me if you change your mind, baby."

He walked soundlessly out of the room and I imagined him entering his room and stripping off his clothes. Would he take a shower before bed? I doubted he would object to some company.

"Ugh!" This time I uttered the exclamation out loud as I dropped my face into my hands. Why couldn't I control my hormones? We were over a week past the last full moon so I couldn't blame it on the lunar cycle. *The baby.* I'd blame it on the baby. *And my cat, the hussy. And Nathan.* This was mostly his fault for being so…so…fucking sexy! Argh! I hated that I felt so drawn to his powerful dominance, but my body didn't give a rat's ass what my brain wanted.

Irritated with myself, Nathan, and my panther, I punched the power button on the remote a little harder than necessary and tossed it into the drawer where I'd found it. I tromped down the hall, paused for half a second at Nathan's door, then shook my head to clear away the fog of lust and continued on to my room. I stifled the urge to slam my door and shut it quietly before falling backward onto my bed.

I sighed as I stared up at the beautiful timber ceiling. The truth was that no-one was really to blame for our attraction. And the only one I could point the finger at for my suffering was myself. Nathan had made it more than obvious that he wouldn't hesitate to take me to bed again. But I couldn't bring myself to do it while I was keeping such a huge secret from him. Besides, letting him ply me with a night of hot fucking and incredible orgasms could potentially have me saying or doing things I would regret later. I'd agreed to stay temporarily, and people said stupid things in the heat of the moment. Right now, I could absolutely see myself being very, very stupid in the throes of ecstasy.

Despite my resolve—shaky as it was—it took a long time for me to soothe my raging desire and fall asleep.

The next morning, food awaited me on the kitchen counter again, along with a now familiar note about Nathan having left for work. Except this one had an added, "Stay."

My temper spiked and I glared at the delicious-looking breakfast, since Nathan wasn't there to scowl at. The next time I saw him, I might let my panther take a swipe just to remind him I was a feline, not a dog. If he weren't so freaking huge, I would've challenged him to prove who was at the top of the food chain… *I'm a badass jaguar, damn it!*

I knew Nathan had a lot on his plate, Pack and Council responsibilities, and I thought I remembered him mentioning his own business. Still, did he think I'd agreed to stay indefinitely? And for shit's sake, we had a killer to find before he found me!

It suddenly occurred to me that he might be investigating the murders without me. *Oh, we'll definitely be having a come-to-Jesus meeting about that the next time I see him.* If he was pulling some protective bullshit, keeping me uninvolved, I was going to play purple nerple with his balls.

Unfortunately, I spent the whole damn day waiting for Nathan to return.

When Beth came over, I was already seething and ready to kill Nathan, but I had this weird need to avoid disappointing Beth, so I put on my best attitude and didn't tell her how big of an asshole her son was.

It didn't take long for her to put me at ease and the afternoon turned out to be more fun than I'd had in a long time.

Nathan's mother was kind and patient—*a product of a hellion for a son, I'm sure*—and it suddenly occurred to me that she was exactly the type of mom I wanted to be.

Which struck me as odd because of her deep ties to her roots, her pack, and her family. Would I feel more like that once I'd had my cub? Perhaps I needed to revisit my idea of building a foundation somewhere near here and making my travel less frequent. I wasn't sure if it would put me in the looney barn or give me a sense of stability that I would eventually appreciate.

It was hard to imagine when I was already itching to be free of my chains. My panther and I were feeling cooped up and in dire need of a run.

When Beth finally left, I considered letting my girl out to get some exercise, but I was afraid I'd miss him if I left, and I was determined to have it out before I went to bed.

So, I did another tiring bout of yoga. It didn't help my mood much. However, I'd been pleased that it hadn't been quite as strenuous as the day before.

The joke was on me because I only managed to stay awake until just after two in the morning before I fell asleep on the couch.

CHAPTER SEVENTEEN

NATHAN

I gently laid Peyton on the bed and stepped back so I could pull the quilt up over her.

The moonlight streamed in through the large window, illuminating her pale skin. Her face was serene as she slumbered peacefully, and I felt a twinge of jealousy. My nights had been filled with tossing and turning, dreams of our night together and fantasies about new ones. I debated with myself about slipping into her bed and seducing her, even going so far as to stand outside her door a couple of times.

In addition to my sexual frustration, and the lack of progress we'd made in tracking the killer, both Councils were driving me batshit crazy. All of a sudden, the representatives from every supernatural species didn't trust anyone besides me, and even that was rocky these days. I'd been breaking up arguments and dealing with accusations and it was making me feel like a preschool teacher with a bunch of kids hyped up on sugar. And besides handling my own pack, there were several Alphas who wanted to challenge another, and mediation had only worked a handful of times. But I would only step in if things continued to escalate like this and I felt the situation warranted it.

Ever since the night Peyton arrived, I'd been inundated with bullshit I had to wade through and constantly putting out fires, so we'd barely crossed paths. Every time I tried to leave KBO to catch her before she fell asleep, I was waylaid by yet another problem, and called in at ungodly hours of the morning for more issues.

The pregnancy had been weighing on me as well and the umbrage I felt at her deception burned hot. So much so that when I'd come home around midnight the other night and found her still awake, I'd chosen to hold off on confronting her until I was sure I wouldn't do or say something I'd regret later.

TRUTHFULLY, the distance between us had given me time to work through the astonishment and resentment from learning the cub was mine. And although my resentment only continued to grow, I had more control over it and wasn't worried about it taking over.

I'd never thought about pups of my own. With no intention to mate, it hadn't even been a question. And I had enough childish squabbling to deal with as the Alpha of the Silver Lake Pack.

That being the case, I hadn't expected my first reaction to be a healthy dose of male pride. The animalistic side of me puffed up over having procreated, a basic instinct for most men, though a great deal of us ignored it. Now that it had happened, those instincts roared to life and I couldn't help but be a little cocky over it.

I was also blindsided by the overwhelming rush of protectiveness and affection, more than I'd ever felt for a child, even the ones in my pack. It was a lot to analyze and understand, which wouldn't be the simplest task because emotions were messy and unpredictable. Learning to control them and filter through what was necessary while throwing out the rest had saved my life over and over.

This was all new territory for me, though. The off-the-charts chemistry between Peyton and I, and now a baby… It had been more centuries than I could count since I'd last felt such uneven ground beneath my feet. But until I figured out how to level it, I didn't think discussing it would lead to anything except angry words and no solutions.

But I was determined to get answers to my questions very soon. Not only did I want to know why she'd kept it from me for so long, I wanted to know what her plans were. Once I knew that, then I would figure out how we were going to proceed. One thing I knew for sure, she certainly wouldn't be keeping me from my pup, or cub's, life.

All the while, my wolf was pissed as fuck at me for the lack of time we'd spent with Peyton. I began to wonder if he would get over his obsession with her. I hated to think about dealing with his crap for the rest of eternity if he didn't. Especially since our lives were forever intertwined through our child.

I'd thought about asking her to mate with me—a solution my wolf kept shoving at me, his desire to claim her constantly filtering through my mind—but the thought of answering to someone else just added to the pounding headache plaguing me. I served enough masters with all of my responsibilities. And with the level of desire already between us, and my glimpses of jealousy and possessiveness, I didn't want to think about how that would all multiply by leaps and bounds with every stage of the claiming that we completed. However, it wasn't as if we were true mates with a soul deep connection, so I assumed the inferno of desire between us would eventually fade. And the thought of coming home to Peyton in my bed appealed to me. We could essentially go about our lives with the benefit of incredibly hot sex and a two-parent home for our child.

Fatigue suddenly caught up with me and I plodded toward the door, ignoring my wolf's howling and growling in protest at leaving Peyton alone. *Relax,* I snapped at him. *She and the cub need rest, damn it.*

He grumbled, then ultimately gave up the fight for the night so that when I climbed into bed, I could fall asleep in peace.

My phone woke me at a little before seven the following morning and I swore a blue streak as I blindly reached for it on the nightstand. Finally locating it, I peeled open my eyes and read the name of the caller through bleary eyes. Usually, when something woke me, I was instantly awake and alert, but after the last couple of weeks, I was so fucking tired. Which put my temper on edge and grated at my patience.

Sighing, I swiped the screen and put the phone to my ear. "What?" I barked.

"The SC wants to call an emergency meeting," Willa informed me in her most professional voice, ignoring my bitter mood.

"Are you fucking kidding me?" I grunted as I flopped an arm over my face.

"Apparently, Xavier is stirring up trouble and it's making the humans in his area suspicious."

"I swear to all that is holy, one of these days I'm going to put that son of a bitch in the ground."

"I doubt you'd hear any complaints."

"No doubt," I agreed. "But it would set a precedent and we'd never be able to put that genie back in the bottle."

"Also, Sam called here asking for you. He wants you to look into the disappearance of an employee. Peyton, I presume."

Willa had been briefed on the situation a few days before, minus the fact that Peyton's baby was mine.

"I'll call him after I speak to the SC." I wanted to reassure him of Peyton's safety and gauge his relationship with her because jealousy had reared its ugly head again.

"Should I tell them you'll come in?"

"No." I rolled my torso up and swung my legs over the side of the bed. "I don't want to be that far away from Peyton while someone is after her. I promised to protect her."

Silver Lake was well guarded. We had inauspicious security booths on all four sides of our land and enforcers made perimeter runs several times a day.

However, it was as much of a fortress as other packs' lands. Mainly because other packs weren't stupid enough to tangle with me or my pack. I had a reputation as a deadly motherfucker, and it had been earned honestly.

But I didn't know what the attacker's story was, what he knew, who he was, anything that would give me a clue as to the best way to keep Peyton safe.

As the Alpha, my home often had a revolving door, especially since I worked from home often. There was a security system, but it was rarely engaged. I'd have to show Peyton how to use it and put in some upgrades.

Willa reclaimed my attention when she replied, "Of course. I'll set up a teleconference."

"Fine. Set up the call with Sam for right after. But we'll do them at KBO. I don't want Peyton stressing over this bullshit." She'd have enough to handle once I came home because our confrontation couldn't wait any longer.

She was so full of fire and so damn stubborn that I knew I would be in for a fight with her. She'd made it clear she wanted to be involved in the search and takedown of her attacker, but that was the last thing she should be worrying about while pregnant. I needed to lay down the law so she understood what would happen from now on and I was sure she'd agree to stay out of it once I pointed out that she needed to rest and avoid stress.

"Set it for ten," I told Willa. I wanted to shower and make breakfast for Peyton before I left.

Willa confirmed and we hung up.

I tossed my phone onto the bed beside me and stood up. I stretched for a couple of minutes, trying to relieve some of the tension in my muscles. My wolf had been feeling cooped up and honestly, we both needed exercise. I promised him we'd take time before the chat with Peyton this afternoon. *I'm sure I'll need it.*

CHAPTER EIGHTEEN

PEYTON

When I woke up in my bed the next morning, my mood had already been in the dumpster. Last night, my dreams of Nathan had been incredibly vivid.

Seriously, this level of obsession with him can't be healthy.

At one point, during a particularly dirty fantasy, I'd been so surrounded by his woodsy scent that when I jolted awake, I would have sworn that if I opened my eyes, he would be right there in bed with me. When I scanned the room and found no one there, I didn't know whether I was relieved or disappointed.

Another morning with breakfast but no Nathan.

As I chomped my way through the delicious breakfast he'd left for me—enjoying it in protest—all alone, *again*, my disposition continued to plummet.

I finished up, rinsed my dishes and loaded them into the dishwasher. When I turned back around, my gaze swept over the wall of glass and soaked in the beautiful view of the land outside Nathan's cabin. Fall on the East Coast could be magical. The colors of the leaves were so bright that even a camera or an amazing artist couldn't capture it completely.

Whenever I found myself out this way, I'd loved going for a run in the crisp air and my panther enjoyed romping in the piles of fallen leaves.

My girl brushed her fur just under my skin, hinting that she would like to be set free to run and play. It sounded wonderful to me too, and I wanted to explore my new surroundings.

Stay.

I snorted. Like that was going to happen. I was done waiting around for him.

I'd had enough sitting around, cooped up in this cage, bored out of my mind and itching to explore my environment. One of my favorite things about moving to a new place was exploring, learning all about it, and discovering all of its secrets. Then when the thrill was gone, and I became bored again, I'd move on to another exciting adventure. Sometimes I stayed only days, and sometimes I settled in for months or a year. I never knew what my future held, and it made every day exhilarating.

If I acted like an invalid and stayed in Nathan's cabin much longer, I'd lose my ever-loving mind. After I showered, I didn't bother with clothes since I would just take them back off when I shifted. As I made my way through the open living room to the back door, I could already feel my tension fading. Then I stepped out into the sunshine and took a deep breath. I felt as if I'd just cut the strings to a corset and could finally fill my lungs with air.

The temperature was on the warmer side for autumn, and I could hear the faint laughter of children playing tag. The joyful sound brought a smile to my face and I lightly touched my stomach, wondering what my child's laughter would sound like. A realization hit me right then. I didn't want my baby to grow up isolated like I had. He or she should have friends to play with and family around to love and care for them. It wasn't something I craved—in fact, it made me feel a little suffocated

—but I wanted my little one to have options, to choose their own path, just as I had.

No matter what happened, I promised my baby that we'd work it out so they spent plenty of time with their dad and his pack. Besides, my cub probably had more in common with the wolves than I ever had, despite my DNA. I kept the knowledge that I was a half-breed locked up tight in a drawer I almost never opened. But a baby changed everything and there were bumps on the road ahead that I'd never expected to deal with. I'd buried the half of me that came from wolves so deep, I had simply assumed my child would be a panther, like me. However, reality busted its way into my mind, and I couldn't ignore the fact that my cub didn't even have half-panther genes. Their father was a wolf, and their maternal grandmother had been one as well.

Long forgotten memories started to surface, and the threat of a serial killer no longer seemed as terrifying as the possibility that my cub would live through the same childhood experiences as me. Suddenly, the need to shed my humanity and let my panther take over, to run and feel the freedom of the wind in her fur, overwhelmed me. She pushed hard to the surface, her protective instincts heightened by the terrible memories cloistering me. I didn't fight her, and she broke free, popping bones and tearing flesh until all that remained was a sleek, black panther.

She leapt off of the deck and raced into the woods, weaving around trees and other obstacles with ease. Euphoria flooded our minds, making our hearts race, keeping time with the light touches of her paws on the ground as she practically flew through the forest. Silver Lake was a gorgeous area and I understood why people would be happy here. We stayed away from the town because Nathan had mentioned that there were humans living among them. But we passed lovely homes all along the lake and even discovered a couple of peaceful clearings.

After a few hours, my panther meandered into a more secluded spot, one with a picturesque waterfall across from it. She stopped at the water's edge and bent to take a long drink. When she finished, she cocked her head and examined her surroundings with interest. The next second she was in the air before diving straight into the clear water. After swimming a small distance, she popped her head back up for air and headed toward the falls.

She went directly under the heavy spray, making a sound that equaled a laugh, then climbed up onto the smooth ledge jutting out from the rock behind the curtain of water. After shaking out her coat, she inspected every inch of the outcropping before lying on her side to rest.

A few minutes later, her ears perked at the sound of another animal approaching. We immediately recognized them as a shifter, but remained wary as a petite, female, golden-red wolf padded onto the ledge from a small piece of land that connected one side of the rock to the grassy bank.

My panther slowly climbed to her feet, alert and slipping into predator mode, which meant appearing relaxed and unimposing. The wolf watched us, her dark eyes so full of pain that I felt the sting in my own heart. My cat immediately backed down and returned to her lazy spot on the ground.

There was a stretch of tense silence, but eventually, the pitter patter of paws sounded as she moved further into the alcove. My panther lifted her head and glanced over to see the wolf still several feet away, but she circled around before lowering to the ground. She curled into herself, a classic "leave me the hell alone" sign, so my panther and I relaxed and gave her space.

After a while, I was tired of doing nothing and nudged my

girl to let me out so I could explore. She huffed in displeasure, mostly because she didn't want to move from her comfy spot but she acquiesced to my request. Once the transformation was complete, I shivered from the cold of the stone beneath my naked skin, but my body quickly adjusted to the temperature.

I rolled up into a sitting position and glanced over at the other occupant on the rock. The wolf watched me curiously, though she remained hesitant, but I sensed it was more of a battle between loneliness and the desire to shut out the world.

I scooted to the edge of the rock and dangled my feet into the foamy water, happy to enjoy the solitude. A few minutes later, I heard the tell-tale noises of my neighbor shifting into her human form, then the soft slap of bare feet on stone as she shuffled closer. She sat a few feet away and crossed her long legs in front of her before brushing her long reddish-gold hair back over her shoulders.

"Are you visiting?" Her voice was soft and sweet, but the angst I'd seen in her eyes was in the undertone.

My head swung in her direction and I met her sad, pretty brown eyes. "Yes. Sort of." She watched me curiously, but I waved my words away. "It's a long story. What about you?"

She paused for so long that I wondered if she'd changed her mind about talking. Then she answered as she faced forward to stare at the waterfall. "I...I just moved here—joined the pack, I mean."

I nodded and placed my palms on the ground behind me before leaning back and raising my eyes to the cliff overhead. "Where are you from?"

Again, her answer was a long time coming. "A world away, and yet not far."

I chuckled and followed the water with my gaze as it fell, splashing into the pool below. "Believe it or not, I know the feeling."

I'd spent a chunk of my childhood with a pack not far from Silver Lake. But I hadn't been back or had contact with anyone since I left for boarding school. Sometimes that time seemed like an out-of-body experience, as if I'd watched it happen but hadn't lived it, which made the place and people feel as if they existed on another plane.

Pulling my feet from the water, I turned to face my companion and tucked my legs around my side. "I'm Peyton," I offered with a warm smile.

The woman's lips curved slightly and some of the darkness in her eyes abated. "Savannah."

"Well, Savannah," I said resolutely, "we're just two fish out of water, aren't we?"

She chuckled and pivoted her body to face me. "I guess we are."

I observed her for a minute, then cocked my head to the side and mused. "A close friend of mine is named Sam. I think maybe I should give you a nickname." I pondered my choices for a minute, before talking through them. "Red seems a little cliché." She nodded with a half-smile. "Bath, however accurate, is too harsh." Her eyes crinkled at the corners as she snickered. When it came to me, I snapped my fingers and crowed, "I've got it! Foxy!"

She laughed again and I felt a little bit of triumph that I'd put a tiny bit of sparkle in her eyes. "Foxy?"

"Yeah, because your hair and fur remind me of a fox's"—I snickered—"and you're not half bad to look at."

Savannah shook her head, even as she gave me a delighted, crooked smile.

There was something in her demeanor that kept calling to me. I felt as if she were pushing against a barrier, trying to break free. She wanted to unburden herself but didn't have anyone to share the load.

This broken woman needed a friend and with all the bullshit currently plaguing my life, I was surprised when I found I liked the idea of having someone to talk to. When the fuck had I become a sharing person? I eyed Savannah speculatively. Was it her? The reason I all of a sudden had the urge to spill my guts? Because it was super weird.

Still… I went for it. "I'll tell you mine if you tell me yours," I said with a wink.

Savannah laughed again, then shook her head.

"Is that a no…?"

"No. I mean it's not no." She smiled and shrugged. "It's just…I haven't laughed like this—or at all really—in ages." Her smile spread a little further. "It feels good."

I let her work through her epiphany and waited until she said, "Okay. You first."

"Well…" I debated how to sum up my fucked-up situation. "I witnessed a brutal murder, fought the guy and he injured me so bad that I almost died. Which meant pain from the stupid human medications and agonizing hours in surgery. Then the night I was released and went home, he came to my apartment to finish the job, but I escaped and ran until I passed out here in Silver Lake."

Savannah double-blinked and her mouth formed an O.

"Also, I had a one-night stand with your Alpha a little over a month ago and I ended up pregnant. He doesn't know it's his, but he's being extremely overbearing anyway and it's driving me crazy. I'm a wanderer by nature and used to my freedom, but he's caged me up in his house like a prisoner. And I get the feeling he's holding out on me when it comes to finding the guy who tried to kill me. All in all, I'm trying to stay alive and out of jail for killing your Alpha."

Her jaw had gone slack, and she stared at me like I'd lost my mind. *Maybe I have.*

"Your turn," I encouraged with a laugh.

"Wow. I mean, your situation is almost as fucked up as mine."

"Let's hear it. We'll see who wins the gold," I teased.

"Well, not too long ago, the man I loved was murdered. Then, when my new Alpha began to investigate, my best friend was killed as a warning to back off. After all that, I was kidnapped and taken to a facility where they began to do painful experiments on me. Once I was rescued, I just couldn't stay there anymore. Nathan was there to help with everything and somehow, I naturally drifted from my pack into his. He agreed to the change and brought me back here."

"Your mate was murdered?" I asked softly. The pain from losing a mate was said to be excruciating, not that I'd experienced it myself.

"No," she clarified. "We were just…I don't honestly know what to call us. Lovers seems so cold." Her eyes were swimming with pain again.

I squinted at her as I pursed my lips. "Hmmmm…sounds pretty even to me, Foxy. I think we need a tie-breaker."

I was joking, but for some reason, I had an urge to confess everything to Savannah. I'd never told anyone about my childhood, not even Sam and Linette, and I didn't understand why I suddenly had a need to share it with someone. This someone. Perhaps because she was easy to talk to, or maybe because she was a relative stranger. I didn't think it was the latter. I felt an odd kinship with Savannah—both of us were slightly broken, though my emotional wounds weren't fresh like hers. We'd both been through enough shit to recognize that we didn't need a hero or to be fixed. We wanted someone to listen and admit that sometimes the world just sucked.

Savannah stared at me while chewing her lower lip, probably contemplating whether she wanted to open up even more. "I, um…" She chewed her lip again, then sighed. "I don't know what it is about you that makes me want to spill all my secrets," she mumbled with a confused frown.

"Kindred spirits?" I suggested, then laughed at the ridiculous notion.

"Maybe." She trailed off and I raised an eyebrow in surprise.

"You believe in predestined relationships?"

She glanced away and took a deep breath, then swung her eyes back to my face. "Where I'm from, a shifter's mate is chosen for them."

"By whom?" I asked, flabbergasted that someone was allowed that kind of power over the packs.

"Fate."

I scrunched my nose and shook my head, feeling as though I was missing something. "Like true mates?"

"No, although I understand your confusion since that's how it works here. We aren't given a choice, you see. Once you've met your fated mate, that's it. There will never be another for you."

"What if you don't want to be with that person?"

She shrugged. "You don't have to, I suppose. But your, um…sexual needs can only be fulfilled by your mate."

"What?" I shrieked. "But—but—" A comment she'd made earlier filtered through my sputtering. "Wait, did you say you had a relationship with someone who wasn't your mate?"

"Neither of us had found our fated mates, so we could be together. But I lived in fear of him leaving me every day. I suppose it was ironic that fate took him from me by death rather than his mate."

I nodded in agreement, still stunned by the idea of the whole fated mate thing. Where in the world did shifters like that exist? Granted, I hadn't spent a lot of time with shifters other than acquaintances and a night of fucking here and there. Still, wouldn't I have heard about it? Savannah was watching me, studying my features like she was waiting for me to work through everything in my mind. Finally, I narrowed it all down to one question. "Where are you from, Foxy?"

"I shouldn't tell you; I'm supposed to keep it a secret. But… I could use a win." Her smile was teasing, and a little light made its way back into her aura. "I'm from another realm. Literally a whole other world."

My first instinct was to laugh, until I realized she was dead serious. *Okaaaay, so I'm not the crazy one.*

However, as I ruminated over her words, bits and pieces of information from my life floated through my mind. My eidetic memory had collected every piece of information I'd ever come across in my life and cataloged them into mental filing cabinets. There'd been whispers and rumors about portals and other worlds. I'd never put any stock in it, dismissing it as crackpot theories and daydreams. But Savannah didn't seem like the type. And I was a pretty good judge of character.

"You're completely serious?"

She nodded. "Please, don't tell anyone."

"I wouldn't," I assured her. We'd crossed into a mutual destruction relationship.

"I didn't think so, but it had to be said."

"Of course," I commented distractedly.

"So I win, right?"

CHAPTER NINETEEN

PEYTON

Savannah asked the question with false brightness, drawing my full attention. Her smile was forced, and I could see that she was emotionally drained.

"I don't know, Foxy…I've got a humdinger for you."

I couldn't believe I was even contemplating telling Savannah about my past. I'd made my peace with it all when I was young, but it was bound to bring back some of the pain for my panther, who was still bitter and angry. I did have a moment's pause at the idea that Savannah might believe the same as my pack had once she'd heard the story. I didn't think it was likely, and I'd learned long ago to let things roll off my back. Even so, if she did, that would totally suck.

Still, I opened my mouth and the story tumbled out. "I understood what you meant about being a world away and yet not far, because I was born into a pack somewhat near Silver Lake."

"Pack?" Savannah asked curiously. "But you're a black panther."

I nodded and kicked my feet in the water, watching it splash and ripple. "My father was a black panther—a jaguar. My mother was a wolf." Damn, that felt super weird to say. I hadn't admitted that to anyone since I'd left the pack.

"It's rare for a panther to settle down, particularly males. And like the animals themselves, my father had one night with my mother, then disappeared. Leaving her pregnant and alone. I know she hoped and prayed that I'd turn out to be a pup. My uncle told me she would have loved me either way, but she knew my life would be even harder if the half-breed was feline."

My girl pushed inside me, not happy about our stroll down memory lane. "I never had the chance to know because she died giving birth to me. My uncle—he was my great-uncle actually, but closer in age to my mother than his brother—he'd never mated and lived alone, so he took me in. Unfortunately, my grandfather was the Alpha of the pack and he blamed me as much for my mother's broken heart as for her death.

"My grandfather demanded the strictest obedience from his pack and kicked out or ostracized anyone who defied his word. He didn't need the hive mind to control the pack, he ruled through fear. That didn't mean he didn't use it though. Particularly with his enforcers. Those guys were practically robots," I said with a roll of my eyes. "My uncle could only go so far when it came to standing up to his brother, partly because he was afraid of what my grandfather might force him to do under his control. So he protected me as best he could." I shrugged and smiled sadly.

My panther whined, pawing at me and making it very clear she wanted me to talk about something else. When we'd traded places, her experiences had been no better than mine, but she'd taken it harder.

"When the Alpha wasn't ignoring me, he treated me like damaged goods, calling me terrible names, and being… physically rough with me. The rest of the pack—well, most of them, especially the kids—did the same. There wasn't much my uncle could do except smother me with kindness within the walls of his home. I think he hoped that by loving me the way a family member should, it would wipe away the pain and humiliation that I suffered outside of the house."

"I wouldn't call that love," Savannah whispered. "He was a coward. If he'd loved you, he would have protected you no matter what."

I shrugged. "My uncle was a submissive wolf. It wasn't in his nature to be confrontational. And there was no way he ever could have fought the Alpha's influence. Besides, eventually, he did what he thought was best for me. And it wasn't easy for him because he knew his brother would be pissed as fuck."

"Did he take you away?" she asked.

"No, he sent me away to boarding school. But under a different name and he paid for it anonymously. I still have no idea where he got the money."

"He just…sent you away? Alone?" Savannah nearly shrieked. I glanced over at her and she had her arms crossed over her chest and a furious expression on her face. Her reaction made me feel a little better, confident that she didn't see me the same way as my grandfather and the rest of the pack.

"He didn't have the strength to leave. It would have taken more courage and determination than he possessed. Don't get me wrong," I hurried to assure her with a wave of my hand. "My uncle was a good man, he was just…a submissive wolf. Weak. And the choice to send me away where my grandfather couldn't find me took everything he had."

"How old were you?"

I tucked my hair behind my ears as I thought back. "Thirteen, I think?"

Savannah gasped, but I felt no indignation on my own

behalf. The past was the past, and even if it hurt sometimes, I couldn't change it, so what was the point of letting it fester?

"I know it sounds harsh, but I'd become difficult to deal with, anyway. When I wasn't acting out, or raging at the injustice of my life, I withdrew and lived deep in my mind where the outside world couldn't touch me.

"It became clear when I was much younger that my instincts were more panther than wolf. I felt as if I were shackled inside a cage by being forced to stay inside so much. I had to contain my urges to wander, to explore, to breathe in the exotic air of new and exciting places. One of the only things that kept me sane was daydreaming about what I would do when I finally escaped that life."

My cat curled into a ball, knowing what came next in the story. "My uncle might have waited until I was a little older to send me away, but there was an incident with a wolf in the pack. He was an enforcer, and at least twenty years older than me. Most of the pack were attending a party in the maid lodge at the back of my grandfather's property, so my uncle gave me permission to play in the woods behind the house.

"The enforcer—Buck—was way over the alcohol limit and must have lost his way because he happened upon me. He grabbed me and told me I'd been a cocktease for too long, and he was going to take what I'd been pretending not to offer." I felt a little nauseous at the memory, but I'd long since stopped remembering that experience with anxiety. I was a survivor, not a victim. "I was small for my age"—I gestured to my body—"something that I thankfully outgrew. So he was able to pin me down easily. One thing I can always thank my uncle for is the self-defense lessons he insisted on—though I wasn't allowed to use them, which I hadn't understood at the time—because size can be deceiving. Yeah, Buck had taken me down, but I didn't have very far to go to put my knee in his balls."

Savannah snorted, then slapped a hand over her mouth, appearing mortified.

"Relax, Foxy," I said with a crooked smile. My response put her at ease, and she dropped her hand into her lap, folding it with the other.

"Anyway, my panther shoved her way to the surface, determined to protect me, but he had a knife I hadn't seen before. Just as the shift was completed, he grabbed her around the neck and tossed her into the nearest tree. It broke several of our bones. When she staggered to her feet, he launched the knife and it embedded deeply into the shoulder. He passed out after that and she limped back to my uncle's home."

I shuddered a little as I told her the next part. "The angle wouldn't allow her to get a good grip and pull out the blade. So—"

"Holy shit," Savannah breathed. "You shifted with a fucking knife in your shoulder?"

"Yeah," I admitted with a wince. "I had no clue what would happen, but my uncle wasn't around, and we certainly couldn't ask help from someone else." I ran my hands through my hair before tucking it behind my ears. "The muscles and bones couldn't shift quite right with an object obstructing their path. So, as they tried to move into position, the knife ripped through them all over again and a few of the bones that broke during the process didn't realign correctly. I was able to remove the knife, but then I passed out from the pain."

"I hope you castrated him," she huffed.

My smile became a little evil as I nodded. "Almost. He had to have surgery to fix whatever I did. My uncle never told me the specifics. He was too busy trying to clean up the fallout anyway."

"Fallout?"

I waved my hand in a careless gesture. "Yeah, Buck cried

foul. Said I'd begged him to help me, lured him into the woods, and taken a bat to his balls."

"That bastard!" Savannah snarled. "You told them the truth though, right?"

"It wouldn't have mattered if I did. As soon as my uncle returned to the house and saw me unconscious on the ground, he took me to a doctor—a falcon from a local flock—who stitched up a few of the sliced muscles. Then he re-broke the bones and aligned them correctly before telling me to shift so I could heal faster. Before I did, I told my uncle the story of what happened. He left me with the doctor to go home and scope out the situation. I think we both knew what would happen, but he hoped he was wrong. When he returned, he told me about Buck's version of events and that he'd gone to talk to my grandfather about it. But the Alpha was already up in arms and demanding I be punished. That night, my uncle drove me to the airport and put me on a plane to France."

"I can imagine the whole situation had you in a freefall," Savannah commented, her eyes cast down and the corners of her lips pinched. "A new place, not knowing anyone, feeling like a fish out of water."

I nodded. "For a while. But one of the best things my uncle ever did for me was choose this school. It was small and, believe it or not, the kids at my boarding school weren't so bad. I'd expected a bunch of rich kids to be uppity bitches and egotistical pretty boys. But most of them were just…normal. Like me, they'd been sent there because they weren't wanted at home. They made the best of the situation and making enemies among such a small group would have just made everyone miserable. I'd learned to close myself off, but that made it easy to build friendships of a sort. They weren't deep or lasting, which meant no one hurt me and I didn't miss them when they were gone. My time there was happy."

Savannah listened carefully, and I sensed the desperate hope in her, but she was terrified. Probably because everything in her life had gone to shit, so why would this be any different?

I reached over and covered her hands with mine. "Give it time, Savannah. And if after a while, you still don't feel at home here, try something new. Hey"—she met my eyes again and I smiled—"you can always fly along with me on my next adventure until you find the right place to land."

Her forehead puckered and she looked away, suddenly uncomfortable.

"Foxy, that wasn't a demand, girl. Just an offer." I laughed and gave her hand a squeeze before pulling back. "I won't be offended if you don't want to go gallivanting all over the world with me."

Her brown eyes swung back to my face. "Oh, it's not that. That would be really fun. It's just…it's complicated. In a way, I'm kind of stuck here until I figure things out. I have to make a choice and it will determine the entire course of my life."

"Does it have to?"

Savannah regarded me curiously, her head tilted to the side. "What do you mean?"

I played with the ends of my hair as I deliberated how to word my answer. "Is there a third option? Or a fourth or fifth?"

"I…" She trailed off, her expression thoughtful, while one of her hands tugged absently on her ear. "Honestly, I hadn't considered it. Where I'm from, your mate is already fated to you from the time you are born. There are few things that affect your life more than a mate, so it often felt as though there was nothing in my control. But here, I can choose my mate, right?"

I nodded, even though I only knew what I'd learned about mates growing up. The process was complex, and I'd never taken the time to learn all the stages and how they were accomplished.

"Even if they aren't my true mate?"

"Yes." That much I knew, but there was a caveat to that. "But from what I'm told, it's not easy to walk away from your true mate. The bond is incredibly strong and"—I smirked—"I'm told the attraction is fiercely hot." After my night with Nathan, I couldn't imagine what it was like for true mates. How they didn't just burn up into a pile of ash was beyond me.

"So, so hot," she sighed as she scrubbed her face with her hands.

My brows hit my hairline. "Have you met your true mate?"

Savannah's cheeks burned and she stared down into her lap. "I'm pretty sure. But…I'm not ready to make the decision—if I want him or not." Her sad eyes met mine. "Does that make me a terrible person?"

"Of course not. Is he willing to wait?" I asked curiously.

She ran her hands through her thick red mane and sighed. "I don't think he's completely figured it out yet. And there are other major complications. Honestly, it gives me a headache just thinking about it. Why France?"

Her abrupt topic change threw me for a second, but I moved on because I didn't want to cause her distress.

"I wasn't sure at first, but another friend of my uncle's met me there and gave me new documents, ones that had my father's last name attached to mine. As it turned out, those were my real legal papers. My uncle had kept them hidden and let my grandfather assume my mother had given me her last name. But what really sent me reeling was when he handed me another set of papers and a new passport. It turned out my father had known about me. I guess he didn't want the family life, but he'd made arrangements for me. Showing love in his own way, I suppose. I have dual citizenship and a trust fund." I held up my right hand and showed her the gold ring on my thumb. "He also left me this. Apparently, it belonged to his mother."

Savannah leaned in and examined it. "What does the engraving say?"

"*Tu es ton propre destin.*' It reminds me that my life is of my own making. My past has shaped me, sure, but I do my best not to let it dictate my future. The truth is, I'm simply more like my father. I crave the freedom to roam, and I get bored easily." I chuckled, then shook my head, my amusement fading fast. "I have to be honest"—I'd shared the rest of my darkest secrets with this woman, why not one more?—"I'm worried about being a mother. I love this little one so fiercely already, but what if…" I sighed and just blurted it out. "What if I suck at it?"

Savannah laughed and I rolled my eyes. "I'm serious, Foxy!"

"I know you are, Peyton," she said, still smiling. "And your doubts are normal. But I've known you for all of, what, an hour? And I already know you're going to be an amazing mother. That cub is going to adore you."

I hoped she was right, but there was still the problem of Nathan. "What if the baby is more like Nathan?"

"How do you mean?" Savannah asked as she unfolded her legs and stretched them out in front of her.

"I told you he's been keeping me locked up, right?"

"Sure. That would drive me crazy, too."

"But that's not all of it. I feel a strange pull to him and it's almost tangible at times, like a tether between the two of us. I'm sure it's because of the baby. We are connected forever through our child now, but this rope feels like it's stronger than that. It's making me worry that the cub feels a stronger kinship with Nathan. That they will be better off living here and putting down roots."

"Are you sure that's not what you want?" Savannah asked softly.

I blew out a frustrated breath and twisted my ring around my thumb. "It's already wrapped around my neck like a noose. It's why I staged a prison break today. I could feel it tightening and I became claustrophobic. And yet, I can't imagine leaving my baby with Nathan while I'm off running all over the world alone. So, how am I supposed to make everybody happy?"

"I wish I had an answer for you," she said, putting her hands out to the sides in a helpless gesture. She was observing me carefully though, and I wondered if maybe she was working through an idea. If so, I was all ears.

A cool breeze swept through the cavern and I shivered, which made me think about the way my body responded to Nathan's touch. The way I craved him still astonished me. I'd never felt such a strong sexual pull to a man.

"It has to be because of the baby," I mused.

"What does?"

I was confused by her question, at first not realizing I had spoken aloud. "This attachment I feel to him," I explained as I gestured to my stomach. "It's the only explanation as to why."

"Is it?"

"Of course," I stated firmly. "But…it doesn't—" I cut myself off as my face heated, both from embarrassment and the tendrils of desire slithering through my body when I thought about the rest of that comment.

Savannah studied my face with interest, amusement dancing in her eyes. "Peyton, are you blushing?"

I waved off her question and mumbled what I'd been about to say. "I can't imagine that's the reason Nathan makes me think of sex all the time." I cut Savannah a look before emphasizing, "*All the time,* Foxy." I ran my hands through my hair before fanning my face a little as I replayed bits of last night's dreams in my mind. "Pregnancy hormones are way worse than people say" I muttered.

"Maybe you need to work it out of your systems," Savannah suggested, sounding dubious despite it being her own idea.

"Nathan mentioned that, too." I pulled my knees up to my chest and wrapped my arms around them.

"Okay. So why aren't you at the Alpha's cabin drowning in orgasms?" Savannah's tone was dry.

"I'm healed and ready to go as soon as we catch this guy," I answered. "Sleeping together could be fabulous, or it could create a twisted mess that would cause pain to one or both of us when we tried to straighten it."

Savannah shrugged. "Maybe."

I narrowed my gaze and turned it back around on her. "Why aren't you rolling in the sheets with your guy right now?"

Savannah stiffened for a second, then relaxed and grunted, "That's fair. Honestly, I hadn't thought about a no-strings arrangement with him before you brought up other options. But you also make a valid point about possible complications."

My stomach rumbled and with the sun well past the highest point of the day, it was clear that we'd been sitting there talking for at least four hours.

Savannah chuckled and moved to stand up. "You should get some food."

I jumped to my feet as well, but stood there for a second, scrutinizing her countenance. "Your eyes aren't quite as sad as they were when you first showed up here," I said with a smile. "I hope talking to me helped, because this was really wonderful for me."

"It did," she confirmed with an answering curve of her lips. "I…I know it's selfish, but I can't help hoping you stick around. It would be nice to have a friend again."

I closed the distance between us and took her hand. "I may

not be around often, but I'll always be available to you, Foxy. Friendships worth nurturing are rare, but I have no doubt ours is one of them."

Savannah's eyes filled with tears. "Thank you. For the first time since Tyler died, I had a stretch longer than a few minutes where I wasn't drowning in sorrow. I don't know if I'll ever be whole again, but this makes me feel like I'll at least survive it."

"Maybe we are kindred spirits, after all," I teased. Except… a part of me started to truly wonder. The only person I'd clicked with faster than Savannah was Nathan. But my friendship with Foxy was a hell of a lot less complicated.

She stepped forward to give me a brief hug and when her hands landed on my back, she gasped and jerked backward.

Oh, crap. I keep forgetting about that.

"Battle scars from the night in the alley," I explained with a wry smile.

"You…you have scars?"

That fact alone gave away a lot.

"I don't want anyone to know he almost killed me," I told her. "Especially Nathan. It would only make him even more determined to keep me in a bubble and out of the hunt." I locked eyes with her and said, "I hope you don't mind keeping it a secret."

Savannah hesitated, then shook her head, though she didn't look particularly happy about it.

"Thank you. Why don't you call…" That's when I remembered I didn't have my phone. *Shit.* Oddly, I remembered seeing a home phone at Nathan's place. "Um, do you know Nathan's home number?"

"Yeah, he keeps it in case the cell towers are ever knocked over in a storm. He requires everyone to have one and the pack pays for it."

"He's a great Alpha, isn't he?"

"Yes," she answered, her eyes far away. "Not necessarily a better Alpha than Tyler, but different." She met my gaze again, guilt swimming in her eyes when she added, "Nathan was born to be an Alpha. It's in every fiber of his being."

"Tyler wasn't?" I knew some Alphas weren't born into the position. Many fought for the right. "Did he challenge the Alpha?"

She shook her head. "Tyler and Alaric were both Alphas, and as it happens sometimes, their wolves couldn't simply coexist; they would always be in a fight for dominance. Alaric chose to leave rather than fight his brother. Nobody questioned it, but after Tyler died, there were whispers. Speculation that Alaric had always been the one meant to lead the Silver Lake Pack in my realm. Tyler knew all along, though, and he'd told me years before. If Alaric had challenged him, he would have been the one to step aside and leave. However, Tyler was a good Alpha who loved his pack. He would have done anything to protect every member."

"What about Nathan?"

Like she'd said, Nathan was destined to be an Alpha. It had been clear from the moment I met him that there was no choice. If he hadn't had a pack, he would have been a loner because his wolf would not have been able to help challenging any Alpha he tried to serve.

"From what I understand, his father was Alpha before him. He stepped down a while back."

Little by little, I was learning about the father of my child. I only wished he'd been the one sharing with me.

My eyes met Savannah's and I wondered what I looked like to her. I could tell she was usually quiet and didn't talk much, but you could read her like an open book. I had no problem talking to people. I could make pointless chitchat all damn day long. But no one saw below the surface.

And yet somehow this woman—someone I'd just met—had managed to draw out all of my secrets. I'd made myself completely vulnerable to this unknown person. There was an odd kinship between us, but it was easy, and uncomplicated. It was so different from the pull I felt to Nathan.

Kindred spirits.

I suddenly felt open to the possibility. Maybe it was wishful thinking, but either way, it made me feel less alone.

We said goodbye and we both shifted but took off in opposite directions. I wandered back toward Nathan's house, grateful for my eidetic memory because otherwise I would have been very lost. Along the way, my panther was sidetracked by a million little things and I enjoyed letting her explore some more. I'd have to do it in human form another time.

She caught herself some lunch and we ended up at another small clearing that had a beach that sloped down into the water. It was more rocky than sandy, but I imagined that didn't stop the kids from having a great time in the summer. My girl curled up in a sunny patch and we both basked in the warmth, losing track of time.

I must have dozed off because it was dark when I opened my eyes. My panther had jumped to her feet—probably what had woken me up—and she was standing, staring into the dark woods, alert and suspicious. After a few quiet seconds, I heard what had put her on edge. A low, menacing growl rumbled from between the trees. The sound was more irate than threatening, but there was no mistaking the danger in the animal's tone.

It sounded slightly familiar and after a beat my panther sensed the same recognition and her muscles loosened a bit. Although she remained tense and poised for a fight.

A ridiculously large, silver paw appeared first, quickly followed by a huge silver wolf. If I was small for my breed, this guy was obviously the complete opposite. I wasn't sure I'd ever seen one his size.

My panther hissed and whipped her head in a haughty motion. *What the hell are you doing?* I snapped. *We probably shouldn't bait the huge fucking wolf growling at us as though he wants to make us his next meal!* My panther purred a little and I rolled my eyes the way she'd taken my warning. *Not like that, you hussy.*

The wolf growled again and slowly prowled toward us. When I met his silver eyes, I knew why he was familiar. This was Nathan's animal.

Damn, I should have figured his wolf would be massive. Sometimes, it seemed like his human half bordered on hulk. My panther's attitude suddenly made sense, too.

Although he didn't have the same reaction to her. He looked mad as hell and when I moved closer to the surface, I saw the molten silver of his eyes harden, giving me a glimpse of Nathan's equally furious gaze.

Under his heavy stare, my panther no longer attempted to be cute and flirty. Nathan and his wolf were an intimidating pair and anyone who was in the sights of their wrath would have to be stupid not to be a little terrified.

I nudged my cat, wondering if we should make a run for it. He might be bigger, but we were faster and could climb trees. *Top of the food chain, buddy.*

As if he knew what I was thinking, the wolf took a step forward and growled, the low warning sending chills down my spine. Then he snarled and jerked his head toward the trees before turning around and lumbering back between them.

He clearly expected us to follow without question, the cocky ass. A howl rent the air and without my consent, my panther took off after Nathan's wolf. *What kind of Alpha female are you?* I mentally sighed.

We arrived back at Nathan's cabin ten minutes later and the wolf was standing on the back porch, staring at us, his eyes still glittering with anger.

Less than a minute later, we were staring at an almost as large, equally pissed off human male.

"Get your ass inside, Peyton," he barked.

I hesitated, not happy about being ordered around, but then his silver eyes turned nearly black and my sense of self-preservation kicked in. I shifted when my panther retreated without a peep, happy to let me deal with the angry Alpha instead of her. *Chicken.* She huffed and ignored me.

"Peyton!" Nathan's bellow made me jump into action and I hurried toward the house. But I glared at him as I marched past, not willing to back down completely.

A gasp burst from my mouth when I suddenly felt a sharp sting on one of my ass cheeks.

What the fuck?

"Don't push me, Peyton," he growled, his tone dark and hostile, sending a shiver down my spine.

CHAPTER TWENTY

NATHAN

Peyton whirled around and glared at me, but her indignation had no effect.

I was too furious with her. She deserved a hell of a lot more than one smack to the ass as far as I was concerned.

"Get dressed," I ordered, then marched down the hall to my bedroom and shut the door. Leaning back against the wall, I took a deep breath and tried to release some of my aggression so that I wouldn't turn right back around and blister Peyton's ass for scaring the shit out of me.

How did this woman strip away years of learned patience and rational thought in a matter of seconds? The woman knew exactly how to push my buttons and I hadn't even known they existed. No one ever made me lose my temper these days. Not for centuries. Even at my most deadly, when I'd faced down the worst evil imaginable, I'd always been cool and methodical. I lived by logic and analytical thinking. But Peyton managed to blow all of it away in one fell swoop.

I'd managed to escape disaster at work for an afternoon and came home early so Peyton and I could talk. When I'd found the house empty, my first reaction had been irritation, especially when I hadn't found a note of explanation from her. I'd specifically told her to stay home and it never entered my mind that she might not obey. People rarely defied me.

Then the fact that she hadn't left a message started to percolate in my mind and I wondered if it was because something had happened to her. My wolf was pacing, his emotions on a rollercoaster like mine, but in a more primal way. He didn't understand why some of my wrath was directed at Peyton, he just wanted to know where the hell she was and that she was safe.

I searched the whole house for signs of forced entry or a struggle and found nothing, but I caught the faintest trace of her scent out back. I walked down to the water and inspected the area for a trail or any indication of where she'd gone.

I could tell she'd been alone from the lack of any other scent, but the brief rush of relief that swept through me had rage biting at its heels.

She'd gone out alone?

I'm going to kill her.

She'd intentionally put herself at risk by going out in the open, alone and unprotected. *And pregnant.*

I'd jogged back to the house, my hostility mounting with every step. What if something happened to her? What if he got to her? Took her? Hurt her?

These questions sparked apprehension and it swirled with my lack of control over the situation. If I wasn't with her, I couldn't protect her. It was what I did. But for some reason, one I'd been trying to decipher, it was different with Peyton. The emotions built on each other until they exploded into the fury consuming me.

I quickly undressed, leaving my clothes in a pile on the ground, and shifted in the air as I sprang off the porch.

My wolf began tracking her, something we were both

extremely skilled at. Our best option was to follow her scent, but we almost lost it a few times because it was so faint. How long had she been gone? Everything I was feeling was amplified with every few minutes that passed.

Her smell eventually disappeared at the lake. *Fuck*. We were going to have to search all over to catch it again because there was no way for us to tell where she'd climbed out of the water. Or if someone had dragged her from it.

Scanning the area, we spotted the falls and I wondered if perhaps she'd gone to the cavern underneath. My wolf had the same thought, and he dove into the water, swimming as fast as he could to the smooth rock ledge behind the crashing wall of water.

A small amount of relief trickled through me when we caught her scent again. Then we returned to our hunt.

By the time we finally found her panther, dark had fallen—it came early in the autumn, so it wasn't all that late, but the time wasn't the issue. The danger lurking in the cover of darkness was.

After a couple hours of searching, my emotions stewing the whole time, seeing her relaxed and asleep on the grass turned up the heat. Knowing she was completely unaware, making herself vulnerable, sent it all boiling over.

My wolf had practically tamed Peyton's cat, and I found myself envious of their simple nature. She didn't follow meekly along, and I had the feeling she wasn't happy to be ordered around, but she didn't fight it. She followed my wolf's lead, submitting to the Alpha. Felines were not easy animals to impress or tame, so her acquiescence was extremely telling.

Our animals felt the same pull, but it concerned me that they might believe there was more to it than a wild attraction. If they became too attached, it would be very difficult to stay away from Peyton without my wolf going mad, and that never turned out well for the animal's human side.

When we arrived on my land she shifted, returning to the stubborn, frustrating, incredibly sexy woman whom half of me wanted to throttle and the other half wanted to fuck. Although doing both at the same time was an interesting idea as well.

Now that I was alone in my room, I expected my emotions to quickly settle down, but it didn't happen. Running my hands through my hair, I exhaled harshly, then stalked to my closet and grabbed a pair of sweatpants. I twisted my hair up at the back of my head and by then I'd gained a little control over myself. My wolf was wary of my attitude, seeming unsure that he wanted to confront Peyton. In his mind, her cat had submitted to him, so the situation had been handled. Unfortunately, I had the feeling I was in for some hissing and clawing from the panther's human.

After opening the door to my room, I walked into the hall and frowned when I scented that Peyton was still in her room. I padded down to her door and rapped on it with my knuckles. "Kitchen," I barked before turning to leave. Then I stopped and turned back halfway. "Don't make me drag your ass out of there, baby," I warned.

I didn't wait for her reply before continuing to the kitchen. My stomach grumbled and I decided to make us dinner. She needed to eat, and I needed something to occupy my hands because the desire to wring her neck—or spank her—was still plaguing me.

About two minutes before I would have gone to get her, she finally trudged into the living room wearing shorts and a loose T-shirt. She looked tired and a part of me wanted to simply let this go and tell her to rest. But that part was shouted down and skulked away.

The gold flecks in her emerald eyes swirled with desire

when they perused my naked chest. Hunger for her welled up inside me, but I refused to give in to it until Peyton and I had reached an understanding. The furiousness in her gaze suggested she wasn't likely to be open to it at this moment, anyway.

I pointed to the kitchen table and commanded, "Sit."

"Sit. Stay," she muttered in a mocking tone. "When are you going to get it through your thick skull that I'm not a fucking dog, Nathan? I'm a panther. A jaguar. A damn cat!" She yelled the last part, but I didn't take the bait because while she'd complained, she'd done as she was told.

"We're going to talk about this," I told her as I filled a plate with chicken, spiced rice, and roasted vegetables. "But you need to eat first."

She looked as though she might argue, but when I put the food in front of her, she licked her lips and focused on the meal.

I joined her a minute later with my own dish and we ate in silence, momentarily ignoring the thick tension in the room. My wolf was pleased to see her eating, especially knowing she was taking care of our pup. But he was every bit aware of the coming explosion and though he was calm, he remained alert.

Once I'd cleaned my plate, I sat back and observed her countenance, noticing a distinct difference. She seemed less heavy than I'd seen since she'd arrived. As if the fresh air had breathed new life into her, taking some of the weight off of her shoulders. This was the Peyton I remembered. Still, it didn't excuse her behavior.

Peyton eventually swallowed the last bite of her second helping and pushed her empty dish away. "You might be a giant pain in the ass, Nathan," she quipped, "but damn, can you cook."

I didn't comment as I cleared the table and loaded the dishwasher. With that done, I didn't have to worry about her being undernourished and could focus on lecturing her about the irresponsibility of her choices.

She stood from the table and crossed the room to one of the recliners, then grabbed a blanket and dropped into the cushy chair.

"Comfy?" I asked, my voice coated in sarcasm.

"As a matter of fact, yes," she replied with an overly sweet smile.

Damn, this woman frustrated me. I still stood on the opposite side of the island, facing the open living area, and I placed my palms on the cool granite, resting my weight on them.

"What did I tell you about leaving the house, Peyton?" My tone was conversational, but I doubted she missed the simmering anger beneath it.

"You didn't *say* anything about it, Nathan." She narrowed her eyes. "You gave me a command and expected to be blindly obeyed."

I contained a frustrated growl and tried to remain calm. "For your own safety, Peyton. You can't go running around alone, out in the open where anything could happen to you." Pressure was building behind my temples, so I yanked the band from my hair and let it fall around my shoulders. "If you wanted to get out of the house, you should have asked me."

"Exactly when would I have done that?" she countered.

Running a hand through my hair, I exhaled slowly. "That's fair. Next time, leave me a note if we don't see each other. If I can't take you out, I'll send an enforcer to escort you."

Peyton's expression darkened and her flat tone was ominous when she spoke. "I agreed to let you help me with my situation. But I am not your prisoner, Nathan King, and I refuse to be treated like one." She dropped her feet to the ground and grabbed onto the arm rests so hard that her knuckles turned white. "I'm a grown-ass woman, Nathan. I can take care of myself. I was doing it long before you and I'll be doing it long after."

I pushed off the counter and marched around it, coming to a stop at the edge of the room. I braced my feet apart and crossed my arms over my chest. "You are under my protection, Peyton. Whether you like it or not. And you *will* follow my rules."

"You are not my Alpha," she snarled as she jumped to her feet. "I'm not your responsibility!"

"Like hell, you're not my responsibility," I stated, my frustration slowly chipping away my control. It didn't help that she looked hot as fuck all riled up. I needed my mind focused and not distracted by her breasts bouncing with each choppy breath, or the sexy fire in her eyes, or anything else that turned me on—which was pretty much everything about Peyton.

"One night together doesn't give you a claim on me, Nathan."

That snapped my attention out of its lust-induced distraction. My wolf had jumped to his feet and growled, snapping his jaw and gnashing his teeth, and I wanted to shout at her that she was categorically wrong, but sensed it would only make the situation worse.

Even if we hadn't created a child that morning, I would still have claimed the right to protect her. Just as I had for anyone who'd needed my help in the past.

However, like in other moments since she showed up here, I was cautiously aware that she was different. The tie between us wasn't something I'd experienced before—not just with someone I was aiding, literally never before.

Normally, I would have made her Tanner's immediate responsibility and stuck to finding the serial killer. And yet here I was, ready to lock her in her room because the thought of anyone else's eyes on her made me want to rip their throats out.

The idea of another man anywhere around her or our baby sent a shockwave of jealousy and rage through me. I would never let anyone usurp my claim on Peyton. My wolf was practically howling in agreement. She was mine to protect and given that she was carrying my child, there was no way in hell I would back down on this.

And there it was. My smoking gun.

I glanced pointedly at her stomach. "You aren't just taking care of yourself anymore, baby." Slowly, I prowled toward her. "Did you think about what could have happened to the baby while you were out gallivanting and making yourself an easy target?"

Peyton was livid, her eyes shooting daggers as she marched to the middle of the room and seethed, "I would never put my cub at risk."

It occurred to me that it might be the perfect time to bring up the paternity of the baby. But I was still battling with my wrath over her stroll in the woods and I didn't want to start that talk until I could focus on it alone. *One angry confrontation at a time.* And in truth, I was still holding out to see if she would finally tell me herself. It was a strange reaction, and I didn't know why it mattered to me.

She took a step another toward me and I couldn't help being a little impressed with her ability to dominate a room, to make her other opponents feel as though she were twice her size. However, I wasn't just any opponent. "I'll give you a few more days," she said. "If we haven't made any progress on finding this guy, I'm done. I'll disappear. I'm very, very good at it."

I raised an eyebrow. The fact that people thought they could run and erase their trail so they couldn't be found was laughable. Even the WITSEC had exploitable weaknesses. But Peyton had never struck me as being a fool, so her claim was surprising.

I didn't bother to refute it because it was moot. I wouldn't let her leave.

"You have a killer gunning for you, Peyton," I growled. At this point, I was only a couple of feet away from her and she instinctively backed up a step, then seemed to realize what she'd done and squared her shoulders, standing as tall as she could.

"And?" she snapped, jamming her hands onto her hips.

"And"—I closed the distance between us by another foot and she retreated another couple of steps—"you can't go running off while some psychopath is intent on seeing you dead." I shook my head and moved forward again, forcing her to back up. When she hit the wall, I closed the gap between us completely.

I pressed my palms on either side of her head and bent forward until we were nose to nose. "You aren't going anywhere, Peyton." *Not you and not my cub.*

My body dwarfed hers and I felt the heat radiating from every inch. She moved restlessly andher nipples brushed up against my chest, our naked flesh only separated by her thin T-shirt. When she opened her mouth, I'd lost my patience with her sass, so I tested my theory for shutting her up.

I grabbed her biceps and lifted her up so we were face to face before I sealed my lips over hers. The instant they touched, lust slammed into me and I lost all sense of reason. Peyton hesitated for a beat, but this insane attraction wasn't the least bit one-sided, and she fell into the kiss.

My hips pushed forward, seeking her heat, pressing her against the wall. Peyton moaned and wrapped her legs around my waist, her heels digging into my ass as if trying to draw me closer. She wrapped her arms around my neck and there wasn't an inch of space between us, but I felt the same need. My body and mind both demanded to be inside Peyton, to consume her being until we were one.

The chemistry between us sizzled and sparked—I wouldn't have been surprised if the air around us combusted. My wolf was pushing me hard to claim her and I barked at him to back off. I would take Peyton, finally feel her hot body wrapped around me again, and mark her from the inside. But biting was off limits. He knew better, yet he still butted his head into me and snapped his teeth.

Peyton wiggled and the sensations shooting through my body distracted me from the argument with my wolf. A groan ripped from my chest as I slipped my tongue into her mouth. It felt like lifetimes since I'd tasted her sweetness.

I kept one hand on her hip and pushed my knee between her legs to support her. With the other, I shoved up her shirt and cupped a full, round breast. Her peaked nipple pressed into my palm as I gently massaged the globe while my tongue explored her mouth. I loved Peyton's scent, but it was even more delicious tasting it in her mouth and all over her body. Like smooth honey and spicy cloves. I couldn't get enough. *Fuck, I need to get inside her.* But first I wanted to see her give herself over to me as she let go and shattered into a million pieces.

I ripped my lips away, gliding them down her throat to her breast. Raising it up, I sucked the tip into my mouth, feeling myself swell uncomfortably when she moaned and arched her back. She moved restlessly on my leg and I thrust it up, then rubbed it against her pussy.

"Nathan!" she cried out, tangling her fingers in the hair at the nape of my neck. The bite of pain from her firm grip shot bolts of pleasure straight to my shaft and I groaned.

I worked her on my leg while I gave her other breast the

same attention. When she was writhing on my thigh and trying to get herself off, I stilled and lifted my head. I waited until her passion-glazed eyes slid open before I growled, "You know the rules, baby. I decide when you come."

Her emerald pools darkened, and the gold flecks swirled with a mixture of lust and defiance. I loved the way she turned into a wildcat and fought for dominance. It made winning so much more worth it. Especially when she finally gave in and let herself submit to the rapture like she really wanted to. It was so fucking hot.

"Listen up, you son of a—oh, fuck!"

I'd shoved my hand into her shorts while she'd been cursing, and I drove two fingers into her tight, wet channel. I caught her mouth in another sizzling kiss as my fingers pumped in and out, without touching either of her most sensitive spots.

"Nathan!" she shouted as she pulled away. But her hostility melted into a ragged moan when I curled my fingers inside her.

"Do you want it, baby?" I purred.

"Yes," she panted.

"You know what to do, Peyton."

She shook her head even as she tried to rock on my hand and gain the friction she was desperate for.

"Too bad," I sighed as I began to withdraw.

Her fists tightened in my hair and she was practically yanking it out when she clenched her jaw and grated out, "Please."

I barely managed to contain my climax. It was hot as fuck when she begged.

With my mouth at her ear I crooned, "Such a good little kitty cat." Then I grinned into her hair when she stiffened and hissed. But her tense muscles only exploded that much harder when I pressed the heel of my hand to her bundle of nerves and curled my fingers into the sweet spot inside her.

Her head dropped back and she screamed while her body shook from the force of her orgasm.

I watched her with awe. The last time we'd been together, it had been the hottest, most incredible sex I'd ever had. But somehow it seemed even stronger now, the burn between us becoming a full-blown forest fire. Was it simply because I couldn't recreate how amazing it had been in my head? Or had it really amplified to this intense, incredibly powerful release?

With all of my blood in my cock, my mind only retained one thought. To find out if it would be as earth-shattering as last time when I was buried inside her.

I kept Peyton in my arms as I turned and started toward the bedroom.

"What?" she asked as she peered up at me dazedly. "Where are we going?"

"Bed," I grunted.

"No." Her tone was flat and final.

I stopped in my tracks and dipped my head down until we were nose to nose. I couldn't keep the fury out of my voice, especially with it being fueled by my hunger for her. "What the fuck do you mean 'no'? I just watched you fall apart in my arms and I can smell how much you still want me. I know you're still feeling the ache, the need for release. Tell me why I shouldn't march you right back to my bedroom and give us both the relief we need.?"

She shook her head and looked away. "It's just…"

I dropped her feet to the floor but kept one hand at her waist while cupping her neck with the other. Forcing her gaze back mine, I searched her face for a hint of what could be holding her back. What was the point? Maybe if we lost some of this sexual tension, we could concentrate on the situation at hand without everything exploding from our pent-up hormones.

I would never force a woman, but my nerves were raw and

on edge from being denied when I was so fucking hard and hungry for her. My words were sharp and meant to cut. "Afraid you won't live up to that night together?" I taunted. "Don't worry, baby. I'll pretend you're still a shiny new toy."

She threw me a withering glare and I could tell she was about to attempt to pull away.

I was on edge from the hours spent fearing she had been hurt or taken, and with the sexual aggression building inside me, I was close to losing complete control. I was suddenly really fucking pissed that Peyton still hadn't told me about the baby.

"Give me one good reason to back off, Peyton. It's not like I could get you *more* pregnant," I said in a tight voice.

I held her a little tighter, the hand at her neck delving into her hair and clenching it in a fist. "Is that it, baby? Afraid I'll fuck you so hard I'll turn the one pup I gave you into two?"

Peyton's eyes went wide and her lips parted in a silent gasp. I waited, letting her work it out in her mind, and trying to find the last shreds of my control.

After a minute she swallowed hard and croaked, "What?"

"You heard me," I growled.

"How do you...why do you think...?" She wouldn't meet my eyes and when she tried to move away again, I let her. I didn't trust myself with her while I was pumped full of adrenaline from lust and animosity.

"Once I learned the time of the full moon that weekend, I suspected."

Peyton twisted the ring on her thumb and stared at the floor.

"I'm right, aren't I?" When she didn't answer fast enough for me, I stalked over to her and caught her chin between my thumb and index finger. "Look me in the eyes and tell me the baby isn't mine, Peyton." She blinked a few times and my impatience—not to mention my jealousy—got the best of me. "Did you hop out of my bed and straight into another man's?" Just the thought was tinting the edges of my vision with red, and my wolf was trying to shove to the surface to hunt down the faceless motherfucker.

CHAPTER TWENTY-ONE

PEYTON

I wouldn't lie to Nathan. One could argue that was exactly what omission was, but I felt differently. However, I hadn't been prepared to have this discussion with him, so it caught me off guard and I became flustered.

When he'd believed the baby wasn't his, he'd implied this same accusation, that I'd slept with another man right after he'd left my bed. I'd understood it before—it seemed a rational thought. But this time, it burned in my stomach, making me mad. It was probably the stress of the evening, all the fighting and the orgasm—which had left me feeling empty and desperate for more. The over-stimulation put my nerves on edge and suddenly I was offended that he would think that about me. My panther wasn't happy with the tone of Nathan's inquiry and she paced inside me.

The insane thing was that his jealousy was turning me on even more. I tried not to focus on the tendrils of desire traveling through my body, making my nipples harder and drenching my already ruined underwear.

I shook my head to try to clear away some of the fog, but it didn't help when Nathan's nostrils flared and his eyes melted into molten silver. "Technically"—my voice caught, and I cleared my throat before continuing—"*you* hopped out of *my* bed."

Nathan was not amused. He gripped my chin a little harder, then dropped it and stepped back as though I'd burned him. He ran his hands through his hair, then hung them at his sides where he clenched and unclenched them repeatedly.

"Peyton," he grunted impatiently. I shouldn't have said what I did about you being a shiny new toy. Not that you weren't, but that doesn't mean you aren't every bit as amazing now as you were that night. Now it's your turn. Tell me the truth."

The look in his eyes as he waited for me to answer told me he already knew. He wanted me to say it, to admit it out loud. I expected it had a lot to do with the fact that I hadn't told him myself. It dawned on me that I'd shaken the trust he put in me, and my guilt at keeping the secret intensified.

"No. I haven't been with anyone since you. You're the father."

Nathan nodded and closed his eyes as he slowly exhaled. When he opened them and pinned his silver gaze on me, I shifted my weight restlessly from foot to foot. "Now, answer my other question," he demanded.

I raised an eyebrow, not sure what question he was referring to.

He took a long, deep breath in, keeping his eyes locked with mine. It felt as though he could see right through me, but I wasn't a member of his pack, so I knew he couldn't dig through my mind. However, after taking in the scents around him, his orbs turned dark and heated. *It's pretty much the same thing,* I grumbled to myself. He didn't have to see inside my head to know I was primed and ready for another mind-blowing orgasm.

"The last thing we need right now is to complicate things

with sex." I didn't admit that I was also afraid for him to see my scars. Somehow, he'd missed them under my hair when he'd smacked my ass, and earlier while we'd gotten hot and heavy, he'd kept one hand on my hip while the other had explored my breasts and between my legs.

It wasn't vanity that worried me, though—okay, it wasn't *only* vanity. Now that he knew about the baby, I was worried that his overprotective instincts would go into hyperdrive. It was just how wolf shifter males were. If he saw the slashes on my back, he might go ballistic and lock me in my room. They were fully healed, but like the scars on his arm, their presence alone indicated just how life-threatening my injuries had been.

It didn't change what had happened. He already knew I'd fought the killer and been chased out of town. The fact that the bastard had almost killed me shouldn't make a difference to Nathan's attitude. But again, this was a male wolf, and an Alpha to boot. The scars would remind him every time he saw my back—even if he couldn't see them through my shirt—that he hadn't been there to protect me.

It wasn't rational, it made no sense, but it was in their DNA.

Wolves were loyal and protective by nature, and mated for life, which was probably why the process of breaking a mating bond was so physically and mentally painful. If the couple had gone deep enough into the mating stages, it usually drove them mad or killed them.

Nathan's chemical makeup would make him even more determined to keep it from happening to me again, which would translate to me losing my mind and foaming at the mouth to be free.

"Complicated," Nathan responded, his face and tone deadpan.

I nodded and twisted my hands in my shirt to keep from reaching for him.

He shook his head and when his eyes landed on me again, they were cold and hard. "Sex is the only time you are honest with me, Peyton. It's the only uncomplicated thing between us."

I didn't miss the barb and it hurt when it hit. I'd spent my life letting things roll off my back, not thinking twice about what people thought of me. Too busy living my best life. Yet, as I watched him leave the room, I stood rooted to the ground, stunned by the tear that escaped my eye and slowly rolled down my cheek.

A LOUD, jarring noise woke me from a dead sleep and I shot up in bed, terrified and confused. It took a few seconds to put together that the sound was coming from me. I was screaming, soaked in sweat, and my body shook violently.

In the next second, Nathan burst into the room, claws extended and his eyes sweeping the space for a threat. When he didn't spot a threat, he rushed to the bed and took me in his arms.

My screaming had died down, but it had evolved into big, choking sobs and an endless river of tears. I clung to him, resting my cheek on his warm chest and trying to calm my racing heart.

"It's okay, Peyton," he murmured as he brushed my hair back from my heated face. He threaded his fingers into the tresses and continually ran them through my hair. "You're safe, baby. Try to calm down for me. It's just you and me here. You're safe."

I cried for a little longer, but his soothing tone and gestures helped to bring me out of the terrified fog I'd been captured in. *Holy shit.* In all my years, even with my fucked-up childhood, I'd never experienced a nightmare like that.

"Nightmare?" Nathan asked softly and not for the first time, I wondered if he could read the minds of shifters outside his pack.

I pressed my face a little harder against his firm, warm skin and nodded.

"Do you want to talk about it?"

I shook my head and my cheek rubbed over his chest hair. He had just enough to look like a real man and I'd loved the way it had felt against my breasts when we'd slept together. But now, it helped to draw me out of my terror, reminding me that he was there and would protect me.

He sat with me for another few minutes until I stopped shaking and finally lifted my head to wipe my blurry eyes. "Are you okay?"

"Yeah," I whispered. "I don't know what happened."

Nathan canted his head and scratched his beard. "I'm a little surprised it took this long," he said.

I blinked a few times, not sure I'd heard him right. "Pardon?"

"I've been expecting this to happen. Most people who go through a trauma like that have nightmares." He shrugged. "Not always, but I slept lightly the first couple of nights you were here because I kept expecting to be woken up. When they didn't come, I slept a little harder, so I guess the joke was on me because you scared the fuck out of me tonight."

My lips tipped up at the corners and he used his thumb to swipe under each of my eyes, clearing away the last remnants of moisture.

"Are you sure you don't want to talk about it? It might help."

Hell, no. No, I did not want to talk about the fact that I'd been reliving the moment a monster had dug his claws into my back and ripped away the skin and bone so deep that it exposed my spine and ribs. "Could you get me a glass of water, please?"

"Sure, baby." Nathan gently took his arms from around me and I immediately wanted to dive back into them again. But I needed a moment alone and I really wanted to change out of my sticky shirt. I was stunned when he brushed a kiss over my forehead before walking out of the room.

Um… I shook my head and blinked a few more times, then climbed out of the bed. As I took the few steps to my dresser, I stripped out of my shirt and dropped it over the edge of the hamper, wanting it to dry before adding it to the other clothes.

I'd just yanked a clean tank top over my head when—

"What the fuck are those?"

Nathan's roar made me jump so hard I lost my balance and since I was tangled up in my top, I began to tumble to the ground. He was there in a flash, grabbing my elbow and steadying me on my feet.

He slammed the glass on the dresser, spilling a great deal of water, which made me frown because I was really freaking thirsty.

I reached for what was left, only to have my hand swipe air when he spun me around so I was facing the bed, presumably so he had room to examine at my back. The overhead light turned on and I squeezed my eyes shut against the brightness.

"Are you trying to blind me?" I snapped as I tried to break his hold on me.

He released it, only to curl his arm around my waist and haul me closer. Then he firmly pushed on my shoulder so I bent forward. He gently brushed my hair away from the scars, moving it so it fell over one shoulder. I felt the tips of his fingers probe the puckered skin that was all that remained of the deadly slashes on my back.

"When did this happen?" Nathan asked in a voice that sounded almost clinical.

I raised my brows, even though he couldn't see the gesture. Had I been wrong? Was he actually going to be calm and rational about this? "I'd rather not talk about it," I murmured. I was still shaken from the nightmare.

"Too fucking bad," he growled.

Ah, I spoke too soon.

"The night of the murder." I sighed.

His arm tightened around me and he traced the scars this time.

I felt like a complete idiot for wondering if he thought they were ugly, if they changed the way he saw me, if...if they turned him off and he didn't want me anymore. I'd been the one putting the brakes on sex anyway, which made me an even bigger idiot for caring about whether he was still attracted to me.

"Tell me exactly what happened, Peyton," he commanded in a stern voice that made me aggravated and hot at the same time.

I knew he wouldn't let it go though, so I gave him the short version of the part I'd previously omitted from the story.

It wasn't easy, going back to that night. The distress. The agony. It was all the more difficult considering I'd just re-lived it in a nightmare. The healed lacerations pulsed with phantom pain, but my panther brushed her fur under my skin, trying to give me comfort, and it helped ease my overwhelming emotions.

Nathan's mounting fury didn't help my anxiety level though. It saturated his scent and filled the air with a palpable tension.

So I hurried to finish my tale. When it was over he remained silent and still, with the exception of his fingers, which continued to run over the wounds with a surprisingly gentle touch.

Eventually, they stopped and tangled in my hair, then he curled the fingers into a fist before pulling my head back a few inches.

"Why didn't you tell me about this, Peyton?" His tone had gone dark and even. The lack of inflection was his tell. A warning that his fury had become animalistic and barely leashed. I'd seen this side of him when we'd spent the night together, but it had been different. His raw, primal instincts had taken over, the desire to sexually dominate his partner and gain their submission.

This time, he was trying to control his feral instincts. The need to hunt down the threat and kill them would be his sole focus. His grip on it, as well as its existence, proved his true Alpha nature. It emphasized his power and just how deadly he could be.

My panther and I both responded to his display with passion. Our primitive traits recognized him as a worthy mate. Luckily, I wasn't ruled by the part of me that wanted to be dragged back to his cave and ravished.

I shoved an elbow back into his chest to get him to loosen his arm around me so I could slide out of his hold. He didn't even exhale from the blow, much less move a damn inch.

Instead, his arm tightened, and he collared my neck with his hand, pulling me up so my back was against his. "Why?" he asked again.

"What would have been the point? It won't help us find him."

His fingers flexed around my throat and his other hand left my hair to splay over my stomach. "Because he almost killed you. Almost killed my pup. Because when I find him, I'm going to make him bleed and make sure he suffers unimaginable pain before I end his pathetic life."

Chapter 22
Nathan

I REMOVED my hand from Peyton's throat to push the back of her shirt up again and stare at the scars. I touched one of the claw marks that went from her shoulder to her hip. They had been so fucking deep. The pain she must have been in… *Fuck.* The thought of something happening to Peyton, it was unimaginable. I'd never experienced this level of blind rage, been this close to losing my control. I felt it deep in my soul and when I touched the puckered skin, something inside me quivered, as if it were stifled and needed to be set free.

My wolf was practically foaming at the mouth, snapping viciously, demanding to be set free so he could protect what was his. He was so close to the edge of savagery that keeping him contained took a great deal of effort.

"Why the hell are you reacting like this, Nathan?" Peyton groused. "I get that you have some kind of hero complex, but you're flipping your shit over something that happened to a relative stranger." She sounded genuinely confused, as well as supremely pissed.

I didn't have an answer for her, nor was I interested in giving one. There were more important things to discuss.

In some rational part of my brain, I understood Peyton's reluctance to share the part of the story, but I also wanted to punish her for it. To force her to stop holding out on me, to let me keep her safe. I wanted to lock her in a room and make sure no one but me ever touched her again. I wanted her all to myself. *All of her.*

"Is there anything else you want to tell me, Peyton? Are you finally done keeping secrets?" I snarled.

"You're acting as if it's your right to know everything about me, Nathan." She shrugged again in an effort to get away, but I held her even higher, my hand returning to her throat. I squeezed just enough to let her know who was in charge.

"I have every right, Peyton," I declared. "You are mine."

Then it happened.

The quivering stopped and a seal broke, flooding me with the sure knowledge that Peyton was my mate. My true mate.

Holy shit.

Everything between us began to fit together and make sense. The heavy pull, the overwhelming attraction, the possessive tendencies, the primal need to protect her. They had all been pointing to the truth, but I hadn't even considered it as an option, so I'd missed all the signs.

I might not have wanted a mate, but I had one now and that was that. Honestly, I didn't see how it would change much anyway. My path for the future remained steadfast, but now it included Peyton, which meant making a few adjustments. I could stop worrying about her leaving now, which would take at least one load off my shoulders.

Thinking about the fireworks between us, I admitted that having her in my bed every night was a plus for this new situation. And once we mated, I would become her Alpha, and thank fuck for that because I was sure she would be less defiant.

It also meant our child growing up in a home with both parents. That alone was worth mating with Peyton.

"How do you figure that?" she asked dryly, snapping me out of my epiphany. "You have no claim on me, Nathan. We've been over this. So how about you let me go before I let my panther out and she makes you."

A laugh rumbled in my chest, surprising me since I was still fuming over her injuries, as well as stunned by the revelation of what we were to each other.

I gave her what she wanted for the moment. When I released her, she yanked her top down and wrapped her arms around herself. She'd seemed so confident and emotionless when she'd told me about the fight that it hadn't crossed my mind that she would still be tortured by it. Over the nightmare or relaying the story, I wasn't sure. But she was my mate, so I figured it was my duty to care for her.

I put our discussion on hold, as well as what we were to each other, until tomorrow.

"Are you all right?" I asked, genuinely concerned.

"I'm fine. You can go."

I wanted to help her, but I didn't know how, other than comforting her with my body. That seemed like the best option for both of us, so I opened my mouth to tell her that. Except I spotted the nearly empty glass on the dresser and wondered if she might still be thirsty.

"Would you like another glass of water?" Seeing as how I was still strung tight over everything, I tried to push back my natural gruffness and be soft with her.

Her eyes narrowed and she twisted the ring on her thumb with her index finger. "No, thank you." Her proper tone grated on my nerves because I'd come to know her well enough that it meant she was shutting me out.

She was scared and distressed, so I told myself to give her a little leash on her attitude. "Why don't I stay and…comfort you?"

"I'm fine. Thank you for offering."

I ground my teeth together and tried another tactic. "You are scared, Peyton. Let me do something for you, damn it."

Peyton's brow rose and she looked at me as if I had two heads. "What's with you all of a sudden? You're acting weird."

I grunted in frustration. "Trying to do something nice for you and be less of an asshole is weird?" I gave up on my attempt to be less gruff with her.

"It is if you suck at it."

Clearly, this mate thing was going to test my patience and I'd had enough of that for now. Although, letting it go gave way for all of the other shit I'd been consumed with earlier. The outrage at Peyton for wandering off and putting herself at risk, for keeping secrets—*which is going to stop right fucking now*—and my homicidal drive to gut the motherfucker who'd nearly killed my mate. They were boiling back up and I clenched and unclenched my fists, trying to keep a lid on it.

I needed to find an outlet for this shit and if it wasn't between Peyton's thighs, then I'd go on a hunt, though I would stay close to keep an eye on Peyton.

Without another word, I turned and strode from her room. *Her room, for now.*

Once I'd stripped, I went out onto the porch and finally stopped holding my wolf back. I shifted in seconds—after living for so long, I barely noticed the bones breaking and muscles tearing as my body realigned its skeleton—and he took off to find some unsuspecting animal that would hopefully help sate our lust for blood. At least for now.

It didn't take long for us to rein in our emotions and apply rationale to everything that had just happened. With anyone else, this would have been my state of mind throughout the conversation with Peyton and the realization that we were mates. And though all of those feelings would still be there, I would have kept them tightly leashed.

Peyton's ability to make me lose my cool, to react emotionally rather than with conscious consideration and purpose, drove me mad. And pissed me the hell off. Was it because we were mates? Or had I simply never come across someone I clashed with so completely? Other than physically, because we were more than compatible when the only words coming out of her mouth were said with mindless passion.

My wolf trotted back to the house and we shifted when we reached the bottom steps. As I made my way back to my bedroom, I paused for a moment at Peyton's closed door. It was quiet and still, so I continued down the hall and shut myself in my room to lie down and go to sleep.

Unfortunately, it eluded me, filled with thoughts of Peyton, worrying over whether leaving her alone had really been the right decision. After an hour of tossing and turning, I threw back the covers and stood. Once I made a decision, I wasn't one to question myself, so the fact that I stood there debating with myself annoyed the shit out of me. The sound of a soft whimper floated to my ears and I pretended not to be relieved that the decision had been made for me.

Peyton made another distressed noise as I padded over the thick carpet and I picked up my pace. When I reached her door, I opened it silently and observed her sleeping form. She flipped from one side to the other restlessly, then curled herself into a ball. Her expression wasn't peaceful the way it had always been whenever I checked on her before, and it caused a sharp pain to pulse in my chest a couple of times. Instead, her lips were pinched, her brow knitted and drawn low, and her cheeks glistened in the moonlight.

Shit. I should have forced her to let me stay. As much as Peyton frustrated me, I didn't like seeing her hurting. As her mate it was my job to protect her from anything that harmed her, and that included the things in her dreams.

I crossed the space to her bed, drew the quilt back, and slid in beside her, careful not to jostle the bed too much. I reached out to take her in my arms and she came willingly, almost eagerly, and cuddled up against me so I was wrapped around her from behind. She released a slow exhale, as if she were expelling her fear and tension. By the time she took another breath in, she'd relaxed, and the peaceful expression had turned to her face.

As my mind finally began to stop spinning and sleep approached, I wondered if all mates found this kind of ease and contentment in each other's arms. If this was what it would be like to hold her every night, especially after an explosive round or two of sex, it would be no hardship.

My wolf completely agreed.

CHAPTER TWENTY-TWO

NATHAN

I removed my hand from Peyton's throat to push the back of her shirt up again and stare at the scars. I touched one of the claw marks that went from her shoulder to her hip. They had been so fucking deep. The pain she must have been in... *Fuck*. The thought of something happening to Peyton, it was unimaginable. I'd never experienced this level of blind rage, been this close to losing my control. I felt it deep in my soul and when I touched the puckered skin, something inside me quivered, as if it were stifled and needed to be set free.

My wolf was practically foaming at the mouth, snapping viciously, demanding to be set free so he could protect what was his. He was so close to the edge of savagery that keeping him contained took a great deal of effort.

"Why the hell are you reacting like this, Nathan?" Peyton groused. "I get that you have some kind of hero complex, but you're flipping your shit over something that happened to a relative stranger." She sounded genuinely confused, as well as supremely pissed.

I didn't have an answer for her, nor was I interested in giving one. There were more important things to discuss.

In some rational part of my brain, I understood Peyton's reluctance to share the part of the story, but I also wanted to punish her for it. To force her to stop holding out on me, to let me keep her safe. I wanted to lock her in a room and make sure no one but me ever touched her again. I wanted her all to myself. *All of her.*

"Is there anything else you want to tell me, Peyton? Are you finally done keeping secrets?" I snarled.

"You're acting as if it's your right to know everything about me, Nathan." She shrugged again in an effort to get away, but I held her even higher, my hand returning to her throat. I squeezed just enough to let her know who was in charge.

"I have every right, Peyton," I declared. "You are mine."

Then it happened.

The quivering stopped and a seal broke, flooding me with the sure knowledge that Peyton was my mate. My true mate.

Holy shit.

Everything between us began to fit together and make sense. The heavy pull, the overwhelming attraction, the possessive tendencies, the primal need to protect her. They had all been pointing to the truth, but I hadn't even considered it as an option, so I'd missed all the signs.

I might not have wanted a mate, but I had one now and that was that. Honestly, I didn't see how it would change much anyway. My path for the future remained steadfast, but now it included Peyton, which meant making a few adjustments. I could stop worrying about her leaving now, which would take at least one load off my shoulders.

Thinking about the fireworks between us, I admitted that having her in my bed every night was a plus for this new situation. And once we mated, I would become her Alpha, and thank fuck for that because I was sure she would be less defiant.

It also meant our child growing up in a home with both parents. That alone was worth mating with Peyton.

"How do you figure that?" she asked dryly, snapping me out of my epiphany. "You have no claim on me, Nathan. We've been over this. So how about you let me go before I let my panther out and she makes you."

A laugh rumbled in my chest, surprising me since I was still fuming over her injuries, as well as stunned by the revelation of what we were to each other.

I gave her what she wanted for the moment. When I released her, she yanked her top down and wrapped her arms around herself. She'd seemed so confident and emotionless when she'd told me about the fight that it hadn't crossed my mind that she would still be tortured by it. Over the nightmare or relaying the story, I wasn't sure. But she was my mate, so I figured it was my duty to care for her.

I put our discussion on hold, as well as what we were to each other, until tomorrow.

"Are you all right?" I asked, genuinely concerned.

"I'm fine. You can go."

I wanted to help her, but I didn't know how, other than comforting her with my body. That seemed like the best option for both of us, so I opened my mouth to tell her that. Except I spotted the nearly empty glass on the dresser and wondered if she might still be thirsty.

"Would you like another glass of water?" Seeing as how I was still strung tight over everything, I tried to push back my natural gruffness and be soft with her.

Her eyes narrowed and she twisted the ring on her thumb with her index finger. "No, thank you." Her proper tone grated on my nerves because I'd come to know her well enough that it meant she was shutting me out.

She was scared and distressed, so I told myself to give her a little leash on her attitude. "Why don't I stay and…comfort you?"

"I'm fine. Thank you for offering."

I ground my teeth together and tried another tactic. "You are scared, Peyton. Let me do something for you, damn it."

Peyton's brow rose and she looked at me as if I had two heads. "What's with you all of a sudden? You're acting weird."

I grunted in frustration. "Trying to do something nice for you and be less of an asshole is weird?" I gave up on my attempt to be less gruff with her.

"It is if you suck at it."

Clearly, this mate thing was going to test my patience and I'd had enough of that for now. Although, letting it go gave way for all of the other shit I'd been consumed with earlier. The outrage at Peyton for wandering off and putting herself at risk, for keeping secrets—*which is going to stop right fucking now*—and my homicidal drive to gut the motherfucker who'd nearly killed my mate. They were boiling back up and I clenched and unclenched my fists, trying to keep a lid on it.

I needed to find an outlet for this shit and if it wasn't between Peyton's thighs, then I'd go on a hunt, though I would stay close to keep an eye on Peyton.

Without another word, I turned and strode from her room. *Her room, for now.*

Once I'd stripped, I went out onto the porch and finally stopped holding my wolf back. I shifted in seconds—after living for so long, I barely noticed the bones breaking and muscles tearing as my body realigned its skeleton—and he took off to find some unsuspecting animal that would hopefully help sate our lust for blood. At least for now.

It didn't take long for us to rein in our emotions and apply rationale to everything that had just happened. With anyone else, this would have been my state of mind throughout the conversation with Peyton and the realization that we were mates. And though all of those feelings would still be there, I would have kept them tightly leashed.

Peyton's ability to make me lose my cool, to react emotionally rather than with conscious consideration and purpose, drove me mad. And pissed me the hell off. Was it because we were mates? Or had I simply never come across someone I clashed with so completely? Other than physically, because we were more than compatible when the only words coming out of her mouth were said with mindless passion.

My wolf trotted back to the house and we shifted when we reached the bottom steps. As I made my way back to my bedroom, I paused for a moment at Peyton's closed door. It was quiet and still, so I continued down the hall and shut myself in my room to lie down and go to sleep.

Unfortunately, it eluded me, filled with thoughts of Peyton, worrying over whether leaving her alone had really been the right decision. After an hour of tossing and turning, I threw back the covers and stood. Once I made a decision, I wasn't one to question myself, so the fact that I stood there debating with myself annoyed the shit out of me. The sound of a soft whimper floated to my ears and I pretended not to be relieved that the decision had been made for me.

Peyton made another distressed noise as I padded over the thick carpet and I picked up my pace. When I reached her door, I opened it silently and observed her sleeping form. She flipped from one side to the other restlessly, then curled herself into a ball. Her expression wasn't peaceful the way it had always been whenever I checked on her before, and it caused a sharp pain to pulse in my chest a couple of times. Instead, her lips were pinched, her brow knitted and drawn low, and her cheeks glistened in the moonlight.

Shit. I should have forced her to let me stay. As much as

Peyton frustrated me, I didn't like seeing her hurting. As her mate it was my job to protect her from anything that harmed her, and that included the things in her dreams.

I crossed the space to her bed, drew the quilt back, and slid in beside her, careful not to jostle the bed too much. I reached out to take her in my arms and she came willingly, almost eagerly, and cuddled up against me so I was wrapped around her from behind. She released a slow exhale, as if she were expelling her fear and tension. By the time she took another breath in, she'd relaxed, and the peaceful expression had turned to her face.

As my mind finally began to stop spinning and sleep approached, I wondered if all mates found this kind of ease and contentment in each other's arms. If this was what it would be like to hold her every night, especially after an explosive round or two of sex, it would be no hardship.

My wolf completely agreed.

CHAPTER TWENTY-THREE

PEYTON

After my night started out like utter shit, I couldn't believe how well I slept when my memories stopped assaulting my dreams. In fact, I was enjoying a spicy dream about Nathan, getting all hot and bothered, when something woke me up. My lips curled down in a frown when my movements were constricted by something. I dragged my eyes open and gasped. Nathan was lying half on top of me with one of my legs between his and the other hooked around his thigh. One of his hands cupped a breast and his very impressive morning erection was snuggled right up against my center.

Uhhhh… I wasn't sure what to do about this. My body was highly in favor of turning up the heat and my panther was right there with it, purring and panting after the feel of Nathan's hard body. To make matters worse, the big, sexy man was completely naked, and my sleep shorts and tank top were not worth a damn as a barrier.

My nipples pebbled and I cursed them when Nathan's hand flexed around my breast. He had been facing in my direction, but he was so freaking huge that I still had to look up to see him.

His eyes were on my face, molten silver pools that sent sizzles of heat over my skin. "Good morning, baby."

Before I knew what was happening, his mouth had taken control of mine. He rolled me beneath him, settling back between my thighs, making me hot and needy. The kiss was full of fireworks and dark passion at the same time. I had no idea how that was possible.

I was having trouble remembering why I kept putting the brakes on sex. Especially now that he knew the baby was his. Then again, it was hard to think about anything else when he was touching me. One of his hands traveled down to my thigh and he hiked it up. The shift in his position opened me up so he was wedged even more firmly in the apex between my legs. I moaned and dropped my head back as he began to kiss his way down my throat.

Then he placed one more kiss on the corner of my mouth and pulled back, gazing down at me with an unreadable expression. I frowned as I remembered our conversation about honesty. He was one to talk. I knew he was keeping plenty of secrets from me. Granted, I doubted there was anything quite like waiting to tell him about his kid. But I needed a reason to be indignant about something, or I would drag him back down and beg him to fuck me.

"How are you feeling?" His voice was rough with morning grit, but I could tell his question was genuine. I didn't understand why he was trying to be…sort of sweet? *Or his version of it,* I thought.

"Um. Fine. But what are you doing here? You don't belong in my bed," I admonished.

He didn't respond at first and didn't hide the fact that his mind was working through something. Eventually, he flipped us over so he was on his back and I was sitting astride him, his hands resting lightly on my hips. *Oh, right…he's naked*, I thought distractedly.

"You're right," he said with a nod.

That definitely caught my attention. At first, I felt relief that he was finally going to stop trying to seduce me. I'd never had trouble moving on to a new place, but there was something about Nathan. He'd continue to strengthen that tether if I let him, but if I stayed, it was more than likely that I'd end up resenting him for it someday. Especially since I was already linked to him and Silver Lake through our child.

However, that didn't mean I didn't feel regret every time I said no. Who wouldn't? Nathan was the hottest man I'd ever seen, and I knew exactly what it felt like to have his hands all over me, his mouth on me, him moving inside me.

I opened my mouth to reply, but before I could, he'd curved his arms around me and jumped out of bed. He stalked out of my room and down the hall to the master where he went to the bed and unceremoniously dumped me onto it.

I glanced around with confusion. "I thought you said I was right."

He nodded as he climbed onto the huge bed and covered my body with his own. "You are. I don't belong in your bed." He jerked his chin up toward the headboard. "You belong in mine."

I snorted and tried to push him off me with my hands on his chest, even though I knew it was a futile endeavor. "I don't belong in anyone's bed but my own."

He took a hold of my chin and stared down at me with a frown. "You belong in my bed, Peyton. End of story."

"And what makes you think that, exactly?" I couldn't wait to hear his reason. I was sure it would have something to do with giving me orgasms…which would be very convincing.

"Because you're my mate."

I almost swallowed my tongue and choked for a minute

before I burst out laughing. "Okay, that's an original one. I'll give you that." Nathan just stared at me and my amusement faded out. "You can't be serious."

His eyes flashed and his wolf glared back at me before Nathan pushed him back. "You're my true mate. Do I seem like the type to joke about this, Peyton?"

"Well, no, but…" I couldn't help it when another chuckle escaped. Nathan's wolf flashed in his eyes again and I frowned. What was he so pissed about? My cat wasn't any happier about the animal's attitude. "That's ridiculous!" I insisted.

"Is it?" he replied, raising a single eyebrow. He captured my wrists and moved them up to hold them over my head. His legs locked around mine, pinning me to the bed so I couldn't move. "You can't tell me you've ever felt the intense attraction we have with anyone else."

"Well, no, but—"

"If you weren't my mate, do you really think we'd be drowning in our need for each other? There's no full moon right now, Peyton. But I can't go five minutes without thinking about fucking you. I've never come so hard as I did with you. And I know it's the same for you."

I scowled, not wanting to admit it, but I also didn't want to taint the one place that Nathan actually trusted me. "True. But—"

Nathan's mouth shut me right up when he slammed it down on mine and kissed me deep and thorough, turning me into a puddle of desire.

"Fuck," Nathan grunted. "I'm dying to be inside you again, baby. It's been way too fucking long."

I loved his filthy mouth, but it didn't chase away my doubts about his claim. I struggled against his hold, but he wouldn't let me go.

Is that the point? Is he making a statement, warning me that he has no intention of letting me go?

The thought brought panic barreling through me and I broke the kiss to try to suck in great big gulps of oxygen. I struggled hard and with one look at my face, Nathan released me. He rolled to the side and I sat up, relieved when I was finally able to fill my lungs.

"You're crazy, Nathan," I snapped when I'd composed myself enough to speak. "All that proves is that we have exceptional sexual chemistry. And aren't a woman's hormones all hyped up during a pregnancy? None of that proves I'm your mate."

Nathan laughed this time, but there was only a hint of humor in it. "The pregnancy?" he asked with another chuckle. "You're grasping at straws, baby."

I turned to face him, moving my feet under me so I was sitting on my heels. It brought our height almost even. "Nathan, I can't be your mate."

He scowled at me and stood, facing me with his arms crossed. "Enlighten me."

I stared. Damn his stupid gorgeous, distracting body with that sexy beard and beautiful hair. His nakedness should not have been so distracting. We were shifters, for crying out loud. Nudity was just an everyday occurrence.

"Peyton." Nathan's voice grabbed my attention, and I ignored the cocky smirk on his beautiful lips.

"I'm a black panther, Nathan," I answered in an insolent tone, earning myself a glare of warning. "We don't mate."

Nathan uncrossed his arms and bent to press his fists into the mattress, leaning over so our faces were only a couple of inches apart. "Yes, *we* do."

CHAPTER TWENTY-FOUR

NATHAN

Peyton's refusal to accept what was right in front of her was starting to get on my nerves.

"Seriously," she said, ignoring my declaration. "Panthers, jaguars, we don't have mates."

I scoffed and stood to my full height, pinning her with a stare that suggested she not push me. "That's bullshit and you know it, Peyton," I vented, my temper rising. "Not only do I know plenty of leopards and jaguars who have found their mates, but your closest friends are a mated leopard couple."

"They made the choice to mate," she replied stubbornly. "And it's rare."

I shook my head, both at her incorrect statement and her obstinance. "It happens more than you think, Peyton. You only know what happened with your parents—of course, I'm guessing since you never want to talk about yourself—and what you've seen in your limited experience despite all of your travels. I'm head of the fucking SC. Trust me."

"Still," she argued. "We don't have 'mates' like you. Sam and Linette, they chose each other and decided to mate."

She wasn't wrong about her friends. They hadn't been

destined to be together, like many other mates, even plenty of wolves. They'd claimed each other through the mating process.

Yet I knew without a single doubt that Peyton was my true mate. I wasn't sure how. Some true mates had no clue and were under each other's noses for years, sometimes even mating others before they figured it out. I assumed plenty of shifters never figured it out and some just never met them. But we were different. I hadn't figured out how or why yet. Apparently, I needed to convince my obstinate mate of the truth before I figured out the rest of it. I wanted to get my mark on Peyton as soon as possible. That thought sparked a memory and—*holy shit. Could it be that simple?*

I climbed onto the bed and grabbed Peyton around the waist, dragging her over to me. I gathered her hair away from her neck with the other hand, then grabbed the neckline of her shirt and jerked it away.

How the fuck had I missed it all this time?

Peyton had a very clear bite on her neck. My bite.

No wonder the pull between us had been so strong, even before she'd showed up at my door. It was also the most likely explanation for how I'd figured out we were true mates out of the blue.

Technically, we were already in the first stage of the mating process.

An arrogant smirk graced my lips. "Told you we were mates, baby," I said smugly.

Peyton's expression suggested she thought I'd lost my mind, then she tried to see what had my rapt attention. Obviously, her head didn't bend that way. I swept her into my arms and took her into the bathroom to set her on the counter. I used her hips to turn her to face the mirror, forcing her to cross her legs in front of her. I pulled open one of my drawers and grabbed a hair band, then gathered her hair up into a ponytail.

She watched me curiously until I grasped her shirt again and ripped the neckline to expose her whole neck and shoulder.

"Hey!" she snapped, turning to glare at me, rather than in the mirror. I put a hand on each side of her head and redirected her gaze before letting go. She stared at herself with a frown. "What am I supposed to be seeing?"

I gently pushed her head to the side, fully exposing her neck.

"What the fuck is that?" she exclaimed as she leaned forward to inspect it from a closer angle. "Is that from when you bit me?"

Curling an arm around her middle, I hauled her back against me, then gently traced the mark. *My mark.* "You didn't reject my claim, baby," I murmured into her ear. "I wonder why that is."

"I…" Her expression was genuinely puzzled, and I frowned, not happy with her reaction. "I…I honestly forgot about it. With the pregnancy and everything…"

The fact that it was still there meant that her panther hadn't forgotten, and Peyton might not have consciously remembered it, but if she'd truly intended to reject the claim, she would have. Although something hadn't quite fully clicked into place or she would have already become a member of my pack. But she wasn't anywhere in the web in my mind.

The fact that she hadn't remembered it was there irritated the fuck out of me. I stalked to my dresser, pulled out a pair of loose shorts, and yanked them on. As I left the room I muttered, "You won't forget it again. I'll make damn sure no one else ever misses it."

I headed to the kitchen to make some breakfast for Peyton before I left for KBO. My home office was usually where I preferred to work, but I'd been at KBO because if I stayed home, I'd have talked Peyton out of her panties the first day and we wouldn't have left the bedroom since. And I didn't want Peyton stumbling across anything I found out about the serial killer. She was pregnant and had enough stress to deal with.

Perhaps that was why she hadn't been applying rationale to our situation. I'd learned a lot about her in the short time we'd known each other. She was extremely intelligent, seemed to be practical, and despite her stubborn nature, I had the impression that she usually approached things similarly to the way I handled things. However, I had a suspicion that I pushed her buttons just as she pushed mine.

Honestly, I wasn't sure we were a good match from a practical standpoint, but fate had paired us together and that was enough for me. I was also confident that Peyton would come around. Once she did, we could start to make plans for the future. We'd need to move all of her things here and...

While I cooked, my mind worked, making lists and arranging information in a way that made sense to me. When the meal was done, I went to find Peyton and heard the shower running in the hall bathroom. It was hard as fuck to walk away when images of a wet, naked Peyton assaulted my imagination.

I knocked and called through the door. "Breakfast is in the microwave. I need to get ready for work."

She said something unintelligible, then shouted, "Okay."

I stared at the door for another moment, bothered by the tone she'd used when she'd mumbled whatever it was. But I shook it off and headed to my room to get ready.

When I reemerged, showered and dressed in jeans and a white short-sleeve T-shirt, Peyton was sitting at the kitchen table with an empty plate, staring at the wall thoughtfully.

I walked over and kissed the top of her head before taking her plate to the sink. "What has you thinking so hard?"

"Nothing."

"Peyton!" I barked. She jumped and spun around to stare at me. "I'm your mate. You do not shut me out."

"First of all, even if I was—"

Before she'd finished saying something that would've almost certainly pissed me off, I scooped her up and carried her to the large island. I set her on the counter and used a method that had been proving to be very useful. I shut her up with my mouth.

I only meant to kiss her hard and fast, just enough that she would forget what she was about to say and tell me what she'd been thinking about. Unfortunately, realizing we were mates and that she still wore my mark had only intensified my hunger for her. She'd put on a pair of skinny jeans that made her long, toned legs look amazing, with a yellow, light, long-sleeved T-shirt. I wedged myself between her thighs and grabbed her ass, dragging her forward until we were practically glued together at our centers.

My hands seemed to have a mind of their own. By the time I let her go, her jeans were on the floor and she was spread out on the counter, panting and unable to move. I licked my lips, savoring the last of her taste and already craving more. Moving over to the sink, I rinsed off my beard, then grabbed her jeans and helped her put them back on. I tugged the elastic band from her top knot and winked at her as I used it to twist my hair up.

I kissed her again, keeping it brief this time. "Stay home," I ordered. "No wandering off."

I left her in stunned silence and headed into the KBO offices.

Tanner was in his office, bent over his desk frowning at a stack of papers.

"Come up with anything?" I asked.

He shook his head and continued to study the documents. "The ME's reports are useless. The only thing we know is that he's a wolf, and we already fucking knew that. How the hell has this guy not left even a single fingerprint anywhere?"

I sat on his couch and spread my arms out along the back. "I talked to Scott yesterday."

Tanner's brow rose. "What made you finally call him?"

My fingers flexed as I debated whether I was ready to share my newfound knowledge in regard to Peyton. It wasn't that I wouldn't have done as much for anyone else as I would for Peyton, but I'd always been methodical, patient, willing to take the slow route if it meant guaranteed success. I felt the pressure of a timetable with Peyton's case. I wanted this done and over so we could put all of our attention into working out the personal shit. I also had a feeling that I'd only be able to distract her from asking about the investigation for so long.

I knew Tanner would be more helpful if I didn't hold back information, but I did it grudgingly. "You figured out the baby is mine," I surmised and he nodded. "There's more to it."

He grinned and I gave him a curious look, but he just smiled wider. "Go ahead."

"She's my true mate."

Tanner laughed and leaned back in his chair. "It's about time you figured that out."

"You knew?"

"Yeah. I would have put some money on it—and made a fortune—but I didn't think you'd want me spreading it around."

"Wait," I said, holding up a hand. "Go back to 'you knew'."

Tanner shrugged. "It was pretty obvious when you told me about her the first time. But you know how it is about seeing what's right in front of you."

I leaned forward and put my elbows on my knees, my hands hanging in between. "You want to explain why the hell you kept it to yourself, Beta?" My tone warned that he should be very careful with his answer.

"That's something people have to figure out for themselves. If you'd gone back to her with that option on your mind, you would have started analyzing every little thing for proof that she was or wasn't. You might have convinced yourself that I was wrong."

I stroked my beard and chewed that over for a minute. "I see your point. I rarely get involved with mate situations for the same reason." I thought about Asher and Savannah and stared at the ceiling for a moment. "Even if they are both being stubborn as fuck and refusing to admit it."

As my Beta, Tanner was privy to almost everything pack related, unless it was something the pack member had specifically asked to be kept between them and their Alpha. I'd debated telling Tanner when I discovered that my head enforcer, Asher, and our newcomer, Savannah, were true mates.

"He'll get his head out of his ass eventually. She's not ready yet, anyway."

I met Tanner's perceptive eyes and inclined my head in acknowledgement of his assumption. "I should have known you'd already have it figured out."

Tanner had an uncanny ability to sense things, like true mates, but we kept it between us, or everyone would be beating down his door to find their mates and anything else he could sense about their lives.

"Anyway"—I redirected the conversation from the tangent and back to the original subject—"Scott said they've hit a wall with the case. They're staking out Peyton's apartment though, so we'll have to figure out how to move all of her things here without tipping them to the fact that we know her whereabouts."

"Move her stuff?" Tanner repeated, his tone questioning.

"Of course," I said absently as I thought through our options for her apartment.

"She's agreed to move here?"

I glanced at Tanner with a frown, wondering why he was stuck on this point. "She's my mate."

He seemed like he wanted to say something else, but after a minute, he shook his head. "Have they reached her place?"

I nodded, allowing the subject change since we had more important things to talk about. "But they didn't find enough evidence to assume he'd killed her. They think she's either hiding or he's taken her."

"Were our guys able to get in there before?"

I sighed and ran a hand over my beard. "Yeah. But other than being more familiar with his scent now, there wasn't anything new."

"What a fucking mess," Tanner mumbled.

"No shit." I scrubbed my face with my hands, then rolled my shoulders and neck. "Still no connection between the victims."

"Oh, shit," Tanner breathed. "I'm such an asshole." He shuffled through the stacks of paper on his desk until he found the one he was looking for and shoved it at me. "I don't have solid proof yet, but I have a hunch it's going to pan out."

"No fucking way," I said in shock as I read through the paper. "Same facility?"

"Nope. That's why I missed it at first. I decided to start with the first victim and follow their footsteps with a fine-toothed comb for the four weeks before their murder. Since that's his time frame, I felt like it was a safe bet with victim number one. But we still don't know what made him choose those particular people as his victims. Or what his purpose is for the way he leaves them."

According to Tanner's research, every single one of the victims had donated their DNA to a lab within the four-week window before their murder. One was a student and had donated to her science department, one was a twin and had donated to a study for identical pairs, another had submitted their DNA to find out if they were genetically disposed to any diseases, it went on and on. Different reasons, different facilities—the act of donating and the time frame were the only discernible connection. I had no clue how this guy had access to all of this information, but if he did, this was most likely how he'd chosen his victims.

"You have a list of the facilities?" I asked. Tanner handed me another sheet of paper. Hacking into some of these databases would be a bitch. A few of them were like Fort fucking Knox and I wasn't sure even I could crack the security on them.

We had other items to discuss at the moment and this would take time. I'd have to dig into it more later, so I set the papers beside me.

I turned my attention to the missing Council members, of which now totaled three. "Any progress on the search for Melinda or Fenn?"

I couldn't dig into the circumstances of all three at once so I'd focused my attention on the missing shifter, Beau. The other two were representatives of different species. Melinda was a vampire from the New York coven, but she was Lucien's cousin, which meant he'd been up my ass about her. Fenn was a Fae representative. His king wasn't happy with me either.

Apparently, absent the real villain, they had no one to blame, so they'd aimed it at me. I was used to it, though, so their displeasure barely registered.

However, despite their disgruntlement, they'd each agreed to assist my agents at KBO in discovering the whereabouts of their respective ISC members. The last time I checked in with Willa, there hadn't been any updates.

Either the three of them were very good at disappearing, or whoever had taken them was the one with talent.

"Actually, Phillipé popped in yesterday while you were... handling your mate."

I snorted at his very inaccurate description. "No one 'handles' Peyton."

Tanner fought a smile, a very smart decision when I was in a shitty mood. "He heard whispers that might be related to whatever is happening with the Councils. He said they are exploring it."

Phillipé was the prince of Monarchie du Sang. But he spent a large portion of his time in New York handling their properties here. I'd hoped the whispers that made their way through their club would pay off.

"Do you think..." Tanner hesitated, and I waited patiently for him to figure out what he wanted to say. "I don't believe that the Council disappearances and the deaths of the shifters are unrelated."

I nodded. "I agree."

"Do you remember about twenty years ago we had that small religious faction that was picking off animals and lone shifters?"

Leaning back on the couch, I resumed my position with my arms spread out and my legs stretched out in front of me, crossed at the ankle. "Of course." They'd been a particularly sick group of humans. Somehow, they'd come to believe that shifters were real. However, they had their facts all wrong. They'd managed to eliminate some packless wolves and a few other shifters who didn't have a family unit. The only reason we'd figured it out was because they'd killed more innocent animals than actual shifters.

When they'd realized they hadn't taken out a supernatural creature, they'd made the mistake of ditching the carcass. Local packs had brought it to my attention after finding more than a dozen dead animals. When we'd found the first body of a shifter, we'd hunted the group responsible and, while not many knew what had happened to them other than that they were gone, the truth was that I'd made them pay and collected the names of every member and accomplice in the process. Then we'd wiped them out.

"Something about all this… I don't know why, but my brain is trying to connect the two."

"You think we missed some members of the group?"

He shook his head and scratched his dark, thin beard. "My gut says no. It's more like a shared purpose. As if someone knew the details of the situation and picked up where the others left off. But with a much more sophisticated, well-executed plan."

My brow furrowed deep over my eyes. "Only a handful of people knew the details. All shifters."

Tanner's dark eyes met mine and he nodded solemnly.

"You think it's shifters behind this?" His speculation threw me for a loop. Not that there weren't plenty of evil sons of bitches who were leaders in the shifter communities. But by interfering with the ISC, particularly snatching its members, they could start a war.

"I'm not sure yet. I do think they are involved though."

"Put Lisa on it," I instructed. "Have her dig into all the local Alphas for now and see what they've been up to." I pulled my hair down and ran my hands through it, relieved when it released some of the tension building behind my eyes. "I want you working on the Council members. I haven't had time to delve into emails and phone records of the members. Find out if anyone is being blackmailed, influenced, whatever. I want to know why the fuck there is so much infighting going on and why the votes are coming up split ninety percent of the time."

I blew out a frustrated breath, knowing it was a lot to heap onto Tanner and Lisa, but I didn't have much choice. They would have help from the other tech team members, but their abilities were far below what was necessary to really offer much aid. "I have to deal with the Peyton situation." I knew she was going crazy cooped up in the cabin, so I'd decided to work for a couple of hours, then take Peyton on a run before coming back to work.

"I've got this," Tanner assured me.

CHAPTER TWENTY-FIVE

PEYTON

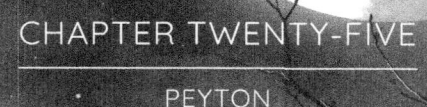

He *did not just say that to me.*

"Don't wander off" was a little better than "stay." But it was like graduating from dog to toddler.

Honestly, how did he think I'd survived for over thirty-two years without accidentally maiming myself?

I wanted to run off just to be defiant, but then I reminded myself I wasn't a rebellious teenager.

Fine, if he wants me to be safe, I get it. I'll just stay home.

An hour later I was bored out of my mind. I'd also been out of touch with my life for too long. Nathan had told me he'd been in contact with Sam shortly after I arrived here, so I knew he wasn't worrying about me. But had Linette had the baby? I'd promised to be there. I hadn't had a chance to erase my details from the hospital and police records yet, either. I couldn't remember the last time I'd been separated from my laptop for so long. And without even my phone, I'd had no contact with the outside world. If Nathan had had his way, I wouldn't have even met Savannah.

As I wandered around the house, I wondered what Savannah was doing today. Nathan had his home phone, but I didn't know anyone's phone numbers. I ended up standing in the doorway to Nathan's study. He'd said I had free rein of the house, that nowhere was off limits. But I hadn't ventured in this room because it had felt a little like violating his privacy.

Thinking about the events of the morning, particularly before he left for work, I snorted. At this point, he'd spent plenty of time invading my "privacy." With that rationale to back me up, I stepped into the office and snooped around. The room reminded me of him—masculine and a little old-fashioned with the dark colors and beautifully carved wooden furniture and bookshelves. I ran my fingers along the cool, shiny surfaces and scouted his book collection. It was an interesting mixture of fiction and non-fiction. He clearly had eclectic tastes. As I approached the desk, I spotted his computer sitting on top.

I hurried around and plopped into his big, leather chair. I rolled my eyes when my feet didn't touch the ground and the chair nearly swallowed me whole. Grabbing the desktop, I hauled the chair forward, then opened the laptop and waited for it to turn on.

When the screen lit up and the sign-in screen popped up, I hit a few commands to bypass it, but it didn't work. *Encryption. How cute.*

I dug into the encryption and with every layer, I became both more impressed and more wary. Whoever had done the security for this laptop was incredibly good. But what I really wanted to know was why Nathan needed security like this. They kept the heavy-duty Council files in a SCIF room at the HQ. I knew because I'd built the encryption system for it. Not that anyone knew that because I'd done that work under my hacker persona. I had layers upon layers of bullshit between me and that "person." It went so deep that I almost felt like if they managed to get through it all and connect me to my alter ego, I freaking deserved to be caught.

I tried another bit of fancy finger work and hit yet another layer of security. Would pack files and records really need this level of protection? Something wasn't sitting right. I leaned back and stared at the black screen with the single blinking cursor and wondered if it was worth it to keep going. The encryption would probably take me a few hours to crack, but did I want to? *Ignorance is bliss, right?*

The question was taken out of my hands when I heard a soft knocking on the glass at the back of the house. I quickly erased any digital evidence that I'd been on the computer, shut it down and trotted through the cabin. A giant smile split my face when I saw Savannah standing there waving. I hurried to the door and opened it. "Hey, Foxy."

"Foxy?" someone repeated with a laugh.

My head whipped to the left and I spotted a woman who was quite a bit taller than me, with flowing emerald-green hair and a lean, athletic body. She had gorgeous features, eyes that matched her hair, high cheekbones, and full, maroon-painted lips. She wore a T-shirt and shorts that showed off a badass assortment of tattoos. There was a beautiful and intricate design on her right forearm, another on her biceps that disappeared beneath the short sleeve of her T-shirt, and several black bands on both arms. She also had a tiny red heart tattooed on her right cheekbone, just beneath the corner of her eye, which would have been ridiculous on a lot of people, but she pulled it off with flair.

"Emerald, this is Peyton—she's a black panther," Savannah introduced. "Peyton, Emerald."

I raised an eyebrow at her spot-on name.

"Another transplant," Savannah added, speaking to me again.

"Is that so?" I glanced warily at Savannah and she put her hand on my shoulder.

"She's got her own secrets to protect. You don't have to share with her, but I thought we could both use another friend."

Hadn't I explained to Savannah that I didn't do friends? She and Sam and Linette were huge exceptions.

"My stay here is temporary, too," Emerald piped up with a smile. "Don't get me wrong, a pack of hot wolves isn't the worst place to be hiding out, but I've got shit to do elsewhere."

"I know the feeling," I said with a little more ease.

Savannah gestured to the trees behind the house and said, "We thought you might like to get out and go for a run." A smirk popped onto her lips. "I may have been paying attention to when Nathan left."

I laughed and nodded. "Are you a shifter?" I asked Emerald curiously. She didn't smell like one.

"Vampire slayer by birth, human tattoo artist by choice."

"But she's in sick shape," Savannah informed me. "She keeps up with me when I run."

"I'm impressed," I said.

Emerald held out her hands and grinned. "Don't be. I can't help it if I'm awesome."

I laughed and stepped out onto the porch, giving her a wink. "Ditto."

Emerald pointed at me and grinned at Savannah. "I dig this chick."

Savannah smiled happily. It was nice to see her with a little less sadness lurking in her eyes.

"Somebody needs to explain the 'Foxy' thing, though. I mean, Savannah is hot, sure, but I have a feeling there's a story there."

I quickly explained my logic for the name and Emerald threw her head back and laughed—a full, rich sound.

"I don't know another Peyton," she said when she stopped. "But I think I'm going to call you Tabitha."

I rolled my eyes but laughed. "A little cliché, don't you think?"

Emerald tapped her chin, looking thoughtful. "You're absolutely right." Her eyes lit up after a couple of seconds. "Schrödinger!"

I scrunched my nose. "As in Schrödinger's cat?"

"Yeah, because with one foot out the door, you're neither here nor there!"

Savannah giggled.

"Next," I said dryly.

Emerald chuckled. "How about we just go with Nomad? Savannah tells me you're a wanderer."

I mulled it over and nodded. "I can feel that one."

Emerald clapped her hands excitedly. "Perfect!"

"Should we stick with the nickname Emerald?" I asked.

Emerald shook her head and pointed at herself with both thumbs. "That's my real name. Part of being born awesome."

"No way," I replied with a chuckle.

"Way."

Savannah smiled at us both, seeming happy, and a little smug, that we were getting along. "Ready to roll?"

I nodded. "I'm game, but let's not go too far and I can't let my guard down. Nathan was beyond pissed at me last time, especially when he found me asleep by the lake."

Savannah tilted her head and watched me with a calculating gleam in her pretty brown eyes.

"What?" I asked.

She shrugged. "He just seems awfully overprotective with you."

I frowned, thinking about his unexpected claim that we were mates. Not ready to talk about that yet, I waved off her observation. "I'm sure any Alpha male would be overbearing and obnoxious when it came to the mother of his child."

It was Emerald's turn to raise an eyebrow. "You're knocked up? With Nathan's kid? The Alpha?"

I nodded, once again wary because I didn't know what she would do with the information.

"Good fucking luck with that one," Emerald teased. "I've seen how possessive my friend's mate is of her and she's not even carrying his pup."

Savannah laughed. "I think his overprotective instincts might have more to do with Rowan's tendency to run headfirst into dangerous situations. That chick is a badass and a warrior, but she's also a little crazy."

Emerald laughed and tapped her chest over her heart. "That's why I love her."

Savannah snorted this time. "Don't pretend you aren't just as crazy."

"I prefer the term quirky, if you must label me."

I couldn't help the smile that grew on my face. These two were funny. Their lighthearted banter was such a change from the mood in Nathan's house. Suddenly, the claustrophobia of being cloistered in this house, in this town, made my panther and I desperate to run. I wasn't stupid enough to take off while someone was hunting me when Nathan could help track the asshole, but if I did what he demanded, I would lose my ever-loving mind.

"Let's get out of here," I jumped in eagerly.

"Dope," Emerald replied with a nod.

Savannah and I started to undress and Emerald snickered as she bent to tie the shoelace of her beat-up old sneaker. "Good thing I don't have a hangup about nudity or living here would be much more awkward."

I laughed as I shifted. Savannah had reason to gloat.

Emerald was the shit and she helped to push away some of the stress that had been slowly crushing me.

"Race ya!" she yelled and took off.

My panther chuffed, her version of a laugh, and I felt her take the challenge right before she jumped off the back deck. Everything became a blur as she flew through the trees, blowing past the other two without even nearing our top speed. Although they kept up to a certain extent and my panther was very impressed. She'd already bonded with Savannah's wolf, but her respect notched up and she accepted Emerald as a friend.

After thirty minutes, my girl slowed to their speed and we all ran together.

We didn't stray far from Nathan's house, but apparently it was too far for Nathan. Not ten minutes later, a massive, silver wolf stepped out of the trees, directly in our path. Fury radiated from him and his silver eyes were almost black, their icy stare sending a shiver through my panther.

All three of us came to an abrupt halt. Emerald and Savannah crowded next to me, showing their support, but despite not being a member of Nathan's pack, I felt the heaviness of the Alpha vibes he directed at the red wolf beside me. I didn't blame Savannah's wolf for yielding to his power, even if he hadn't been her Alpha. She slouched down and leaned her head to the side, baring her neck in a sign of submission.

He growled and jerked his head to the left. Savannah's wolf bowed her head, threw me an apologetic glance, then trotted off in the direction Nathan's wolf had directed.

Emerald placed her hand on my head and my panther swung her head around to meet concerned, emerald orbs. "Should I stay?"

Her willingness to stand with me against Nathan—for

someone she'd just met—overwhelmed me. I hated being ruled by emotion. It was one of the reasons I kept people at arm's length. But I should have seen it right away. Emerald had the ability to bust through walls without even trying. We'd bonded and I knew I'd never shake her from my life. Surprisingly, I found that I didn't want to.

The silver wolf growled aggressively, staring at Emerald with a dark, warning gaze. I knew he wouldn't physically hurt Emerald on purpose, but I didn't want her getting in the middle of things and risking accidental injury. And I didn't want to make things even more tense with the person who could have her tossed out on her ass. This was my fight. My panther didn't know the words Emerald spoke, but their meaning was still clear, and she agreed with my assessment. Except her attitude toward Nathan definitely didn't mesh with mine.

She shook her head and nudged Emerald's shoulder in a gesture of thanks and affection. Emerald's green orbs bounced between Nathan and me a few more times, then she muttered, "Get word to me if you need me to break your ass out of jail." Then she ran off, leaving me alone with a very big, very angry, wolf, who looked like he just might kill me.

He rumbled with a low growl and turned to head back to the house, expecting me to follow. However, my small taste of freedom had made me a little salty when he cut it short, and I wasn't about to let him have his way all the time. It took some convincing for my panther though, because she just wanted to be with the big, powerful wolf that made her all hot and bothered. His display only made her even more attracted to him.

I glanced to my right and spotted a big-ass tree that would be way out of reach for a wolf but was easily scaled by a jungle cat. My panther fought me, but I somehow convinced her that the wolf would see it as…foreplay of a sort, I guess.

Finally, she leapt onto the tree and gracefully made her way up to a cluster of thick branches that made a perfect spot for her to curl up on. Nathan's wolf seemed to sense something was off almost immediately—probably because I was up high enough to make my scent much lighter.

The wolf glanced around, then his head slowly lifted, following the trunk of the tree up to the branches. I was feeling a little smug over the fact that I was a badass jaguar who could run faster and climb trees. But when he spotted us, I suddenly wondered if I'd just made the stupidest choice of my life.

He was *really* fucking angry.

Even my panther shrank back from the waves of rage coming off of him.

I guess we live here now.

To my surprise, he shifted into human form.

A human Nathan, staring at me with an icy glare and shaking with rage, wasn't much better.

His whole countenance changed, becoming soft and affectionate. "Hey, pretty girl," he crooned, shocking the fuck out of me.

My panther perked up and scooted a little further out on the branches to get a clearer view of the ground.

"You're amazing," he praised with a voice dripping in pride. "Can I talk to Peyton, sweetheart?"

What the hell is happening right now? My panther retreated a fraction and I shoved her forward again. *Don't you dare.*

"Please?" he cajoled.

My girl dropped back inside me and forced me to the surface. *Traitor!* I shouted at her. She ignored me, not at all interested in what I wanted.

The abrupt shift caught me off guard and as soon as my bones and muscle had fused back together, leaving me in human form, I lost my balance and tumbled out of the tree.

"Peyton!" Nathan shouted.

Before he could catch me, I landed gracefully on the ground. I was a cat after all. Even in human form shifters shared a lot of the characteristics of their animals. Nathan looked stunned and I took the opportunity to run. I needed time to figure out how to deal with his bullshit before the unavoidable confrontation. I barely made it a single step when an arm banded around my waist, jerking me to a stop like the cartoons that are hooked by a cane and pulled off stage.

He didn't say a word, he just tossed me over his shoulder and stalked in the direction of the house. I started to protest, but he slapped my ass hard enough for the pain to steal my breath a little. "Stop doing that!" I gasped when I could inhale again.

He repeated the action on my other butt cheek and barked, "Quiet!"

My mouth snapped shut and I let him take me back to the cabin without further comment.

CHAPTER TWENTY-SIX

NATHAN

What the fuck had I done in my life to be saddled with Peyton as a mate?

Is this the universe's idea of a joke?

I'd only been gone a few hours and when I came home to take Peyton on a run, what did I find? No Peyton. No note. Just a pile of clothes by the back door.

Like the last time, worry over her safety washed over me and ignited the simmering anger at her flagrant disobedience. Did the woman have no fucking regard for the fact that she was in the crosshairs of a serial killer?

I picked up the other two scents as soon as I stepped outside. Emerald and Savannah. The fact that she hadn't gone out alone should have soothed some of my ire, but I was just too fucking pissed to be placated. I shifted, not caring that it shredded my clothes, then my wolf stood still and focused, his mind probing through the pack until he latched onto Savannah. As I'd suspected, she was in wolf form. It was a little easier to connect with members of my pack in their animal form once I'd shifted into my wolf. I paid attention to what she was seeing, and it only took a few seconds to recognize their location and the direction they were headed. I knew every inch of my pack's land.

My wolf grunted in irritation and took off to a spot where we would cut them off. They weren't far from the cabin, but my temper had been unleashed to its fullest extent and I was being ruled by it. When we brought them to a sudden halt a few minutes later, I sent Savannah on her way with a command from her Alpha, then Peyton wisely encouraged Emerald to leave while I stared coldly at the both of them.

Then, after turning to lead her home, my wolf froze when her scent grew weak. In all honesty, I was kind of impressed to find her up in that tree, but at that moment, it was just another thing that stood between Peyton and my wrath.

Her panther's interest and desire hadn't escaped my notice, so I opted to throw a Hail Mary. I shifted and convinced her panther to change. However, I hadn't expected Peyton to lose her balance and fall. My heart stopped as images of her broken body on the ground filled my mind. I ran to catch her but found myself standing in astonishment when she landed with the grace and agility of a cat.

Sadly for Peyton, that scare just added to the storm brewing inside me.

I'd had enough, so when she attempted to run, I threw her over my shoulder. If she'd only stayed quiet and given me the walk to calm down...Instead, she poked at me and I lost my temper. Not that she didn't deserve the spanking, but it irritated me yet again, that I didn't have complete control over myself.

Now that Peyton and I were mating and she was staying, I was determined to stop allowing her to get under my skin. How she'd accomplished it when I'd spent two millennia mastering self-control was beyond me. My best guess was the mate thing, but the electricity between us would surely fizzle eventually.

Once we were in the living room, I dropped her into her favorite recliner and began to pace in front of her.

"Nathan—"

"Shut it, Peyton," I snarled. "I swear to all that is holy, if you talk right now, I will lose my shit. And your ass will pay the price."

She closed her mouth and sat back in her seat, but her expression made it very clear that she was silently cursing me.

"I don't understand how this happened again. What did you not understand about our last discussion on your safety and leaving the house alone?"

When she didn't answer, I stopped in front of her and waited with a deep frown.

"Oh, can I speak now?" she asked sweetly.

My eyes narrowed in warning, but I gestured for her to go on before crossing my arms over my chest.

"First, I never agreed to stay inside, you just assumed I would obey your order—frankly, I'm a little surprised you haven't figured out that I don't follow anyone's rules but my own."

My mouth flattened from repressing the urge to cut her off because I wanted to hear what she had to say for herself and if I pushed too hard too fast, she'd close herself off and I'd get no-fucking-where.

"Second, I wasn't alone. And we didn't go far. The fact that I considered your demands, *at all*, is rare for me. Take the win, Nathan."

I swallowed hard, repressing my desire to shout at her, and instead spoke in a cold, even tone. "You really thought Savannah and Emerald were sufficient protection, Peyton? Savannah is a submissive wolf, not a fighter. And while Emerald has been trained to kill vampires, she's been out of the game for a long time."

"I can take care of myself," Peyton insisted again.

I ran a hand through my hair before pinching the bridge of my nose in an effort to stave off the growing ache in my temples. "You wouldn't have just been protecting yourself—and I'm not just talking about the pup," I spit when she opened her mouth. "You would have ended up protecting Savannah and Emerald, too. Do you not fucking remember what happened the last time you fought this motherfucker?" By the time I finished, I was shouting.

Peyton was quiet for a while and I wondered if I'd finally gotten through to her. Until she muttered, "I remember every time I get a glimpse of my back or feel the scars pull. I remember every time I close my eyes. I remember *all the damn time*, Nathan. But I can't live my life in fear. I refuse to let you coddle me and treat me like a child."

"Then stop acting like one!" I yelled before picking up my pacing again. I was filled with energy and while pacing didn't help free it, it kept me from taking Peyton to the ground and releasing my aggression by fucking her long and hard.

Peyton stood and walked over to her clothes. I turned my head when she bent to pick them up because it only pushed me closer to the edge. After a few seconds of listening to the fabric rustle, she appeared in front of me. "What's the solution here, Nathan?"

"Other than chaining you to my bed and wearing you out so you don't have the energy to be a pain in my ass?"

Her contemptuous glare made it clear that if I tried to follow through with my suggestion, I'd be risking my life, or at least my balls. "Other than that," she hissed.

"I'm going to put a couple of enforcers on you," I announced. My wolf wasn't happy about other men watching our mate, but he understood the necessity when we couldn't be with her. And we couldn't catch the killer if we were with her all the time. Especially with what I'd learned the day before. I needed KBO's supercomputer and other resources.

Peyton played with the ends of her hair for a minute. "Okay," she agreed.

My wolf nudged me, wanting me to go after her, but I just watched her walk away, wondering if I should be worried about how easily she'd accepted my decision.

When the enforcers called the next day to report that she slipped her tail and I had to track her ass down, *again*, I had my answer.

"Why won't you stay where you're put?" I demanded after returning to the cabin and dumping her onto the couch.

She snorted and rolled her eyes, jabbing a thumb at her chest. "Panther." Then she pointed to the butterfly tattoo on her inner wrist. "I'm a free spirit, Nathan. Nobody 'puts' me anywhere. When are you going to accept that I don't fit in the damsel-in-distress box you keep trying to shut me in?"

"I'll stop treating you like a helpless damsel when you prove you have some sense of self-preservation," I grunted.

"Is that so?" she asked, her gold flecks glittering suspiciously.

A warning sign flashed in my head. *It's a trap! It's a trap!* But I foolishly stepped right into it. "Yes."

"So you'll tell me what the hell is going on with the investigation into my situation? Because I'm pretty fucking confident that in all the time I've been here, you have to have discovered something."

Yeah, I'd stepped right into that. "Baby…"

She jammed her hands on her hips and aimed a deadly glare at me. "Don't 'baby' me! Turnabout is fair play, Nathan. If you don't want me to lie to you, don't lie to me."

"I haven't lied to you," I stated firmly.

Her green eyes flashed gold—both she and her cat were calling bullshit. "According to you, omission is still a lie."

I had to be careful how I approached this. I had the feeling she wouldn't see this as a gray area like I did.

She probably thought she could help. Shortly after she showed up at my door, I'd done a full dossier on her. Among other information that needed further research after we put this asshole in the ground, I knew she had a degree in cybersecurity engineering, but from what I could tell, other than her internships during college, she hadn't done anything with it. And so much of the information we needed required stealth and in-depth skills that she didn't have.

"Baby, when I have something significant to share, I promise to tell you," I vowed, walking a very thin tightrope. As far as I was concerned, she didn't need to know any of the gritty details of the investigation. Especially if we had promising leads that didn't pan out. Which had been the case a few times. The only thing that mattered was when we caught the guy and until I could tell her that, I didn't have anything important to share with her.

Peyton stood still and silent, her face completely masked and unreadable.

"I'm going to get dressed and make you some lunch. Then I need to get back to work."

She still didn't say anything, so I started toward the hallway. Right before I left the room, I called over my shoulder, "And, baby, if I have to drag your ass back to the house one more time, I will break out the cuffs. And don't think for one second that I won't follow through with my threat to give you a proper spanking." Then I strode to my bedroom, a corner of my mouth kicking up when I heard her litany of curses. I was dead serious, but still, she was cute when she was pissed. Fucking sexy, too.

When I returned to the kitchen she wasn't there, and I assumed she'd gone to her room to dress as well. I was nearly done with our meal when she wandered into the room in an oversized T-shirt and tiny shorts, her hair down and her feet bare except for their blood-red toenails.

Another outfit I approved of when we were alone, but I'd have to tell the guys on her detail not to look inside the house and just watch for people coming and going. Better yet, I had a few female enforcers and plenty of female operatives at KBO whom I could assign to her.

My wolf brushed his fur under my skin and urged me to go to her, to touch her, just be near her. But I had work to do, and I wanted to have a conversation with Peyton first. If I went near her, we would not be talking.

She sat at the island where I indicated by sliding her plate in front of it, then she quietly ate.

I watched her for a few minutes, trying to figure out how to proceed. Maybe if I extended an olive branch we could come to some kind of agreement. Every time she'd run off, I'd had the impression it was because she didn't have anything to do. So I'd been ruminating over options and was confident I'd found one that would work out well for both of us.

"I've been thinking," I started, my own lunch forgotten in front of me. "I know you're bored. Now that you're the Alpha female of the pack, there are responsibilities you could take over if you'd like."

Her head popped up at that and I expected to see a smile of gratitude for giving her something to do and a way to begin becoming a part of her new pack. Hopefully, as soon as she started to feel at home here, the first bond would finally snap into place and she'd show up in the web with all the members of my pack.

Instead, she was glaring at me, her eyes sharp and icy. Her

tone was equally cold when she snapped, "I am *not* the Alpha female of this pack. We are *not* mates. And I will *not* be staying here indefinitely."

I sighed and opened a drawer, grabbed a hair band, and slammed it shut. After putting my hair in a top knot, I dumped my food in the trash and put the dish in the sink. When I felt I had a handle on my temper, I turned back to her. "You're going to have to accept this eventually, baby. If you think about it logically, it's what makes sense. We have similar personalities and"—I smiled, trying to draw her out of her shell—"when you're not pissing me off, I enjoy your company. The chemistry between us is hot as hell. We burn up the sheets like nothing I've ever experienced in the bedroom. What's more, you're having my pup. It's the best scenario for all of us."

"Is it?" Peyton hopped off the stool and stared at me, her face completely unreadable, more closed off than I'd ever seen her. I was floored when she spoke again, and her frosty tone actually sent a shiver through me. My wolf growled in frustration, not happy with the deep freeze he felt radiating from his mate. "If the time I've been here is any indication of what a future with you would be like, then you've lost your fucking mind if you think I'd consider it for even a minute."

I grabbed onto the edge of the granite countertop and squeezed so hard I wouldn't have been surprised if it cracked. I searched inside myself for my patience, but the slippery motherfucker kept evading my grasp. "I know you—"

"I don't think you do," Peyton interrupted. "The truth is that we barely know each other, Nathan. You assume that I've been going out for a run because I'm bored. Did it ever occur to you that this goes against my very nature?"

I frowned, not quite understanding her point. "Staying inside?"

She crossed her arms over her chest but remained hard and

stiff. "Staying *here*. Not the house, although that certainly hasn't helped. Here, as in Silver Lake, New York, sometimes even the whole freaking United States!" Her mask cracked and revealed a glimmer of panic in her eyes. "The longer I stay here, in one place, the more claustrophobic I feel."

Peyton walked forward and leaned on the island across from me, her emerald pools swirling with gold flecks and flashing with her panther every so often. "Listen to me, Nathan. Eventually, every breath will feel as though it's choking me. You don't get it because you were born to be an Alpha, to settle down, have a family, all that domestic stuff that makes me feel like I'm wrapped in chains just thinking about it."

I could see the truth in her eyes, but while I knew that was what she *believed*, I didn't buy it. Not completely anyway. I was beginning to see that there would always be a part of Peyton that would need to break free for a time, to be unbridled. But no matter how deeply hidden it was, I'd seen the glimpses of another side of Peyton. In her relationship with Sam and Linette, her interaction with my mother, even in the very brief moment I'd spent with her, Emerald, and Savannah. Neither of those two would stand with someone they didn't have faith in. But more than anything, I knew Savannah wouldn't be able to handle losing another friend. Something had happened between her and Peyton. They'd forged a bond that neither one was willing to relinquish, and it was one more string connecting Peyton to Silver Lake.

Sam had mentioned that Peyton was from somewhere upstate, and that NYC was her...home base, he'd called it. Even though she didn't recognize it as such, she'd given herself a place to land, somewhere that was the center of her world. Then she flew from there and while she didn't return in between every move, eventually, she returned home. Perhaps the first step was to convince her to make Silver Lake the new center of her universe. Savannah and Emerald might be willing to help me with that, but it would have to wait.

This conversation definitely hadn't gone as I'd expected, and it wouldn't do any good to continue until I'd had time to study it out in my mind. Peyton didn't appear to be in any mood to listen to reason anyway.

Before anything, I needed to make sure she was safe.

But there was one thing that couldn't wait. "What about the baby?"

Peyton's hand went to her stomach and rested there. "I will never keep you from our child, Nathan."

I canted my head and narrowed my eyes. "And how exactly would that work if I'm here and you're off who knows where? Because I don't intend to be the 'every other weekend and one month in the summer' kind of dad. And I don't see you as the type to abandon your child."

"Of course not," she snapped.

"So, if you're not staying, have you thought about how that would work?"

"Believe it or not, I have, Nathan. I'm not so callous that I would make a decision like that without considering you and talking to you."

My eyes roamed her beautiful face and I wondered, if we had a daughter, would she be as gorgeous as her mother? I needed to be around to protect her, just as I needed to keep Peyton safe. I refused to live without either of them. For now though, it was enough to know that she was planning on making the decisions for our child together.

"We can talk about this another time," I said, breaking a long silence that had built between us. "For now, will you please either stay on my property or take an enforcer with you so that I know you are protected?"

Peyton's hard exterior melted a little and she nodded. "I

promise. Thank you for asking and not demanding for a change."

I hadn't registered that I'd softened my language. Maybe I needed to reconsider the approach I'd been taking with Peyton. People might say you couldn't teach old dogs new tricks, but when it came to immortal dogs, the one lesson we all learned if we were to survive was to adapt. More to think about when the time was right.

I nodded in acknowledgement, then I did something I rarely ever did—I acted without thought. Moving around the island, I walked up to Peyton and brought her close with a hand on her shoulder. Then I pressed a kiss to her forehead.

"I'll probably be late." I was about to tell her to let me know if she needed anything when I suddenly felt like a complete jackass. "If you need me, you can hit #2 on the phone in the kitchen. It will connect you directly to my office. I'm sorry I didn't think to tell you before." She nodded and her head bumped my chin. I placed another kiss on her crown before walking to the kitchen counter closest to the back door. I'd thrown my keys there when I'd stormed into the house earlier.

"Nathan."

I turned my head to see her sitting on a stool, watching me with wariness and…regret?

"I've been this way since I was a kid. Restless, for lack of a better way to describe it. My uncle always told me I inherited it from my dad since I'd turned out to be a panther. It didn't help that I was cooped up and alone so often. When I left for boarding school, it was the first time I felt like myself, because it was an adventure. So many new places to explore and things to try. Then I managed to get through college, with several study-abroad programs and internships. But when I graduated, I started wandering and never stopped. I love my life."

She was trying to tell me that her desire to leave had

nothing to do with me, and maybe it was true. But I had every intention of being the reason she stayed.

I lifted my chin in farewell and she gave me a little wave.

As I drove to KBO, I went over what she'd said several times. I'd been collecting bits and pieces from her, but this was the first time she'd shared something substantial enough to begin sorting everything.

When I'd had time to really study her dossier, there had been a fuck ton of red flags. Her childhood information was almost non-existent before she'd arrived at boarding school at thirteen. Other than her birth certificate—which confirmed the date and the place as New York City but somehow didn't have names for her birth parents—and her passports—I'd been surprised to see that she had dual citizenship in France and the US—there was no other documentation. And no evidence of family.

Even information about payments to her boarding school had been purged from the system. Although, right around the same time that she'd arrived in France, she'd started making withdrawals from an untraceable account with more than three million dollars in it. She'd used it to pay for college, but since then, she'd only added to it—and yet there was no record of any jobs other than small things here and there, like waitressing at The Spot. Her deposits were always in cash and never big enough to require any kind of paperwork, which meant I had no way to trace it unless I could get my hands on the serial numbers for the bills. And even that would very likely be a dead end.

Now I had a few more facts to add to her story and dig into. The key to convincing her to stay might be in the details of her old life.

I eventually learned it was the key to everything.

CHAPTER TWENTY-SEVEN

PEYTON

After Nathan left, I felt drained. Not tired, just…drained.

I hadn't hidden the fact that I planned to leave eventually, so he'd really shocked me with his assumptions. And damn, I rarely became that angry. I would have bet money that he'd made me angry more in the week that I'd been in Silver Lake than I had been in the last five years.

Maybe I shouldn't have been surprised. Nathan analyzed things with the mind of a man who'd seen enough lifetimes to predict the most sensible and successful outcomes. Except no one could predict human behavior and I had a feeling he forgot that sometimes.

My panther was off sulking, because she didn't like it when I pushed Nathan away, but I pretended that if she knew why we'd been fighting she would have been on my side. It was sad that I didn't know if that were true. The girl seemed to be buying into this whole mate thing, no matter how many times I reminded her that she was not a wolf.

I was too tired to pick my conversation with Nathan to pieces or deal with my pouting cat, so I trudged back to my room to relax and read a book. I'd grabbed a mystery novel that sounded good from Nathan's library earlier, so I stretched out on the bed and cracked it open, careful not to crease the spine too much. I was immediately sucked into the story and couldn't stop turning the pages.

It was dark in my room when I opened my eyes, and I glanced down at the book lying open on my chest. *Oops.* I guess I'd been more tired than I thought because when I peeked at the clock on the bedside table, it turned out I'd been asleep for a couple of hours.

My stomach rumbled and I wandered out to the kitchen to make myself a sandwich. I polished off two while I dove into the book again.

A knock on the front door startled me and I hesitated, then rolled my eyes at myself. Nathan's overprotective paranoia must have worn off on me a little. Besides, I had babysitters.

I opened the front door and screamed.

Then I jumped into Sam's arms and he laughed as he nearly fell over. Next, I spun to his side and hugged Linette, though I was much gentler considering she had a little bundle in her arms.

"I can't believe you're here," I exclaimed, "Come in, come in!"

I led them into the open space and over to the couches. Sam plopped down in one while I stuck out my hands to his mate and said, "Gimme!"

Linette laughed and carefully transferred the little person wrapped in a blue blanket into my arms.

"You guys," I breathed. "He's so perfect." Tears filled my eyes, and I examined the sweet face that seemed like a perfect mixture of my friends'.

"Isn't he?" Linette agreed, her voice choked up.

Sam laughed and grabbed Linette's hand to pull her down beside him. "He's a stud all right. A chip off the old block."

I chuckled but kept it soft so I wouldn't jostle the sleeping cub as I lowered myself into my favorite chair. "I'm so sorry I missed his birth."

"We understand," Sam said with a wave of his hand. "We're just glad you're safe."

"What's going on with the investigation, anyway?" Linette asked.

I shrugged. "Nothing as far as I know. I'm not sure they've gotten anywhere with it."

"That's odd." Sam scratched his chin thoughtfully. "When I called Nathan to ask if we could bring the baby to see you, he said they thought they finally had a break in the investigation."

My heart skipped a beat. I must have heard him wrong. "He said what?" I asked in a mild tone, not wanting to tip Sam off that he obviously wasn't supposed to share this with me.

"I guess Tanner finally came across a link or something."

It was a good thing I had a baby in my arms, or I would have jumped to my feet and taken off to find Nathan so I could kill him. *Nothing to share? I call bullshit, Mr. King.*

"Anyway, he also asked me to run by your place and see if it was still being staked out by the police. Which it is, by the way."

"Why?" This news distracted me from the elaborate murder I was plotting in my head.

Sam shrugged. "My guess is because you are the only witness they've ever had for this guy. They are probably hoping you've gone into hiding and they'll be able to bring you in if you try to sneak back to your apartment. Just a guess, though."

"How do they know…shit!" I cursed and immediately froze, afraid I'd scared the baby.

Linette laughed. "He could sleep through a freight train blowing its horn in his room. Don't worry about him, but what's wrong?"

"With everything that happened, I never had a chance to wipe out my digital records at the hospital. My nurse shredded the paper files and put off the police interview for me, always telling them I was too ill. So I forgot about their records."

"It's understandable that you forgot about it when you got here," Linette sighed. "Give yourself a break, Peyton. You can do it when we leave."

"I don't have my computer, tablet, or even my phone."

"Oh, I didn't think of you leaving everything behind," Linette mused. "Nathan doesn't have one you could borrow?"

I must have been too wrapped up in all the other stuff to notice it before that moment, but once I sat and thought about it, I found it a little odd that Nathan had never offered me the use of a phone or computer.

"Does he know what you do for a living?"

"Of course not," I denied, wrinkling my nose. "I barely know him."

"And yet you're carrying his cub," Linette remarked dryly.

"Why do you think he'd try to keep me from a phone or computer? I haven't seen a tablet around, and his computer... damn, there are so many layers of security on there, if I didn't have an eidetic memory, I might have wondered if I'd designed it and forgot."

"Well, that makes sense, though," Sam said as he settled back into the couch and pulled his mate into his side.

"What does?" I certainly didn't understand.

"The security. Between the security company and council responsibilities—"

"Security company?"

Sam's head reared back a little and he gawked at me. "What the hell have you two talked about in the last week? It's like you know nothing about each other."

"I guess we don't." I wasn't sure why that bothered me so much.

"Oh! I have my laptop in the car!" Linette exclaimed.

"I don't know, babe," Sam hedged, glancing at me. "If Nathan doesn't want her to—"

"Sam," I warned in a steel tone. "If you say another word, I will kick your ass back to New York City." Then I gentled my voice. "Linette, may I borrow it, please?"

She looked between Sam and me twice, then seemed to decide I was more deserving of her support at the moment because she scampered off to the front door.

Reluctantly, I passed their tiny cub into Sam's arms so when Linette returned, I could take the computer. It didn't take me long to erase any traces of myself in the hospital database, then I cleared any record of me in a few other places. Then I moved on to the police files. While in the system, I scanned all of the reports pertaining to my "incident." As I read, my eyes grew wider, and rounder, and my temper bubbled under the surface. My panther went on alert at the volatile emotions churning inside me, ready to pounce if I needed her.

Not that she would be much help once she figured out who it was I wanted to rip to shreds.

They had labeled my attacker a serial killer. The woman I'd tried to save had been his seventh victim, as far as they knew. There didn't appear to be a lot of details—they either didn't know much, or they were incompetent. *Could be a little of both.*

Nathan filtered into my mind and the shock began to give way to the molten fury below my surface. How could he have kept all of this from me? *Nothing to share?*

"Did you know about all this?" I asked my friends before giving them a super-fast rundown on what I'd learned.

Both shook their heads.

But Nathan does.

That reminded me. I did a quick search of Nathan and found only a cursory explanation of his company, KBO Consulting—I couldn't find what that stood for anywhere—on social networking sites for professionals. When I searched for a website, all I found was KBOC.com and it was password-protected.

"What is KBO?" I asked aloud.

"You should ask Nathan," Sam replied cagily.

"Are you his friend or mine?" I huffed as I glared at him.

"Both. I've known Nathan even longer than I've known you, P. He does the security for the club."

My lips curled down. "I had the impression that it was a much bigger deal than small-time security gigs."

Sam rolled his eyes. "Gee, thanks for that positive assessment of my life's work, but also, he does it as a favor, because we are friends."

"So what you're saying is that he isn't ignorant to all of this information, he's just been lying to me about it."

Sam moved uncomfortably in his seat.

"I can't believe you won't spill the beans, Sam," I griped. "You're basically choosing him over me."

"Do you want to know what we named the baby?" Linette piped up all of a sudden.

"Good grief, I can't believe I forgot to ask." I shut the computer, distracted by fun baby stuff.

"We named him after his godmother," she explained as she gazed down at her son fondly.

"Godmother?"

Sam nodded, as he studied the baby's cute little face. "We named him Peyton."

I gasped and my eyes welled up with tears while a giant smile split my face. I all but snatched the little boy from his father's arms. "I forgive you," I said to Sam before giving the baby my undivided attention.

I barely noticed Sam standing and slipping away, assuming he'd gone to find the bathroom. When he came back into the room, I frowned when I saw him slipping his cell phone into his pocket.

"Who were you calling, honey?" Linette asked curiously. *Thank you, friend.* He was much more likely to answer his mate than me.

"Checking on something," he answered with a smile. "There's a storm cell coming in. We should probably get going."

I sighed, already lonely as they took back their little bundle of joy and readied themselves to leave.

After shutting the door behind them, I marched into the kitchen and over to the phone hanging on the wall. I debated for a good ten minutes before deciding that I wanted to have this conversation in person.

I didn't want to wait around for him any more—it was setting a bad precedent. But I had no clue where he worked, and I doubted my babysitters would be any help.

My furiousness continued to build throughout the evening, and by the time I gave in and went to bed, I was feeling bloodthirsty.

He liked my wildcat? I hoped so, because he was about to get real up close and personal with her claws.

CHAPTER TWENTY-EIGHT

NATHAN

A knock on my door dragged my attention away from my computer as Asher and Ephraim—another enforcer—strolled into my office.

"Alpha," Asher greeted as he took a seat in one of the chairs flanking the small table with my other chess set. Ephraim nodded and leaned a shoulder against the wall by the door.

These two were complete opposites. Asher had joined the Marines at eighteen and in his time he'd seen and done some intense shit. Only I knew the full extent, because he'd allowed me to see into his mind before I made him head enforcer. I'd needed to make sure that his head was screwed on tight and he was up for the job. The skills he'd learned in the military had also earned him a place as an instructor with KBO operatives. He had no problem speaking up and had the ability to talk himself in and out of most situations. And though he had strong opinions, he was also open-minded and willing to consider every avenue to a situation. People had to work hard as fuck to earn his respect, but once they had it, he had unwavering loyalty.

Ephraim was the quiet one, preferring to observe rather than ask questions. He rarely spoke, so when he did, people listened. He'd been with KBO as an operative since he was twenty—arguably my best tracker—and he'd only left covert operations when I offered him a position as an enforcer. Though I still tapped him for KBO from time to time. He was fiercely loyal and extremely protective. If someone crossed him, particularly if it put his family in jeopardy, they had a death wish.

They worked well together because their strengths complemented each other. Especially if they were in a situation where both stealth and distraction were necessary. Which was why I'd called them in.

"What can we do for you, Alpha?" Asher queried, relaxing into his seat and propping an ankle on the opposite knee.

Before I sent them on their task, I needed to know. "Who do you have on Peyton?"

"Jase and Amanda."

"Put Jase on something else and assign Sabrina," I ordered tersely.

If Asher had an opinion about my request, he kept it to himself. "Done."

I nodded, then picked up a sheet of paper from my desk and handed it to Ephraim, who was closest to me. "I need you both to go to that address and pack it up, then bring everything back here. But you'll have to do it while avoiding the NYPD stakeout teams."

Ephraim raised an eyebrow, but Asher asked the question. "Isn't this a residential address?"

"Peyton's place."

Asher cocked his head to the side and frowned. "How exactly are we supposed to pack up an entire apartment and transport everything under the noses of the cops? I'm fucking awesome at what I do, but I'm not invisible."

My seat creaked as I leaned back and propped a hand on the

arm. "She doesn't have much. I'd guess not more than a couple suitcases' worth."

"At her apartment?"

I nodded and stroked my beard. "She's a loner. Doesn't stay in one place long enough to accumulate possessions."

"Why are we bringing everything she owns to Silver Lake?" Ephraim spoke up, his eyes scrutinizing me. With that one inquiry, he was asking why the police were involved, what she meant to me, if she was staying, and how a loner would integrate into our pack.

As I was their Alpha, it was their duty to do what I asked without question and I contemplated whether to exercise that power or to answer Ephraim. Part of me simply didn't like the idea of discussing Peyton with two unmated males. But the bigger issue was that my situation with Peyton was still precarious at best and spreading the news that I'd found my mate would throw Peyton in the spotlight.

However, my enforcers knew better than to flap their mouths and these two, in particular, were used to a life of secrets. And she *would* be their Alpha female, so I explained.

"She's my mate."

"You've mated her?" Asher blurted in disbelief.

"That's not what I said."

"She's your true mate," Ephraim concluded, his voice giving no indication of his thoughts.

I nodded. "She witnessed a murder, and the cops want to talk to her, so they are watching her place with the hope that she'll return. Until we have more information about the killer, I don't want them to know where she is."

Ephraim's gaze was probing, trying to discern what I wasn't saying.

"I don't know what's going to happen, but at the moment,

we will work under the assumption that she is staying indefinitely."

Tanner appeared in my open doorway, his expression concerned. "We need to talk."

I nodded before lifting my chin at Asher and Ephraim, dismissing them.

"We'll let you know when it's done," Asher assured me before they both exited the room.

Tanner shut the door and paced in front of it for a tense minute.

"Anytime, Tanner," I grunted, anxious to return to the work I'd been doing before my enforcers arrived.

"I had a theory this morning and took another gander at the police report for Peyton's incident."

"What did you find?"

"It's not what I found, it's what I didn't find."

I crossed my arms over my chest, my mind whirring with possibilities. "The files are gone?"

"Not the files, but almost all the references to a witness. But Peyton's name and address specifically were wiped from the reports. I even went a little broader, checking the entire database. She is nowhere in their system."

My face formed a scowl as I digested Tanner's discovery. I'd been over the case myself and I knew for a fact that Peyton's information had been in there when I did. Someone had gone in and done the deed. "You're sure it wasn't us?" We hadn't tasked anyone with the job, but sometimes our people took initiative. Not that it always panned out.

"Positive. I tried to find a trace of the hacker, a fingerprint, familiar code, anything, but they were damn good."

I ran my hands over my hair, stopping before I dislodged the high bun on the back of my head. "I suppose it works to our advantage for keeping her hidden, but I doubt the hacker's reasons were altruistic. We need to figure out their endgame."

"I agree, but that's not all."

"What the fuck else?" I snarled.

"I had a hunch, so I checked a few other places. She's all but disappeared from the digital world. Her hospital records were gone, the lease on her apartment has a different name—utilities too. Even the address in the DMV is different from the one in her dossier. It's like someone is trying to wipe her out of existence."

"Maybe." Something felt off about this. I had nothing to back it up, but I wasn't convinced it was her attacker. "What about her birth certificate? Passports? Social security?"

"Those don't appear to have been tampered with."

Not recently, anyway.

"It sounds to me like whoever did it was focused on anyone being able to find her in New York."

My phone rang and I ignored it so we could continue our conversation without interruption. But when it ended and started ringing again immediately, Tanner gestured to it and said, "Probably should answer it."

He was right. My first thought was Peyton, but it wasn't the extension for my home phone. After a second, I recognized the number as Sam's and I immediately picked it up. He was with Peyton. Something must have happened. "Is Peyton all right?"

"Yeah, man. She's fine. It's you who should be worried."

"Excuse me?"

Sam sighed. "You didn't tell me that you were keeping Peyton in the dark about everything. I caught it pretty fast, so I didn't tell her anything specific. But she's not stupid, Nathan. She knows you're hiding shit."

Just fucking great. The last thing I needed right now was

another thing for us to fight about. "She doesn't know anything though, right?"

Sam's silence was more telling than any words.

"I thought you said you didn't tell her anything," I growled.

"I didn't. But she...she stumbled upon some information about the case. Details about the attack and the parallel between the man who hurt her and the serial killer you've been hunting. I tried to backpedal when I mentioned you do the security for the club, but... Anyway, I'm pretty sure she's in the other room plotting your death with my mate."

"How the hell did she see any of that shit? She doesn't have —" I stopped as soon as it hit me. "You let her use your computer, didn't you?" There was a deadly edge to my tone that suggested he better find an explanation that would keep me from kicking his ass.

"Not me..." He paused, clearly reluctant to divulge the details. I wasn't his Alpha, so I couldn't demand his answer, but there were many ways I could make his life miserable. Finally, he spoke, but his voice held as much warning as mine had. "It was Linette."

My eyes rose to the ceiling and I tapped into my patience before responding coolly. "How did that happen? Seriously, Sam. You need to get a handle on your woman."

Sam scoffed and muttered, "If you think that's ever going to happen, you don't know Linette or Peyton very well. Good luck. And don't say I didn't warn you." He hung up, leaving me glaring at the phone as if my wrath could reach through and strangle Sam. I'd deliberately kept Peyton away from anything connected to the outside world so that she wouldn't stumble onto something that reminded her of her attack. Plus, I'd figured it would help her to settle here if she didn't have other people and places coloring her view of a future with me.

I'd even been reluctant to allow Sam and his mate to visit.

Until it dawned on me that Linette was hoping something would develop between Peyton and me. I'd figured it couldn't hurt if Linette gave her a little push.

"Did he say details of the attack?" Tanner asked, having overheard the entire conversation. He'd moved to sit on the couch under the window and leaned forward with his elbows on his knees.

"Yeah," I answered distractedly, still stuck on the fact that my bright idea had backfired spectacularly.

"Nathan," Tanner pressed, demanding my attention. He waited until our eyes met before continuing. "The details of the attack were never released. She was the only one there and with her injuries, I doubt she was aware of much. I can't see details being leaked by the paramedics or hospital staff, and the serial killer angle isn't public knowledge either. The detective didn't want to tip him off that we'd made the connection."

Son of a bitch.

"Do you think Sam…?" Tanner wondered.

I shook my head. "He wouldn't cross me, and he'd never do anything to hurt Peyton."

My mind cycled through more questions. Did she know someone who would have divulged the details? Was this person behind the hacks? If she was still hiding shit, especially if it had to do with the night she almost died, I might finally give her the spanking she'd been begging for since the day we'd met. The threat of locking her in my room wasn't out of the realm of consideration either.

"Then how did she find out?"

"I don't know," I gritted out through a clenched jaw. "But I intend to find out how and who the fuck is digging into her and purging anything with information on her." I pushed my chair back and stood. "I think my mate and I need to have a chat."

"Perhaps we should chat first, Nathan," a suave, musical

voice said from my door, which had been closed until a second ago.

A tall, pale man with sleek, white-blond hair that hung just past his shoulders lounged against the jamb, his piercing, sky blue eyes trained on me. He had an angular face with high, sharp cheekbones, a straight nose, and a perpetual smirk on his mouth. In black slacks and a black dress shirt—complete with French cuffs and diamond links—with the regal way he carried himself, and the air of superiority that surrounded him, he was the poster boy for aristocracy.

"Phillipé," I greeted the French vampire prince.

"*Salut, l'ami,*" he responded in kind.

"What can I do for you?" I asked impatiently.

"I have news on the leads you requested I follow."

"You couldn't have called?" For him to have come all the way here didn't bode well.

"I felt it was more appropriate to speak in person. I'd rather not risk a leak."

His explanation made sense, so I pushed away some of my impatience and nodded for him to go on.

"Melinda?" Tanner asked, and Phillipé inclined his head in the affirmative.

"Her body was left at the steps of The Crimson *Calice* last night."

"Fuck," Tanner grunted.

I watched Phillipé carefully when I asked, "Do you have any leads?"

Phillipé stepped into the room and strolled to one of the chairs in front of my desk. He sat and crossed one leg over the other. "Not at the moment." He didn't exhibit any signs that he was withholding anything. "However, it was the way they found her that I thought you should know."

He described a scene that matched those of the other victims attributed to the killer we were hunting. Except…

"A vampire?" I mused aloud. "It's always shifters and the timing is all wrong. From the profile we've built of this guy, he doesn't deviate from his pattern."

"Never?" Phillipé raised a perfectly groomed eyebrow. "Was there not an incident recently that interfered with his planned attack? One involving the woman you are currently harboring?"

My eyes locked with Phillipé's, and I knew he was staring back at my wolf. I gave my animal a minute to convey his own warning and when he faded back, I dropped all pretenses. I let him see just how deadly I could be. The killer that lurked inside me and would decimate anyone who threatened my mate.

"I don't know how you found out, but if you breathe a single word about Peyton, I will hunt you down and let my wolf rip out your heart and feast on it while you slowly slip into oblivion."

"Relax, *mon ami*," Phillipé said evenly, holding his hands up in a gesture of surrender. "I have no intentions toward your woman. I have a specific reason for bringing her up in this conversation."

"How did you even find out about her?" I growled. Besides the few in my pack who were aware of her, the only other people who knew her location were Sam and Linette, who would never betray Peyton.

"I cannot share my source. However, I can assure you they have nothing but her best interests in mind and they only brought this to me because of the similarity."

"We will come back to this 'source'," I stated in a tone brooking no argument. "But first explain this similarity."

"I am given to understand that you have not met Melinda?"

I shook my head. She hadn't had her position in the ISC

more than a few weeks before she'd disappeared and I hadn't had the opportunity to meet with her yet.

"I have," Tanner interjected, and I glanced at him. He had a shell-shocked expression on his face. "Shit." Then his eyes met mine. "She's tall, athletic, long dark hair, green eyes."

My brow furrowed and I grunted, "The resemblance could be a complete coincidence. We don't even have proof that she was killed by the same man."

"There aren't enough details available for a copycat, Nathan," Tanner argued.

"There's something else," Phillipé announced. Both Tanner and I leveled him with hard stares. "Melinda had an injury that wasn't prevalent on the other victims. Her back had been slashed diagonally from shoulder to hip."

I blanched at the description. "Son of a bitch."

I sat in stunned silence until Phillipé added, "I didn't know about Peyton's injury, but my...contact brought it to my attention, and I felt you should be aware of the full situation."

My wolf snarled and snapped while I glared daggers at Phillipé. "Who?" I demanded. The rising aggression inside me and the power I exuded would have most people shrinking back and telling me whatever the hell I wanted to know.

Unfortunately, Phillipé wasn't one of them. He'd also shared this information without coercion when he had no responsibility to do so. He wasn't on the ISC, primarily because French vampires were not known for involving themselves in situations that did not affect them directly—such as helping Dimitri reclaim his throne.

However, through money and a lack of scruples, Lucien and Phillipé had built an empire in New York City. They'd proven to be powerful allies in the vampire world and assisted us on occasion. But when it came to Peyton, I didn't give a fuck about propriety, relationships, or burning bridges.

Phillipé shook his head. "It's not up for discussion, Nathan. Move on."

"Is there anything else you can tell us?" Tanner asked while I ground my teeth practically into dust.

Phillipé stood and tugged at his cuffs before flicking an imaginary speck of dust from his pants. Then his icy blue eyes observed me, and he appeared to be contemplating his next move. "I don't have anything substantial to back up my theory, but I do not believe Melinda's death was as simple as killing your woman in effigy. I think she was chosen for more than her appearance."

"Do you have a theory as to why?" Tanner asked. I let him take the lead in the conversation while I tried to calm the hell down. My wolf's agitation wasn't helping the situation.

Phillipé drew his fingers through his hair and sighed. "Not yet. But...I think there is more to all of this than anyone has puzzled together yet." He walked toward the door and stopped, staring at me over his shoulder. "If I were to hazard a guess, I'd say a war is brewing."

CHAPTER TWENTY-NINE

NATHAN

After Phillipé dropped his bomb and disappeared, Tanner and I stared at each other for a time. Neither of us seemed to know how to digest everything we'd just learned.

However, my wolf snapped me out of it when he shoved hard against me and his desperation to check on Peyton flooded my mind. I yanked the receiver from my desk phone and put it to my ear before dialing the extension to my house.

When no-one answered, I jumped to my feet, barely noticing that my chair flew back and crashed into the wall. "I need to go. Do a deep dive on Melinda and get your hands on all the information surrounding her death. Call me when you have updates." I grabbed my keys, wallet, and an item I'd been debating about giving Peyton. Ultimately, I figured I'd rather she have access to the outside world if it meant I would be able to get in touch with her at all times.

Tanner nodded and I took off.

Despite the darkness around me, the late hour didn't register until I walked into a quiet, still house. I made a beeline for Peyton's room and when I saw her asleep in her bed, I released my first easy breath since I'd left her earlier.

I backed out of the room, shutting the door behind me. But before it closed, I paused, then pushed it open again. The moonlight was streaming through the window, making her pale skin glow and her inky black hair shine. She was so fucking gorgeous. And she was mine. I knew I would do whatever it took to keep her.

After another minute, I forced myself to leave her and went to ready myself for bed. Sleep eluded me for a couple of hours until I ultimately gave in and slipped out of bed. I padded down the hall and silently entered Peyton's room.

She barely even twitched when I scooped her into my arms and carried her back to my bed. I set her in the spot I'd vacated and pulled the quilt up over her. Then I rounded the bed and climbed in beside her.

That was when I noticed my cell phone blinking with a message on the nightstand. I picked it up and swiped it to open the message. It was from Ephraim.

Ephraim: Done. Almost there.
Me: Leave everything in the garage.
Ephraim: Will do.

Moving all of Peyton's belongings here had been a bold decision because I had no way to predict her reaction. I presumed it would be best to keep it out of sight until I'd talked her around to the idea. At least this way, it would already be done when she eventually capitulated.

I curled myself around her and contentment stole over me, allowing sleep to finally overtake me.

Peyton was still sleeping like a rock when I woke up the next morning. She had mentioned being a night owl, but she went to bed earlier these days because the pregnancy sapped her strength. Even so, she still slept late in the mornings, whereas I'd always been an early riser. So it was barely seven in the morning when I glanced at the clock.

During the night, Peyton had flipped around and snuggled into me so that she was now wrapped around me as if I were her own personal body pillow. Not that I had any complaints about it. Other than the fact that she had one of her legs thrown across my hips. I was a big man, everywhere, so it didn't take much for my morning erection to be pressed into her thigh. Her full breasts were crushed against my chest, and her head was buried in my neck. Each soft, warm breath that blew across my skin sent more and more blood straight to my shaft.

I debated teasing her sweet spots into becoming so hot and bothered that she'd be begging for my cock once she knew what was happening. All the sexual tension between us boiled to the surface and my lust was bound to overpower my brain soon. One right move from her and I'd be buried inside her before either of us knew what had happened.

I nearly gave in to my urges, but when I lifted Peyton's face for a kiss, I spotted the deep purple bruises under her eyes. She clearly hadn't been sleeping well and waking her up just to keep my balls from turning blue would be a real asshole move. Instead, I gently rolled her over and extricated myself from her embrace.

I had hoped to talk to her today, to hash some things out and deal with the fallout from Sam's blunder. However, Tanner messaged me while I was in the shower, telling me he had news and I'd probably want to come in for it.

Me: Emergency?

Tanner: Not urgent, but not something we want to sit on for long.

Me: Be there in an hour.

Tanner: I'll be in the SCIF room.

I dressed and went into the kitchen to make Peyton breakfast, hoping she'd be awake before I left. However, even after pushing it to an hour and a half, I forced myself to leave her a note and go meet with Tanner. I'd brought home a burner cell from KBO and set it next to the paper.

Please keep your sexy ass in the house or hit speed dial 4 on the phone and Sabrina or Amanda will shadow you on a run. I'll be home to make dinner and we'll talk. —Nate

At the last second, I added,

Thank you for staying where you were put yesterday.

I stared at the note and shook my head with a self-deprecating chuckle. I wasn't sure how I felt about the man I was becoming around Peyton, but that was something to ponder another day.

I checked on her one last time before heading back to KBO.

CHAPTER THIRTY

PEYTON

Nathan's spicy, woodsy scent was all around me and I inhaled deeply, wondering if I smelled it long enough, I could imprint it in my lungs. My eyes slowly opened, and I felt disoriented for a minute, not recognizing my surroundings. A quick scan revealed that I was in the master bedroom. *What the hell am I doing in Nathan's bed?*

I turned to demand an answer, but the rest of the bed was empty and though the pillow had a dent from his head, the spot had long since cooled.

A little growl escaped my lips, and I renewed my determination to confront the overprotective, controlling, lying jackass.

Nathan and I seriously needed to have it out. I was done being kept in the dark, done being lied to, just…done.

Rolling over, I curled up into a sitting position, then scooted off the bed. I padded down the hall to the kitchen and spotted the usual note and plate of breakfast waiting for me.

Snatching it up, I almost laughed at the last line. If I weren't so unbelievably furious with him, I might have thought the note was sweet. The phone, though...I wasn't sure what to think about it.

I put the note in the pocket of my sleep shorts and sat on a stool to eat. I'd given up pretending not to enjoy his cooking, but it didn't diminish my desire to kick his ass.

Curiously, I turned on the phone and recognized right away that it was a burner. Interesting that he happened to have one of those lying around.

The contacts had three names—Nathan, Savannah, and Lizabeta.

Once I'd eaten every bite of the breakfast, a bowl of fruit, and some toast, I jumped into the shower. Afterward, I dressed in a pair of yoga pants, a light pink bra, and an oversized yellow tunic that slid off one shoulder.

I thought about going for a run and returned to the kitchen to grab the phone so I could call one of my babysitters to accompany me. Maybe I could convince her to take me to Nathan afterward.

The phone wasn't on the counter when I walked into the kitchen area. I frowned, positive I hadn't taken it with me into the bedroom.

The cell phone suddenly appeared in my vision, held in a hand that I vaguely recognized. "Looking for this?" a calm, melodic voice asked.

My stomach rolled at the sound as recognition slammed into me. The hand. It sported scars that had been made by my claws.

A scream tried to rip from my lips, but nothing came out because a hand came from behind me and clapped over my mouth.

"Hello, puss."

Read the next book in Nathan & Peyton's story!
Available Now!

Read the conclusion to Nathan and Peyton's story!
Available Now!

Curious about Asher and Savannah's story?
A Promised Claim, book 4 of the Silver Lake Shifters
Coming March 2022
Preorder it now!

ALSO BY ELLE CHRISTENSEN

Silver Lake Shifters

An Unexpected Claim: Nathan & Peyton (Book 1) – Available Now!

An Uncertain Claim: Nathan & Peyton (Book 2) – Available Now!

An Unending Claim: Nathan & Peyton (Book 3) - Available Now!

A Promised Claim: Asher & Savannah (Book 4) - Preorder Now!

A Forbidden Claim (Book 4) – TBD

A Vengeful Claim (Book 5) – TBD

The Slayer Witch Trilogy

The Slayer Witch (Book 1) - Summer 2022

The Wolf, the Witch, and the Amulet (Book 2) – Summer 2022

Stone Butterfly Rockstars

Another Postcard (Book 1) – Available Now!

Rewrite the Stars (Book 2) – Coming 2022

Daylight (Book 3) – TBD

Just Give Me a Reason (book 4) – TBD

All of Me (Book 5) – TBD

Miami Flings

Spring Fling – Available Now!

All I Want (Miami Flings & Yeah, Baby Crossover) – Available Now!

Untitled – TBD

Ranchers Only Series

Ranchers Only – Available Now!
The Ranchers Rose – Available Now!
Ride a Rancher – Available Now!
When You Love a Rancher – Available Now!
Untitled – TBD

Happily Ever Alpha

Until Rayne – Available Now!
Until the Lighting Strikes – Available Now!
Until the Thunder Rolls – Coming 2022

Standalone Books

Love in Fantasy – Available Now!
Say Yes (A military Romance) – Available Now!
Bunny Vibes – Available Now!
Fairytale Wishes (Mermaid Kisses Collaboration) - Available Now!

The Fae Guard Series

Protecting Shaylee (Book 1) – Available Now!
Loving Ean (Book 2) – Available Now!
Chasing Hayleigh (Book 3) – Available Now!
A Very Faerie Christmas (Book 4) – Available Now!
Saving Kendrix (Book 5) – Available Now!
Forever Fate: (Book 6) – Available Now!

The Fae Legacy (A Fae Guard Spin-off)

Finding Ayva (Book 1) – Coming 2022

Books Co-authored with Lexi C. Foss

Crossed Fates (Kingdom of Wolves) – Available Now!
First Kiss of Revenge (Vampire Dynasty Trilogy Book 1) - 2022
First Bite of Pleasure (Vampire Dynasty Trilogy Book 2) – TBD
First Taste of Blood (Vampire Dynasty Trilogy Book 3) – TBD

Books Co-authored with K. Webster

Erased Webster (Standalone Novel) – Available Now!
Give Me Yesterday (Standalone Novel) – Available Now!

If you enjoy quick and dirty and SAFE, check out Elle Christensen and Rochelle Paige's co-written books under the pen name Fiona Davenport!

Website

ACKNOWLEDGMENTS

It's been more than three years since Nathan and Peyton introduced themselves to me. Their story would never have been told if it weren't for the amazing people in my life.

My greatest thanks are for my husband and baby girl. They put up with so much from me. I love them more than life.

Ro, the Thelma to my Louise, the Ethel to my Lucy, the Dr. Phil to my crazy person. You have a part in every book I write. Thank you for always being there no matter what.

Hannah and Cassandra, you are amazing. Thank you for helping me to polish this story.

Thank you so my editor, RJ Locksley! You put up with my crazy deadline and last minute manuscript and still did an awesome job. Lol. I promise to be better prepared next time (No, my fingers are not crossed behind my back…)

A major thanks to KD from Story Wrappers. The covers for this series are brilliant! Just brilliant!

Many thanks to all of the authors who have helped me along the way.

A special shout out to the authors of Writing Instalove. This book would probably still be in chapter five if it hadn't been for you. Not only were you moral support by simply sprinting with me all the time, but you have no idea how much you encouraged me. Your excitement is contagious and your dedication is inspiring. Here's to many more books brought to you by the Instalove Sprinters!

To my readers. For those of you who have stick with me for

the last four years, I have no words to express my gratitude. Life hit me with curveball after curveball and I only now feel like I'm inching up my batting average. Lol. Thank you for always being there.

And to my new readers, I hope you enjoyed the story and will keep walking these crazy book journeys with me!

ABOUT THE AUTHOR

About Elle Christensen

I'm a lover of all things books and have always had a passion for writing. Since I am a sappy romantic, I fell easily into writing romance. I love a good HEA! I'm a huge baseball fan, a blogger, and obsessive reader.

My husband is my biggest supporter and he's incredibly patient and understanding about the people is my head who are fighting with him for my attention.

I hope you enjoy reading my books as much as I enjoyed writing them!

Join Elle Christensen's newsletter to receive a couple of updates a month on new releases and exclusive content. To join, all you need to do is click here.

Website
Newsletter Book+Main

Printed in Great Britain
by Amazon